Running Around

(and Such)

A novel based on true experiences from an Amish writer!

LINDA BYLER

Running Around

(and Such)

LIZZIE SEARCHES *for* LOVE
· Book 1 ·

Good Books®

Intercourse, PA 17534
800/762-7171
www.GoodBooks.com

Running Around (and Such) includes material originally published by the author as these books: *Lizzie, Lizzie and Emma, Lizzie's Carefree Years, Lizzie and Mandy*, and *Lizzie's Teen Years.*

Cover design by Koechel Peterson & Associates, Inc.,
Minneapolis, Minnesota

Design by Cliff Snyder

RUNNING AROUND (AND SUCH)
Copyright © 2010 by Good Books, Intercourse, PA 17534
International Standard Book Number: 978-1-56148-688-5
Library of Congress Catalog Card Number: 2010010347

Library of Congress Cataloging-in-Publication Data
Byler, Linda.
Running around (and such) / Linda Byler.
   p. cm. -- (Lizzie searches for love ; bk. 1)
   Summary: A hot-tempered, high-spirited teenaged girl who hates house-
work, dislikes babies, and loves driving fast horses tries to fit in among the
members of her Amish community. Based on the true experiences of the
author's extended family.
   ISBN 978-1-56148-688-5 (pbk. : alk. paper) 1. Amish--Juvenile fiction.
[1. Amish--Fiction.] I. Title.
PZ7.B9882Ru 2010
[Fic]--dc22   2010010347

Table of Contents

The Story   1

The Recipes   325

The Glossary   341

The Author   345

Other *Lizzie Searches for Love* books   346

Chapter 1

LIZZIE GLICK NOTICED THE CHANGE IN DAT one evening when he came in from checking things over at the pallet shop one last time before bed. He stood at the sink, washing his hands much longer than usual. Lizzie watched her father from the corner of her eyes, knowing something was about to give.

Things had been tense between Dat and Mam for more than a week, ever since Dat had announced he wanted to move to the new settlement and try his hand at farming. Mam most decidedly did not want to go. Her despair and total dislike of the whole idea had turned the usual peaceful, happy atmosphere of the Glick home tense.

Lizzie and her sisters had done the best they could to keep the peace, trying to understand Dat's ambition to become a farmer like his father and brother-in-law, even as they knew Mam didn't want to move again.

Lizzie thought she knew how Dat felt. There wasn't much of a challenge in Jefferson County anymore. The house was almost paid for, there were few financial concerns, and the pallet shop made an easy living. Dat was bored.

"Annie," Dat said.

"Hmm?"

Lizzie's heart leaped to her throat at his tone of voice. Dat meant business. Here it comes, she thought wildly. We're moving.

Dat dried his hands on the dark green towel, then turned to face his wife and daughters before he sat down opposite Mam at the kitchen table. He took a deep breath.

"Annie," he said a second time. "Doddy Glick and Daniel were here at the pallet shop this afternoon again."

Mam stiffened, her fingers working the straight pin in and out of her dress, which she often did when she was nervous.

"And?"

Lizzie bit down hard on her lower lip, drying a plate over and over again.

"They want me to go along over to Cameron County to look at a farm. It's only about two miles from Daniel's place and four or five from Doddy's place."

"I'm not going, Melvin."

"Ach, Annie, I thought you said the decision was up to me. If I make a choice, can't you find it in yourself to honor it?"

"I didn't say I wouldn't move. I said I'm not going along to look at the farm. You know I don't want to move, Melvin, but I have no choice if you decide to go."

"Annie, why don't you want to?"

"Melvin, think a little!" Mam's voice rose, desperation almost making her choke.

Lizzie felt like running out of the kitchen, her hands over her ears, far away where she'd never have to hear this painful conversation. Her older sister, Emma, sat quietly at the table, playing with their little twin sisters, KatieAnn and Susan.

Mam continued, "Emma will soon be 16 years old. She has all her friends and interests here. As far as I know, there are no other youth in that...that settlement, Cameron County, whatever you want to call it."

She clenched her hands.

"Another thing, Melvin," she continued. "We've talked of this before. How do you know we can make a living farming? You've never farmed. You don't know the first thing about it. Even if Uncle Eli gives you a good price for the pallet shop, the cost of starting up, with cows and equipment plus the farm itself, is completely frightening."

Dat sighed. He pleated the tablecloth with his fingers, then he sighed again, watching Mam's face as she stared at the floor.

"Where's your faith, Annie?"

Mam made a sound much like a snort. "I guess I don't have any where Cameron County is concerned.

I'm so afraid we're making a big mistake. The *Ordnung* here is plainer; our young people are well behaved—"

Lizzie thought of high heels and ice cubes in the refrigerator and gas stoves with a broiler to make toast. "Do they wear high heels in Cameron County?" she blurted out.

Dat glared at her, clearly perturbed that she should even think of anything like that at a time like this. Mam tried to hide her smile, but Lizzie could tell she had to laugh.

Lizzie had loved heels forever. Ever since Mrs. Bixler had stopped in for a visit with Mam when Lizzie was five years old, Lizzie had wanted to grow up to wear shoes like Mrs. Bixler had—shiny and white with high heels. Maybe Cameron County was her chance to wear fancy things.

Watching the brief smile on Mam's face, Lizzie said, "Because if they do, I'm going to wear them."

Mandy, Lizzie's younger sister, yelled out from the living room, "Me, too!"

There was silence for a while, and not altogether a comfortable one. No one was smiling about wearing high heels anymore. Mam and Dat both looked desperately unhappy again. Mam broke the silence with a sigh.

"Well, Melvin, you know I am supposed to submit like every good Amish wife should. And I will go along if that's your decision." That was said in a much softer tone of voice, but there was a line of steel running through it, too.

Dat looked at Mam, then looked away. Lizzie knew that her mother thought Doddy Glick was responsible for all this. Dat always wanted to have his father's approval and praise. It was just how Dat was, Lizzie realized.

"I need a challenge again," he said. "Besides, I farmed growing up. I know how to milk cows, load hay, plow, and till the soil. I know plenty."

Suddenly enthused, excitement lighting up his blue eyes, he said, "Well, I'll tell you what, Annie. I'll go look at the farm, and if it's alright, I'll come back, and you and the girls can look at it before I buy it, okay?"

Mam didn't answer.

"I want to," Lizzie said. Emma and Mandy nodded.

"It's 120 acres. Can you girls imagine how much you would have to do? There's a large creek bordering the property and hills to sled-ride! Doddy said it would be perfect for you girls."

"It sounds exciting," Emma said politely, but her heart clearly wasn't in it.

Dat's smile folded up like an unplayed accordion. The light went out of his eyes just as quickly, leaving his face a picture of disappointment mixed with false bravado. His shoulders sagged, and he turned to go into the living room, first looking searchingly at Mam, who would not return his gaze.

Lizzie felt sorry for Dat, she really did. She knew how much it meant to him to be able to buy a farm and live in a new community. She wished Mam wouldn't act so stubborn and would be nicer to Dat about moving.

Later that evening, lying in the bed that they shared in the little room at the top of the stairs, Mandy told Lizzie, in her wiser-than-her-years kind of way, that a husband should honor his wife's wishes.

"But, Mandy..." Lizzie said lamely.

"I don't care, Lizzie. I don't care what you say. If Dat loved Mam with all his heart he would not make her move to a place she does not want to go. I pity her so much I can hardly stand to even look at her poor face. Her hair is so gray, Lizzie. She coughs all the time."

Mam's hair was turning completely gray so rapidly it almost scared Lizzie, especially since she so often looked pale and tired, too.

Lizzie rolled over to face Mandy. "Mam is not pitiful. She's stubborn."

"Lizzie!" Mandy was furious. She seized her pillow and flung it at Lizzie.

"You don't know one tiny bit, Lizzie Glick!" she yelled. "You were always Dat's pet. You can read German better, drive ponies better, and you even stole nails out of the nailer and he never blinked. So why wouldn't you pity Dat? Huh? *Huh?*"

Lizzie muffled her giggles in her pillow, but her shaking shoulders gave her away.

Mandy made a fist and got a few good raps on Lizzie's shoulders. "So there. You don't have to have such a righteous attitude about Mam. I pity her. You can just see how hard she's struggling to let Dat have his own way."

She plopped down on her side of the bed, turned her back to Lizzie, and mumbled a "Good-night." It didn't sound like a real "Good-night"; she just kind of swallowed the word till it sounded like "Gnat."

"Gnat!" Lizzie said loudly.

There was a sputter and Mandy burst out laughing. She snorted and laughed, rolling off the bed, hitting the floor with a whump, all the while whooping and laughing. It was so infectious, Lizzie stuck her head in her pillow and laughed along with her.

"Be quiet!" Emma called from her room.

"What is going on?" came Mam's anxious voice from the bottom of the stairs.

"M-M-Mandy fell out of bed," Lizzie gasped.

"Gnat, Mam!" Mandy called, which reduced them both to helpless waves of mirth.

Mam had flown up the steps to see what was going on. She shook her head and then leaned down and blew out the kerosene lamp that sat on the table next to the girls' bed.

"Sleep tight," she said as she closed the bedroom door.

Soon Mandy's breathing became regular and even, accompanied by soft little snores. But Lizzie lay awake, a thousand thoughts and fears swirling through her mind.

She wondered what God thought about all this. She also wondered if he cared. Surely Dat had prayed for direction. She wondered if Dat and Mam had asked God for exactly opposite things. How could he answer each of them fairly?

Lizzie rolled over and rearranged the blankets. Mam had said there were hardly any young people in Cameron County. What would that mean for Emma and her, so close to 16 but with no one to date? Besides, she had heard that the bishop in Cameron County was strict, so she would probably never have high heels or anything fancy at all, so what did boys matter anyway?

And of course there was the farm, too. What if Mam was right and Dat wasn't a farmer? Then they'd live in Cameron County with no money. She had absolutely no clue what the farm looked like. Dat didn't even know. Why wouldn't Mam go with him to say if she thought it was alright to live there? What if it was so old and tumbledown, it wasn't even fit to live in? What if they had no money to fix it up? Mam would stay angry and grouchy for the rest of her life. It was all too troubling to think about.

Money had been an off-and-on touchy subject for the Glick family ever since Lizzie was a little girl. Even now, Lizzie got sad whenever she thought about Teeny and Tiny, their beautiful miniature ponies. She had been only eight when Dat had sat down at the breakfast table one morning. She knew something was wrong.

"I guess I may as well tell you now, girls," he said.

"What?" Emma asked. She had looked up and smiled.

But Lizzie's heart had sunk way down with a sickening thud. She knew. She knew exactly what Dat was going to say, because she had overheard Mam trying to persuade him to part with Teeny and Tiny, along with the glossy black spring wagon with the golden pinstripes along the side.

"We are going to have to sell Teeny and Tiny," he said.

"Why?" Emma asked, stopping halfway with a bite of potato soup.

"Because we really need the money, and because it costs too much to feed three ponies. Mam thinks it would be best. I do, too, of course, but I wish we could keep them, I really do," he finished.

Lizzie was heartbroken. It was just unthinkable, selling their miniature ponies. They were pint-sized little animals, a perfectly matched team of copper-colored ponies with blond manes and tails that Dat had made a little wagon for. The girls just loved when Dat hitched them to this wagon, and they went clipping down the road with their heads held high.

"When do we have to sell Teeny and Tiny?" Lizzie had asked so she wouldn't cry.

"I've decided we'll sell them soon at Harrison's Horse Auction in Taylorsburg."

Dat had spent several nights teaching Lizzie and Emma to drive the ponies. Lizzie loved the way the two creatures stepped together as if they were one animal instead of two. Their coats had glistened in the evening sun, and their blond manes and tails streamed behind them as their little black hooves pattered.

Lizzie was thrilled to sit on that seat in the little black spring wagon, up so much higher than the ponies, and feel the power of their sturdy little bodies. Driving ponies made Lizzie so happy that she smiled to herself without even realizing it. Dat said he loved it, too, which made her even happier.

The neighbors stopped their work and waved at Dat, calling out to him or shaking their heads in wonder at the size of those miniature ponies, Lizzie remembered. She had tilted her head back to see Dat's face, and he was smiling and waving. He was so proud of this matched pair of ponies and the little spring wagon he had made all by himself.

As they pulled into the gravel driveway, Lizzie said to Dat, "We should get lots and lots of money for these ponies and never be poor again, ever— right?"

"Yes, Lizzie, you're right," Dat agreed.

But Lizzie wondered how Dat could have been laughing so much one minute and sound quite so sad the next. She thought he was probably as sad as she was to be back home so soon after that ride.

❧

Lizzie jerked awake and rolled over. Her throat was dry and her tongue was parched. She needed a drink of water. Shivering, she slid out of bed. She still did not like to go roaming about the house at night after hearing of that creature in Alaska they called Bigfoot. He was as tall as a second-story window, with shaggy hair, and no one had proved yet that he did not exist.

Mam told Lizzie over and over that this was all untrue. God did not make big horrible creatures like that. Lizzie had put Bigfoot to the back of her mind, but she still pulled her blinds the entire way to the windowsill every evening before she went to sleep. She told herself it wasn't because she was afraid or anything; she just felt safer that way.

Lizzie stepped out of her room, half asleep, feeling tired and groggy. Suddenly she stopped and her eyes flew open. Directly in front of her was a huge, shaggy shadow. Its hair stuck out wildly, and the shape of its grotesque head advanced slowly on the wall ahead of her.

Lizzie grasped the door frame, her eyes opening wide with pure terror. Her breath came in ragged gasps as she watched the shadowy creature on the wall. Just when Lizzie could take no more without screaming, cold with fear and her hands pressed tightly to her mouth, a very small voice said, "What are you doing?"

It was her little brother, Jason, stumbling out of his room, his riot of brown curls sticking up every which way. As he passed the kerosene lamp on the hall dresser, his woolly head had been illuminated on the opposite wall, blowing it way out of proportion until his headful of curls had taken on the appearance of a huge creature.

"Jason!" Lizzie gasped. Her knees were shaking so badly, she dropped down to the floor.

"What's wrong with you?" he asked innocently.

"You just scared me, that's all." She couldn't tell him that his woolly head resembled an imaginary Bigfoot. He was self-conscious enough about his thick head of hair without her telling him what it had appeared to be.

"I'm thirsty," he said.

"Me, too. Come with me."

After they each had a cold drink from the gas-powered refrigerator, they made their way carefully back up the stairs. At the top, Lizzie turned to watch Jason walk down the hall to his room, grimacing again when the same shaggy head appeared on the wall as he passed the kerosene lamp.

Still, weak with relief, she turned into her room and quietly got into bed, not wanting to wake Mandy. Maybe that's how it was with her worrying. Everything looked so big and so terribly frightening, but if you refused to let it grow in your mind, it wasn't half as scary as it seemed. A dog barked in the distance, and a chill crept up her spine. She flopped onto her back, seeing again the expression on Dat's face years earlier when she had begged him not to sell Teeny and Tiny.

❧

"Do we…I mean…do we have to, really have to sell Teeny and Tiny?" she had asked, raising her eyes in misery.

"Ach, Lizzie." Dat's face softened, and for a minute Lizzie knew Dat felt exactly the same way she did. Emma stopped brushing Tiny, resting her hand on his back to listen. Dat didn't say more, and Lizzie waited expectantly, brushing back Teeny's forelock. His hair was so soft and blond, and…

"We have to, Lizzie. We need the money, and that's all there is to it," Dat said gruffly.

"Oh," said Lizzie, knowing deep down that Dat was only saying what she knew all along.

When Lizzie drove Teeny and Tiny into the ring, with Emma riding beside her, the crowd had gone wild. People stood up in their seats, clapping and cheering, smiling and waving their hats. The auctioneer could barely be heard above the thunderous applause. He laughed, put his microphone down, and waved his white cowboy hat. Emma and Lizzie had looked at each other and laughed.

Around they went, back to where Dat was standing, shaking his head and laughing, although Lizzie thought he looked as if he could cry at the same time.

"Keep going, Lizzie!" he yelled.

The auctioneer had opened the sale of the ponies at $500. He had to lower it to $300, and Lizzie dared hope that maybe, after all, Dat could not get a good price for them and they would be taken back home. Then the bidding escalated so fast and at such a confusing rate, with the auctioneer talking so fast that his words were a blur. Lizzie just kept driving the ponies steadily, eventually stopping them in front of the auctioneer's stand.

Lizzie remembered hearing the amount of the bid. "Emma!" she whispered. "One thousand dollars!"

"That's a lot, isn't it?" Emma smiled at Lizzie, wringing her hands nervously in her lap.

Dat ran over to hold the ponies' heads, patting their necks as he spoke to them.

"Eleven hundred dollars!" yelled the auctioneer. "Do I hear $1125?" A pause and a resounding, "Sold!" with a whack of his gavel, and the ponies were officially sold to buyer number 520.

Dat looked at the girls, a broad smile on his face and tears in his eyes. Lizzie and Emma smiled back, but Lizzie's smile felt funny, as if it could slide downhill and pull tears along with it, like ice cream melting off a cone.

"Come, girls," Dat said firmly, and they walked away, Dat in the middle with Emma and Lizzie on either side looking straight ahead. None of them had looked back at their ponies — not once. There was simply no use.

Lizzie pulled the covers up and sighed. She had done what she could to help their family have enough money then. And things weren't as tough now as they were once. She would do what she could now to make the move to Cameron County as smooth as possible.

Chapter 2

Lizzie hurried into the kitchen, clutching two pieces of wood that she had collected from the back porch. She lifted the metal handle from its hook on the wall behind the kitchen range and opened the round black lid so she could feed the wood into the fire. But the fire was hot and she couldn't quite arrange the wood so that it would fall in the way it was supposed to. She pulled back as smoke burned her eyes.

"Shut that lid!" Mam said loudly.

"I can't get the wood in right," Lizzie answered.

"Here." Emma came quickly to her rescue. Lizzie stepped back as Emma removed another section of the cast-iron top, and the wood fell to the grate. She quickly replaced the top and turned to wipe her hands on her apron.

Lizzie rubbed the smoke from her eyes. What is ever going to become of us? Lizzie wondered. She dreaded the future, so afraid Mam and Dat would never be the same. Mam had never gotten this upset when they had moved in the past.

Suddenly, Emma squared her shoulders and turned to face Mam, looking directly into her eyes. "Mam, there's not one thing that is going to keep us from moving. I wish you wouldn't be so dead set against it. You're just making it hard for all of us."

Lizzie was shocked to see Mam burst into tears. She lowered her head, bringing her hands to her face and turning away. Emma watched without expression before looking at Lizzie and raising her eyebrows. Lizzie could hardly bear what was happening. She let her eyes drift out the window at the dreary landscape, the dry grass, the pallet shop, and the overcast skies.

After a moment, Mam took off her glasses and wiped her eyes with the corner of her apron. She breathed a trembling sigh, replaced her glasses, and said, "I'm sorry, Emma. I really am. I know I'm acting like an absolute baby. I have to get a hold of myself and stop this bitterness. But we have it so nice here..." Her voice trailed off.

"Mam, I know. I don't want to move either. But we have no choice. We have to be strong and look forward now," Emma said.

Mam sighed. "I've always been able to give up before this and never minded moving so much. But this time, I don't know why, but it's different. My whole being resists this move. I have never *not* wanted to do anything so badly."

Lizzie sat down on the bench opposite Mam.

She put her hands on her knees, leaned forward, her eyebrows raised hopefully. "But think, Mam, it might not be so bad. Didn't you say we can wear a different kind of apron? A bib apron? Do you know how to make them? We could see if we have material, and you could make some for us."

Mam looked at Lizzie, a blank expression in her eyes. "Not today."

That was all she said, but Lizzie knew it would take Mam a while to accept this move. The weight of Mam's struggle would fall mostly on Emma's responsible shoulders since she was older and closer to Mam. Lizzie and Mandy would try to make everything seem normal by acting as if nothing had happened.

The next day, Lizzie and her family piled into the van Dat hired to take them to Cameron County and the farm that Dat and Doddy Glick were buying. The road into Cameron County didn't seem very big, at least not like the four-lane highways Lizzie was used to. She leaned against the cold window of the van Dat had hired to take them to the new farm as they crossed the bridge at Port James. The road wound through the countryside, past mountains, through wooded areas, and along tumbling streams. They passed through a few small towns, but there were no cities or shopping centers—nothing big or exciting.

"Look, girls, there it is," Dat said.

He leaned forward and pointed out the window as the driver slowed the van. Lizzie moved up in her seat so she could see where Dat was pointing. All of a sudden, there it was. The farm. Lizzie's heart sank. She did not dare look at Mam's face, or Dat's, or anyone's. It was so awful.

The barn appeared first on the left, towering over them like a dark, scary thing. There was not a drop of paint on its black weatherbeaten boards. A row of cracked, dirty windows stood along its front.

"That's the cow stable," Dat said.

Lizzie couldn't understand his excitement. A rickety barbed-wire fence made a barnyard of sorts, with sagging locust posts and rusty, broken wire. The barnyard was a quagmire of trampled black mud, with broken concrete blocks, pieces of brick, and old boards scattered through the oozing sludge.

The drive turned up a small slope, and the house was on the right behind a large oak tree. The house itself was brick, with a smaller mismatched brick addition that someone had tacked on as an after-thought. A wide porch ran along the small brick addition, with three or four steps going up to it.

The thing that shocked Lizzie most was the length of the grass in the yard. It looked like a hayfield, but there was no way you could have cut it, there was so much junk in the yard. The porch was filled with old stoves, chairs, boxes, barrels, chicken crates — just about anything you could imagine.

There were a few outbuildings, with broken

weeds left over from the summer alongside them, hanging their heads like tired, sleepy sentries.

Despair washed over Lizzie, enveloping her in a thick cloud. Emma's face was white, and Mandy whispered, "Wow!"

"Here we are!" Dat sang out.

"Melvin," Mam said weakly.

"Now, Annie, I told you it looks bad. It's just their junk, that's all. By the time we get everything cleaned up and painted, this can be a lovely home. I tried to tell you," he pleaded.

"But...but...Melvin, nothing could prepare me for *this*!" Mam gasped.

"Mam, now..." Emma said quietly.

Mam's mouth was pressed into a thin, hard line, and Dat's gaze never left her face as she climbed down from her seat in the van. It was heartbreaking to see how much he wanted Mam to like this farm. But it was so hopeless-looking that Lizzie pitied Mam with all her heart.

Mam stood uncertainly beside the van, her fingers working the straight pin in the front of her dress. She looked as if she could burst into tears any minute but was trying hard to put on a brave front. Dat talked to a small man in at the house for a while before motioning them all to come up on the porch.

The first thing that struck Lizzie was the bare light bulb hanging from the ceiling. It looked so stark and so ugly it reminded her of a prison. The interior of the house looked no better than the porch or the yard with dishes, clothes, boxes, shoes, and toys strewn everywhere.

The living room was an unbelievable mess. Once, when Dat had started the harness shop and things were slow, Mam had spent as much time helping him as she had working in the house. Emma had done her best to keep things clean, but sometimes things got away from her. But things at their house had never been as dirty and disheveled as this. The only thing Lizzie could really see was the television set in the corner. The sofas were sagging with pillows and afghans and two cats, a gray one and a yellow one that was so big he reminded Lizzie of a bobcat. Books teetered on the wide arm of an old brown sofa, with tablets and pencils scattered beside them. Lizzie guessed it must be someone's homework.

Two long, narrow windows looked out over the fields to the south. The walls were papered, or had been at one time. The paper was peeling off in layers but was still intact on some of the walls. Curtains sagged at the windows, which were so dirty Lizzie could barely see the fields beyond.

Lizzie glanced at Mam to see if there was a spark of interest in her eyes. She was talking with the heavyset woman, who still had not introduced herself. Lizzie couldn't tell how Mam felt, so she soon forgot about watching her as they finished their tour of the house.

When they had seen all the rooms, Lizzie and Mandy headed outside and toward the road, looking for bright sun and fresh air. They spotted Dat and Edwin, the small man, coming out of the cow stable. Dat looked happy, talking animatedly and pointing to the distant slopes. The two men walked along the fields to survey the property lines. Mandy and Lizzie turned back toward Mam in the house, hoping that they would soon leave.

Mam was talking to Edwin's wife, trying to keep the twins out of mischief and looking very tired and impatient.

"Where's Dat?" she asked as the girls entered.

Mam sighed when the girls told her he was walking along the property line with Edwin.

"Should we tell him you're ready to go?" Lizzie asked helpfully.

"No."

The girls sat on the porch, mostly because they didn't know what else to do. They both felt awkward because Mam was so impatient and Dat wouldn't be back for a while, Lizzie knew. So they sat side by side on the steps, their chins in their hands, looking out over the muddy pasture that went down to the creek.

Mandy sighed. So did Lizzie. They said nothing for a very long time.

"Mam said we're allowed to wear sweaters here."

"So?"

"Which would be better? Living in a nice house with our cousins and friends in Jefferson County, or living in this...this...ugly place and wearing sweaters?"

"I don't know. Be quiet. That's dumb."

"You're grouchy now."

"Well, you don't have to say things like that."

They sat in silence as the birds twittered high in the old oak tree.

"We have to slap water on our hair and roll it if we live here," Lizzie offered.

"I'm not going to."

"You have to."

"I don't know how."

"You'll learn."

"From who?"

"Mam."

Lizzie felt mixed up. A part of her wanted to live here, to try new and strange things, but another part of her clung to Jefferson County. She felt as if everything secure was being taken away from her, and there was nothing to do but let it go.

Chapter 3

A FEW WEEKS LATER, DAT SOLD THEIR HOUSE and the pallet business to Uncle Eli. Dat couldn't wait to move to Cameron County. He loved change, and this was a brand new challenge, probably one of the greatest ones he ever faced.

Mam did her best to hide her misgivings. She spent lots of time at the sewing machine, making dresses and bib aprons, so different from what they wore now, for the girls. Emma giggled as Lizzie tried to put one on but got stuck. She held the strange apron in front of her, trying to figure out how she could ever get it over her shoulders.

"Here," Mam said, throwing it over Lizzie's head and settling it around her neck.

"Now, stick your arms through here," she instructed.

Lizzie held her arms up, and suddenly the whole apron slid into place. She reached back to tie the strings as she hurried into the bedroom, excited to see herself in the dresser mirror.

"Lizzie's hardly fat at all anymore," Emma whispered to Mam.

Lizzie heard her and smiled as she turned this way and that, swiveling her head to see the back, and adjusting the front, smoothing it down over her stomach. Lizzie hated dieting. Every morning she would get up and vow silently to herself that today was the day she would start her diet.

Mam had even bought diet soda for her to drink, mostly to be encouraging without being rude. But the diet soda wasn't very tasty all by itself. The only way Lizzie could really appreciate her diet soda was with a big, thick sandwich made of ham, cheese, lettuce, tomato, and lots of mayonnaise. And a handful of potato chips, too.

Maybe Cameron County wasn't so bad after all, if the new aprons made her look slimmer. She studied herself in the mirror and sighed. Emma had dark hair and green eyes, with a round cherubic face which made her look a lot like Mam. Lizzie didn't resemble Mam and Emma at all, so she guessed she must look like Dat's side of the family. Her hair was straight and mousy brown, and her eyes were gray.

Since she had slimmed down some after becoming a teenager, her nostrils didn't seem quite as long and slanted anymore. She supposed that when you lost weight, the size of your nostrils diminished as well, which was a very interesting thing. She never read that in a magazine though, or heard of anyone else discovering this fact, but that's how it was for her.

And now, of all the nightmarish fears of Lizzie's 15 years, she was getting blemishes on her forehead. Ugly red pimples that popped if you squeezed them. When the pimples had first appeared, Mam was concerned, peering closely at Lizzie's forehead through her glasses, clucking worriedly as she did so.

"You shouldn't squeeze them," she would say.

Eventually Mam bought her a tube of Clearasil lotion the same color as her skin, and that helped the pimples dry up quickly. It was the single best thing anyone ever invented, Lizzie always thought, because it certainly did make a difference and it was almost like makeup.

Emma and Mandy hardly ever had one pimple, and if they did, it soon disappeared. But they were always careful of Lizzie's feelings, because they knew that Lizzie's skin troubles really weren't fair.

"Do you like it?" Mam asked from the doorway.

Lizzie smiled and glanced one more time into the mirror at her new apron. Now all Lizzie really needed to feel attractive was a nice pair of shoes with heels on them. She was not allowed to wear heels till she turned 16, but that was the one single goal of her life—to wear high-heeled shoes. She often told Emma she wanted some that would make a clacking noise when she walked. Emma said that was *grosfeelich*, or vain, and if that's why she wanted high-heeled shoes, she had better forget about it.

"I love the apron," she said. "It feels so comfortable."

"This style will be ideal for milking cows and carrying hay bales," Mam said.

That was closer to genuine happiness than Mam had come in a long time, Lizzie thought. She knew Mam was trying very hard to accept the move. Lizzie found that it made the future much less frightening if Mam at least tried to be a good sport about moving to the tumbledown old farm.

She turned to smile at Mam as she wriggled out of the apron, handing it back to her. "Now, when are you going to teach us how to roll our hair?" she asked since Mam was almost happy.

Mam narrowed her eyes, looking at Lizzie's profusion of loose waves. "Go wet your hair. The whole top of your head," she said.

"Sopping wet?" Lizzie asked.

"Well, wet."

Lizzie giggled and ran into the bathroom. It wasn't the wet hair that made her laugh as much as the fact that Mam was finally warming up a little bit. Kind of like an ice cube just beginning to melt. But she *was* melting, which made Lizzie's heart feel light.

She pulled the pins out of her covering and laid it on the counter. She took down her bob, or hair bun, running her fingers through her waves as they tumbled down her back. Her hair was getting to be so long and thick she could hardly make a decent bob on the back of her head. She used 10 straight hairpins and still she could hardly keep her hair up till the end of the day.

Quickly she held her hands under the water faucet, ducked her head, and patted the water onto it. The water felt cold as she wet her hair twice before going out to Mam.

"I need a fine-toothed comb," Mam said.

Lizzie returned to the bathroom, found a comb, and came back to sit on a chair. Mam combed through her wet hair, then stopped, and taking both hands, pulled back dreadfully hard.

"Ouch!" Lizzie winced.

Mam laughed, stepped back, and said, "You had better get used to this."

"But it hurts! Look at me. I have tears in my eyes."

"Alright. I'll be careful." Mam started rolling in the wet hair along the side of Lizzie's brow, smoothing it back with her hand as she rolled. She completed the other side before stepping back to see the finished result. Before she had a chance to say anything, Emma and Mandy started laughing hysterically.

"Li-i-i-zzie! You look so—!" Emma tried to say, but she was laughing too hard.

"Homely!" Mandy sputtered between giggles.

Lizzie got up and hurried to the bathroom to look in the mirror. She did look so ugly! Her forehead was twice as wide as it should be, making her eyes appear way too low on her face.

"I look…I look like a drowned rat!" she wailed.

Mam was hanging onto the back of the kitchen chair, she was laughing so hard. Emma and Mandy were sitting on the couch, their heads thrown back as they laughed with Mam.

Mam took a deep breath to answer but was overtaken with a fit of coughing. She leaned over the kitchen table, her hand covering her mouth as spasms racked her body. She clutched the table for several minutes until she could breathe normally again. Finally, she lifted her apron to retrieve the handkerchief in her dress pocket, gasped, and shook her head.

"My goodness, what a cough," she said.

"Mam, you should see a doctor," Emma said, gazing worriedly at her mother.

"I know, Emma," Mam said. "I'll see if the cough gets better this week. If it doesn't, I promise I'll go."

Lizzie shivered. She hoped Mam wouldn't wait too long.

Chapter 4

Mam and Dat had stopped arguing in front of Lizzie and her sisters.

Lizzie knew why.

One of the last evenings the family was in Jefferson County, Lizzie couldn't relax and fall asleep. She lay in bed, thinking once again about all they were leaving behind for Cameron County, when she heard Dat and Mam talking in the kitchen.

Mandy must have left the stairway door open because Lizzie could hear her parents more clearly than usual.

"I still don't want to move," Mam said. "But I won't argue with you anymore."

"Thank you, Annie," Dat said. "I know this has been hard."

"Not just for me," Mam said. "It's hard on Emma, too, knowing that she's moving some place new where there aren't many young people her age to run around with. But there's no point in making it harder for her by arguing, so I'm going to just let it go."

"What about Lizzie and Mandy?" Dat asked.

Lizzie lay very still, waiting to hear what Mam would say.

"They aren't turning 16 yet," Mam said. "Besides, they're like two colts full of life. They don't mind moving. It's exciting to them."

Lizzie rolled over so she couldn't hear anymore of their conversation. Mam had done it again. Emma, Emma, Emma. Poor Emma. Well, what about me? Lizzie thought resentfully. Maybe I mind it more than anyone else. I'm just scared to bring up the subject for fear it will make it harder for Mam.

Lizzie always wanted to be like Emma, but she couldn't seem to be, no matter how hard she tried to be good and sweet like Emma was. Emma loved to cook and bake and try new recipes, even copying a whole boxful of them before she had a boyfriend, which Lizzie couldn't imagine doing. Emma loved to sweep and dust, wash clothes, and sew. She had even started sewing their white organdy coverings, which was a skill in itself.

She had copied every song from the many hymn-books they had, writing them all down neatly in a composition book, so that when they felt like singing they used Emma's handwritten songbook. Emma had first started copying songs in a thick composition book in sixth grade, so now she had a collection of over 100 songs—hymns, school songs, and little funny songs—actually, anything she could learn or that Mam and Dat taught her.

Lizzie often started copying songs, but she never finished any of them. The thing was, it took too long. Her hand got awfully tired of writing, and she became so horribly bored that she felt numb all over, so she never had a songbook of her own.

It had always been like this, Lizzie thought. Even when they were little girls and Dat was under a lot of pressure to have their very first house "under roof," as he said, "before the snow flew."

Emma, Lizzie, and Mandy went off to school every morning, while Mam cared for the twins, who were babies then, and cooked meals for the men who helped Dat build the house. Emma was clearly under plenty of stress, too, coming home from school every day to a sink filled with dirty dishes, and the house strewn with toys, baby bottles, diapers, and loads of unfolded laundry on the kitchen table.

One evening, after Mam had spent the whole day cooking for a tableful of men, the house was such a mess that Emma burst into tears of frustration when she stepped in the door. She tossed her lunchbox on the table, ran into her bedroom, threw herself on her bed, and cried.

Lizzie had looked up from her after-school snack of cold leftover meat loaf with ketchup, chewing methodically.

"What's wrong with Emma?" she asked.

"Close your mouth when it's full of meat loaf, Lizzie. She's just upset because everything is such a big mess. It's no wonder. If you and Mandy would help more around the house, she wouldn't feel quite so responsible. All you do when you come home from school is eat and read the comics in the paper. You're lazy, Lizzie. You're actually getting quite overweight and you are *lazy*." Mam's face had been red with frustration and anger as her voice became louder.

The meat loaf that had been so delicious a moment earlier turned to sawdust and stuck in her throat. Lizzie was shocked. She felt hot all over, her face burning with humiliation.

"I don't mean to be rude, Lizzie. I know I'm losing my temper. But you need to shape up and help Emma and me more over this time. We're building a house and this house is for you, too, so your duty is to help along with everyone else."

Lizzie hadn't said one word. She couldn't. She supposed what Mam had told her was true. She was fat and lazy. The truth hurt so badly, Lizzie felt like crawling under her bed and never coming out again. She would stay under her bed until she died and turned into one big dust ball. They would never know what had happened to her.

That evening, when Emma set the alarm clock properly as she always did, climbed into bed, plumped her pillow, rolled over, and said, "G'night," Lizzie didn't answer. After a while, she said, "Emma."

"What?"

"Do you think I'm fat?"

"Ach, Lizzie, it's mean to say someone is fat. I'm not thin, either."

There was silence as Lizzie stared wide-eyed into the darkness. It was not a nice thought, but Mam wasn't very kind. How could she be so mean?

"Emma?"

"Hmm?"

"Mam likes you a lot better than me, doesn't she? I mean, she likes me as good as you can like a fat, lazy person, but she likes you a lot better. Not just because you're thin and you work harder, but she really, really, really likes you a whole pile more than me."

"Lizzie, now stop it. You know that's not true."

Lizzie sat straight up. "Emma, I know what's true and what isn't. Don't you try and tell me. Mam said I am overweight and lazy, so that's exactly what she thinks of me. And I don't care."

Lizzie plopped back down on her pillow, snorted, and then twisted and arranged herself in a comfortable position before she said, "G'night."

"Lizzie."

"What?"

"You can't go to sleep thinking that. Mam would never love one of her daughters more than another. It's just that you *could* help more since we have the twins. There is about three times as much work now as there was before they were born."

"See?"

"See what?"

"I tried to tell you. What do we want another baby for? And then she goes and has two."

"You think it's her fault? God gave us those babies."

At least Mam had decided to stop being upset about their move to Cameron County. Lizzie wished now that Mam could bring herself to care as much about her as she did about Emma. Dat did, but Mam still seemed to think first of Emma and her needs. Lizzie shifted in her bed, listening to the sound of Mandy sleeping. Maybe when they were little, Emma had been right about Mam loving all her girls the same. But that didn't mean she did now. Lizzie was going to have to do something about this whole dilemma in the morning.

Chapter 5

LIZZIE POUTED ALL THROUGH BREAKFAST, barely touching her food. When someone asked her a question, she shrugged her shoulders and looked at the cold, congealed egg on her plate.

"Alright, what's wrong?" Mam asked finally.

Lizzie blinked her eyes rapidly to hold back hot, angry tears of shame and resentment. She got up from the table. At the sink, she started throwing dirty dishes out of the way and slamming plates on the countertop as hard as she could. She would show Mam and Emma who could get work done around here. She held the bottle of dish detergent upside down and squeezed, producing mountains of white, frothy bubbles. The rinse water was foamy with soap when Mam came back to the kitchen to heat water for formula.

"Lizzie, how many times do I have to tell you? Don't use so much dish detergent!" she said.

Lizzie didn't answer. She turned away from Mam,

blindly looking for more utensils. Just go away, she thought. Go away and leave me alone.

"Lizzie?"

"Nothing." Lizzie kept her mouth clamped shut tightly. She refused to turn around and look at Mam.

Mam sighed and started to clear the food from the table.

CRASH!

Lizzie jumped as the milk bottle she was holding slipped through her soapy hands and landed on the floor. The whole glass gallon jar lay in a hundred pieces on the linoleum as milk streamed in every direction.

"Lizzie! You did that on purpose!" Mam shouted.

"I did not!" Lizzie yelled back. She grabbed a roll of paper towels and dropped to her knees, swabbing at the flow of milk.

"Ouch!" she yelped, as a large chunk of glass embedded itself in the palm of her hand. She sat back on her heels as blood spurted from the wound.

Emma knelt down beside her and calmly wiped up the milk with an oversized towel from the bathroom, absorbing most of it. Mandy gingerly picked up pieces of the glass jar with her thumb and forefinger. Mam bent over Lizzie, her face red, scolding and fussing anxiously. Jason sat on the bench at the table, his curly hair sticking out every which way and said calmly, "This is about a mess."

Lizzie sat with her back against the cabinets,

holding her bleeding hand while Emma filled a bucket with warm, soapy water and finished mopping up the milk. Mam stood up and turned to Lizzie.

"Whatever in the world were you doing? Banging the pots and pans around because you were mad about something again, Lizzie? Well, you just let me tell you something."

She paused and took a deep breath.

"Emma, go get the gauze and tape. Union salve, too."

While Emma hurried to the bathroom, Mam pressed the paper towel down hard until Lizzie winced.

"Ow. Watch it!" she said.

"Oh, sorry. As I was saying, you can just straighten yourself up right this minute, Lizzie Glick."

"I heard you and Dat talking about Emma last evening," Lizzie snapped, pulling her hand away.

Mam grabbed her hand again.

"Well, you're going to have to learn to stop being so selfish. All you ever think about is yourself, and whether or not I like you as much as I like Emma. Now listen to me."

Mam took off the paper towel, releasing the pressure on the wound, and only a small swell of blood seeped out of the cut. She cut off a piece of white sterile gauze and laid it aside.

"As long as you are planning to go through life thinking only of yourself, you're going to have an awfully hard time. I've often told you girls, Jesus

first, others next, and yourself last spells J-O-Y," she
said.

Lizzie shrugged. Emma and Mandy stood in the
doorway listening.

"You know, too, Lizzie, that I've had an awful
time giving myself up to moving to Cameron
County. It's a struggle to think of Jesus first. But if
it's his will that we move—which I hope it is—and if
I don't want to give in to that, then I most definitely
am not putting God's will first. And Dat..." Her
voice trailed off.

Lizzie watched the emotion on Mam's face. She
wanted to be truly submissive, Lizzie knew, but it
was very hard.

"You think it's stupid, don't you," Lizzie asked.

"What?"

"Farming."

Mam held Lizzie's hand tightly as she applied the
dark brown pungent salve before laying the gauze
carefully on top of the wound.

"I shouldn't say this, Lizzie. Especially not to
you. But, yes, it's stupid. Financially, for sure. I don't
know about spiritually. Maybe it will be good for all
of us to do without money again." She tore off a
few lengths of adhesive tape, wrapped them around
Lizzie's hand, and stood up.

"There. No more washing dishes for you." She
bent down, her face level with Lizzie's. "And quit
your pouting."

Lizzie looked squarely into Mam's face before
she said, "I will, if you quit treating Mandy and me

like we're two years old. Mam, I am 15, not four. And I have feelings, too, you know."

Mam laid a hand on Lizzie's shoulder, softly rubbing it back and forth. "Ach, yes, Lizzie, I know. You're just so very, very different from Emma that it seems as if you're younger than you are."

Lizzie swallowed the lump in her throat. She could never understand why she felt like crying when Mam was kind.

But that was often how it was. Maybe when anger dissolved, it brought a lump to her throat and tears to her eyes. Probably.

Chapter 6

WHEN MOVING DAY ARRIVED, LIZZIE WAS glad to see the moving truck pull in. She just wanted to put the worst part behind her, get to the new farm, and begin living her new life in Cameron County.

The sun shone with a golden light on the new spring leaves as they wound their way along the twisting mountain road, following closely behind the loaded moving truck in a van Dat had rented for the day. It was a lovely time of year to move, with a fresh spring breeze making everything seem soft and new. Lizzie supposed the four seasons would be the same in their new home, which was somewhat comforting.

When the van turned down the farm's steep drive, the front door of the house opened and Lizzie's Glick aunts and uncles filled the yard, ready to help unload their belongings and carry them into the house. The yard looked so much better without all the pieces of junk strewn about, Lizzie thought.

Inside the house, the girls ran excitedly from room to room. The place didn't seem nearly as hopeless as it had on their previous visit. Mammy Glick and two of Lizzie's aunts, all of whom lived right there in Cameron County, had emptied the house as soon as the English family had moved out. The tall, old kitchen windows shone, the glass sparkling in the spring sunshine. Even the grayish white tile of the kitchen floor was waxed to a glossy shine.

While most of the family helped unload the van, Dat and his two brothers worked in the kitchen, connecting the gas stove and refrigerator to the propane tank that sat outside the kitchen wall. When they were finished, Lizzie turned the burner handles, one by one, and watched as an even blue flame burst forth. Next she opened the refrigerator door and stuck her head in, enjoying the cold air that brushed her cheeks. Now they could have ice cubes again and ice cream whenever they wanted.

Mam came into the kitchen, carrying a box.

"There is so much to be done," Lizzie said.

Mam nodded. "We could paint for a year and still find something to paint. But that will have to wait till we're settled and everything is put in order," she said.

Lizzie knew that Mam was right. The walls looked dirty, even after Mammy Glick had scrubbed them clean. But at least they had nice things in this new house.

That hadn't always been the case, especially when Mam and Dat had first started the pallet shop. Then, it seemed, they were so poor that all they had to eat was lumpy potato soup.

"What's wrong with Mam and Dat?" Emma had asked one evening back then as she scraped Lizzie's uneaten soup into her own bowl and added the crusts of leftover bread.

"I think we're very, very poor," Lizzie had said as she gathered a handful of silverware from the table and carried it to the sink.

"Why are we so poor?" Emma asked. "I mean, Dat and Mam are always busy in the shop. Dat makes lots of pallets, and the little bell above the door rings an awful lot lately."

"I know," Lizzie said. "But they argue all the time."

"No, they don't, Lizzie. Mam and Dat really like each other, and they don't argue all the time," Emma said.

"I don't care what you say, Emma. I heard them."

"When?"

"One time."

"Lizzie, you stretch stuff. Everything isn't nearly as bad as you make it sound."

"Well," Lizzie sighed, grabbing a washcloth and wiping the plastic tablecloth furiously. There were little rips and holes in the cheap fabric, and Lizzie caught her washcloth in one. "See, if we weren't so poor, we wouldn't have this pitiful-looking, old, torn tablecloth on our table."

"Lizzie, you should be ashamed of yourself. Lots of Amish families have torn plastic tablecloths on their tables. When I get married, I'm not going to go buy a new tablecloth just because it has a hole in it. Everybody has holes in their tablecloths," Emma said.

Lizzie drew herself up to her full height.

"Emma, I don't care what you say. Anyone that has a torn plastic tablecloth on their table is poor. If they weren't, they'd buy a new one. When I'm married, I am not going to keep mine that long. It looks sloppy and makes you look like you're poor, anyhow," she said.

Emma added dish detergent to the hot water in the sink. "Well, I pity Mam."

"Why?"

"I don't know. I just do."

"I pity Dat," responded Lizzie.

"I pity Mam most, because she's always working in the shop and it's just a fright how sloppy this house looks," Emma had said.

Lizzie shook her head, remembering Emma's words and the terror in her own heart. Well, at least they weren't poor anymore. Not yet, at least. She turned to help Mam finish putting the pans away.

"Do you like it here now, Mam? I mean, better than you did that first time we saw the place?"

Mam turned and gazed across the kitchen. "Yes,

Lizzie, I do," she said quietly. But Lizzie heard a sigh in her voice, a kind of hollow undertone that wouldn't quite go away.

"But you're worried about Emma, right?"

"Well…yes, I am. I mean, turning 16 years old is hard enough in a settled community like Jefferson County. But here…I don't know."

"She'll be 16 in six days."

"I know."

"Are we having a birthday party?"

"Who would we invite? There are no young people here." There was an edge of bitterness to Mam's voice.

Lizzie pushed the last pot into the cupboard and then quickly closed the door so it wouldn't fall out.

"Who will Emma marry if there aren't other Amish youth in this area," she asked.

"I don't know. Two new families are moving into the area from a neighboring community, but they have only a girl about Emma's age," Mam said.

"That's nice!" Lizzie said, even though she knew Mam didn't think that was enough to be happy about.

"Yes." Mam opened a new box and started to unpack silverware, placing it into a drawer next to the sink.

"Mam, how does God's will work if there are no boys to marry, anyway? How will poor Emma ever get married? I mean, this is getting serious. She's soon 16, and in a year I'll be, too. What are we going to do?"

Mam put down a handful of forks so she could look at Lizzie. She was clearly trying to muster her own conviction about this subject.

"Lizzie, if you would only read your Bible more and try to be more mature about your faith, you would not be so troubled. If you pray honestly, God will direct you to the right husband. Even if right now you can't figure out how that's possible."

Lizzie nodded, but she couldn't help but wonder how God would direct her if there weren't any boys nearby. Before she could ask Mam more about God's will and future husbands, Mommy Glick called them to dinner. Lizzie followed Mam into the dining room where the table was covered with food.

Mommy Glick had made chicken potpie with large chunks of potatoes swimming in thick chicken gravy. Chunks of white chicken meat were mixed with the potpie squares and sprinkled with bright green parsley. Mommy Glick made her own noodles, too. She mixed egg yolks with flour, and the potpie turned out thick and yellow and chewy. It was the best thing ever to eat with creamy chicken gravy.

Lizzie also admired the baked beans that had been baking most of the forenoon and now were rich with tomato sauce and bacon. Bits of onion floated among the beans, and steam wafted from the granite roaster. Applesauce, dark green sweet pickles, and red beet eggs completed the meal.

Lizzie was so hungry she forgot all about her diet for the day. When they finished eating the main part of the meal, Lizzie and Mandy helped themselves to pieces of shoofly pie and sat on the steps of the porch together. They each bit off the very tips of their pieces.

"No one else in the whole world can make shoofly pies like Mommy Glick," Lizzie said.

Mandy nodded, her mouth full as she ate her way through the whole delicious piece.

"Do you think we'll ever feel at home here?" Mandy asked, finally.

"Probably."

"It's going to take a while."

"I know."

"We can't hear any traffic or see any lights. We don't even have neighbors."

Lizzie pointed toward a white house in the woods down by the creek. "There are people," she said.

"Who are they?"

"Old people, Dat said."

"How does he know?"

"I have no idea."

They sat in silence, the breeze stirring the leaves of the walnut tree beside the sidewalk.

"We can make a nice farm out of this junky place," Lizzie said, even though she wasn't sure that was true.

Mandy nodded.

Chapter 7

Mam came out to the enclosed back porch, her back bent as she coughed deeply, her handkerchief to her mouth. Mommy Glick and Emma followed close behind her.

"Emma, how long has she been coughing like that?" Mommy Glick asked, her brows drawn with concern.

"Most of the winter, it seems like," Emma said, her eyes filling with unexpected tears.

Mommy Glick turned to Dat. "Melvin, I think Annie needs to see a good doctor, and soon," she said.

"I've begged her to go," Dat replied.

"I don't like the sound of that cough," Mommy continued as she helped Mam into a chair.

Mam sat down slowly. One of the twins ran over and buried her face in her apron. Mam stroked her head absentmindedly as she cleared her throat repeatedly. Mommy Glick watched Mam, while

Emma hurried back into the house to get Mam a drink of water.

Lizzie and Mandy huddled together. "I wish Mam would stop coughing."

"She's going to end up in the hospital."

"She can't. We need Mam more than ever now."

Lizzie gazed across the field and the trees beyond that, where the creek ran wide and cold. She shivered. She hoped fervently that God would watch over them way back here on this winding country road in the middle of nowhere. She had never felt quite so alone, or quite as old as she did right this minute, sitting on the concrete porch steps.

About a week after they had settled in, Mam's cough became an alarming rasp. She held a Kleenex to her mouth as she bent over, painfully hacking from the persistent ache in her chest.

She had gone on as best she could, even as her strength sometimes failed her, Lizzie knew. But she worked more slowly every day.

One afternoon, Lizzie was outside pulling weeds around the little log cabin. She was tugging with all her strength on a very stubborn weed almost as tall as herself. She didn't notice Emma running down the sidewalk until she called for Dat in a tone of voice that made Lizzie stop yanking on the weed.

She watched as Dat emerged from the barn and listened to what Emma was saying. When he walked toward the house with her, Lizzie knew there must be something wrong. She wiped off her grimy hands on her apron and hurried up the slope to the house.

As she entered the kitchen, Dat pulled up a chair and sat close to Mam, a concerned look making his tired face seem soft and vulnerable. Mam was struggling to breathe and her complexion was almost blue in color.

"Annie, you should have done something a long time ago," Dat said. "You just go on and on and on, even if you feel so bad."

"Well, Melvin, I can't go on. I need to go to the hospital now. Every breath I take burns in my lungs, so I suppose I have a bad dose of pneumonia. I guess we'll see a doctor first, but who? Everything is so strange and new here."

Dat sat up resolutely.

"No, Annie, you won't go to the doctor. You're going straight to the emergency room in Falling Springs. There are no two ways about it."

"I'm just so sorry. It will cost thousands of dollars if I'm admitted," Mam said anxiously, searching Dat's eyes.

Dat smiled at her tenderly, covering her hand with his own. "What are thousands of dollars compared to losing you, Annie?"

Mam tried to smile at Dat, but her nostrils flared as they always did when she had to cry. Her face turned a darker shade as her tears came uncontrollably.

"Ach, now you made me cry," she said.

"I'll go call a doctor. You get yourself ready and we'll leave for Falling Springs."

Dat glanced anxiously at Emma. Lizzie knew she was the one who would keep everything else going. She would take full responsibility for the laundry, the cooking, and the cleaning. She was naturally a very capable girl for her 15 years, as she had always been, even as a child.

Lizzie met Dat's concerned look and smiled bravely, consoling him with her cheerful appearance.

"We'll be all right, Dat. Please don't worry about us," she said, although Lizzie could see that Emma's smile was a very good cover-up, hiding her own worries. Lizzie vowed to do all she could to be a good helper, working along with Emma, even taking on jobs she didn't want to do.

Chapter 8

Dat left to call a driver, and Mam went to take a bath, even if it was mid-afternoon. Mam was very particular about being clean when you went to see a doctor. Even when she took the twins for a checkup, she gave them a bath in the middle of the day.

Emma hurried anxiously after Mam. "Are you sure you should be taking a bath, Mam?" she asked.

"Why, Emma?"

"Suppose you pass out?"

"I won't. I'll be fine."

Mam always said that. Lizzie twisted her fingers nervously around the small hem of her bib apron. She could not bear to hear Mam coughing from the bathroom, so she hurried outside to the porch. Jason was sitting on the porch swing.

"Is she going to die in the hospital?" he asked, his voice quavering.

"No, Jason. She is just really, really sick. I'm sure the doctors can make her well."

"Are you sure?"

"Oh, yes." Lizzie said this with a lot more bravado than she felt inside. People died of pneumonia every day. That's how Mommy Miller had died. But she didn't say that to Jason. She just pushed the porch swing back and forth with her one foot.

The porch swing comforted Lizzie. It was the one thing that made her feel at home these first days of living on the farm. There was something very soothing about swinging back and forth on it in the clean spring air. Even if Lizzie was troubled, the porch swing always calmed her spirit.

Dat hurried up the sidewalk and into the house without even glancing at Lizzie. Emma called him, and Lizzie heard their low tones as they discussed something in the kitchen behind the screen door. Soon Dat reappeared, looking sternly at Lizzie.

"Where's Mandy?"

"I don't know."

"Well, Emma said she doesn't want to tattle or make you and Mandy angry at her, but you don't always listen to her when Mam and I are away, that you just run off to the creek or go drive Billy, or do anything you can to get away from doing jobs she asks you to do."

Lizzie watched her foot on the concrete floor of the porch, not sure what to say. She knew it was true. There was just something about Emma asking her to do a job that ruffled Lizzie's feathers. She wasn't as bossy as she used to be, but whenever Emma asked, Lizzie always felt like not doing the job Emma wanted done.

"Do you hear me?"

"Yes."

Lizzie wished her toes weren't so crooked. She had the ugliest feet she had ever seen on anyone. She decided then and there that she would never go barefoot except at home. Her toes were hideous.

A dull thump from the direction of the living room and a piercing scream made Lizzie leap to her feet, almost upsetting the porch swing. Dat sprang to the door of the kitchen as Emma screamed again. They yanked open the bathroom door to find Mam in a heap on the floor beside the counter. She had been pinning her apron when she fell. Pins were scattered all over the floor.

Dat cried out as he stooped to lift her, but he wasn't able to pick her up because she was so limp. Her face was so pale, Lizzie couldn't bear to look.

"Emma open the windows," Dat said.

He rolled Mam over.

"Lizzie, go get a pillow. Hurry up!"

Lizzie dashed to the bedroom, her heart racing. Poor Mam! Poor, sick Mam who just went on and on, feeling horrible all week. She grabbed a pillow off of her bed and ran back downstairs.

Dat lifted Mam's head and gently placed the pillow underneath it. Lizzie was terribly alarmed to see how Mam's head rolled around on her shoulders, just like a rag doll's. Dat stood up and held a clean washcloth under the cold water faucet. After he wrung it out, he knelt to bathe Mam's face.

Mam's head rolled to the side, and she moaned as her eyes fluttered open.

"Annie!" Dat touched her face. "Annie!"

Mam's eyes blinked, and she struggled to focus.

"Ach, my," she whispered weakly.

"Annie, you'll be all right. You fainted," Dat said tenderly, as he kept stroking her forehead with the cool washcloth.

"Ach, my," Mam said again.

Dat was just helping her to a sitting position when the kitchen door banged shut.

"Hey," Mandy yelled.

Lizzie hurried out. "Shh!"

"What?"

"Mam passed out on the bathroom floor!"

Mandy clapped a hand to her mouth, her big green eyes opening wide. Hay was stuck in her hair, her face was grimy with dust, and she had torn a big hole in the sleeve of her dark purple dress.

"What happened?"

"Mandy, she's terribly sick. She has to go to the hospital. Where were you?"

"In the haymow. Hey, I found a bunch of kittens. You know all those wild cats around here that have no tails? There's a whole nest full of kittens and *not one* has a tail!" Mandy was so excited, the veins in her neck stuck out like cords.

"Shh! Mandy, calm down! Mam's sick."

"I know. Are they...is she...how are they going

to the hospital?" Mandy asked as she made her way to the bathroom door.

Dat was helping Mam to her feet as Emma hovered nearby, picking up the pillow and comforting the twins who were crying.

Mam sank wearily onto the sofa, just as they heard the crunch of tires in the driveway.

"Your driver's here," Lizzie announced.

Dat helped Mam back to her feet while Emma hurried over with her black Sunday apron.

"Your apron, Mam."

Mam could not answer. Her mouth was pressed into a straight, thin line as she used all of her concentration to stay on her feet. Dat shook his head at Emma as they slowly made their way across the kitchen, through the door, and into the waiting car. This was the first time Lizzie ever saw Mam go away without her black apron, but she supposed it was all right to do since Mam was so sick.

As Mam and Dat got into the car, the twins started crying uncontrollably. Susan wailed steadily, and no one was able to console her. KatieAnn finally sat in her little chair with great sad eyes and sniffled, her teddy bear clutched to her chest.

Emma reached down and scooped up Susan, holding her close until her wails at last subsided.

"Poor little things, Emma," Lizzie said over the top of KatieAnn's dark head.

"I know," Emma agreed. "We just moved from the only home they've ever known, and now Mam leaves them like this."

"Let's rock them on the porch swing," Lizzie suggested.

They took both little girls and held them, gently rocking the old wooden porch swing in the warm spring sunshine. Jason sat on the steps, his curls lifting and falling as the breeze played with his hair. Mandy found a flashlight and ran across the yard to the barn, returning to her newly found nest of baby kittens.

Chapter 9

Emma started humming as she rocked back and forth on the swing. Here they were, way back in the sticks, or so it seemed to Lizzie, the twins crying, Mam sick, Dat on the way to hospital with her, everything frightening and unsure.

Lizzie felt as if her life was a jigsaw puzzle, all finished, each piece fitting perfectly into the next, until now when it seemed someone had suddenly come along and scattered the whole thing. Now nothing made any sense.

She thought of praying, but she didn't really know how to word her scattered thoughts and fears. Would Mam die? Could God be so mean? The thought was so unbearable that she got up from the porch swing and went into the kitchen, balancing KatieAnn on her hip.

Just as she was opening the refrigerator door, she heard the dull, muffled sound of a car engine. Quickly she closed the door of the refrigerator and watched as an old green pickup truck ground its gears to a stop beside the sidewalk. Her heart leaped in her chest as she saw a young man leaning out from the window, his thick, hairy arm bent in a V shape. Huge red, black, and blue tattoos covered most of his arm.

His hair hung straight down over his face. His eyes were half closed. Lizzie clutched KatieAnn so tightly that she began to squirm and push at Lizzie's arms.

"Sorry," Lizzie muttered, without thinking.

Another passenger turned the handle of the old truck and climbed down to stand beside it. Looking more closely, Lizzie saw that this second person was a woman, dressed in ragged jeans and an old, torn T-shirt. Her hair was swept up in a tight ponytail that bounced as she moved.

Finally, the driver opened his door and ambled around the front of the truck. He was very heavy, with holes in the stomach of his shirt, white skin showing through. His hair was just as long and dirty as his companions'.

Lizzie shivered with raw fear. She swallowed, thinking wildly of where she could run. The attic. That would be the best. They would never find her in the attic back under the eaves behind some cardboard boxes.

But what about Emma? Or Jason? She had to stay here. She couldn't leave Emma alone. She wished Emma was not out there on the porch swing. If only she was in the house, they could hide somewhere and those awful people would think there was no one home.

What should they do? Lizzie glanced wildly around the kitchen, still looking for a place to hide. But she couldn't leave Emma alone to talk to them. Who were they? What did they want?

Mustering all of her courage, she made herself walk to the screen door. Her legs felt like wooden stilts, she was so afraid. She was fairly gasping for breath because of the unnatural rhythm of her racing heart.

Without thinking, she prayed in silent little screams. Please, please. Help us, dear God. Help Emma to know what to do.

The dark-haired man stepped up on the sidewalk in front of Emma. Emma stopped the porch swing with both feet. She clutched Susan tightly on her lap, her face very white and as still as a stone. Jason sat beside her, not even a curl ruffling his stillness, his eyes big, round, and absolutely terrified.

"How you?"

Lizzie jumped as the man spoke to Emma in a raspy, deep-throated voice.

Emma's mouth opened, but no sound came from it. She cleared her throat and tried again to speak.

Lizzie pushed open the screen door and stepped out. She did not know if these people were dangerous; she just knew she could not trust them. First of all, they must never know their parents were not at home. The man's eyes were on her. The woman stepped up on the sidewalk beside the man and glanced at the twins that Emma and Lizzie were holding. For a moment, Lizzie thought she would smile, but she didn't. She only lowered her eyelids farther.

"How y' doing?" the man asked.

"I'm fine," Lizzie said, louder than she had wanted to.

"Y' Mom and Dad home?" he asked.

"Y-yes," Lizzie lied.

"Can I talk to 'em?" he asked, eyeing Lizzie suspiciously.

"No. My mom is too sick and my dad is with her. He can't come to the door right now," Lizzie said.

The dark-haired man glared at her, and Lizzie glared back.

"Y' think your dad would let us look for arrowheads along your bottom field, here close to the creek?" he asked, jerking his thumb in the direction of the line of trees bordering the creek.

"What do you mean?" Lizzie asked bluntly.

"These." He came forward, reaching into the pocket of his jeans for a few arrowheads. He held out his hand, showing her pieces of grayish brown stones in the shape of an honest-to-goodness arrowhead.

Lizzie bit down on her lip as she surveyed the stones from her spot on the porch.

She looked at the arrowheads, and then looked up at the man's face. His eyes were chocolate brown and not unfriendly now. She looked at the arrowheads again, and then up at him. What should she do? She glanced at Emma.

"Could...could you come back later this evening?" Emma asked.

The man smiled widely and Lizzie took a step forward.

"Your dad ain't home, huh? Your mom ain't, either," he stated.

Lizzie stepped back. She felt extremely foolish.

"That's okay. We're not going to hurt you. We live a couple miles from here. I own a machine shop in the nearest little town. Everybody knows me, Evan Harper, my wife, and brother-in-law.

"So you bought this farm from ol' Edwin. Don't look the same with his junk gone. We'll be back later when your dad's home. See ya."

He headed down the sidewalk toward his truck with the woman close behind him. The truck starting with an awful-sounding roar.

Lizzie sank onto the porch swing, letting out her breath in a long, slow whoosh. Emma looked over at Lizzie and said, "Oh, I mean it, I was never so scared in all my life!"

"It was awful," Lizzie agreed.

"You lied, Lizzie," Emma said.

"Not really a bad lie, Emma. I was only trying to protect both of us, Jason, and the twins. They looked so...so, well...just like you would imagine kidnappers or thieves might look."

"It was still a lie."

"Emma, now don't scold me. What if they were dangerous, and I would have let them know our parents weren't at home? I couldn't do that."

"He knew you lied."

"So? If he knows, he could wash his hair and cut it and stop acting so big and tough. Then I wouldn't have to lie, because I would trust him in the first place. It's his own fault, not mine."

"You better ask God to forgive you."

"I will."

Dat came home toward evening, leaving Mam at the hospital. As the girls crowded around him, he told them how sick Mam was, how they took X-rays of her chest and admitted her as soon as they could.

Dat said she was resting well, and they had already started medication and it would help her fight the pneumonia.

"The doctors said that Mam is very, very sick and it will take a few days to tell which medication works best," he said with tears in his eyes.

"Is...is she in pain?" Emma asked.

"No, not really. Only when she coughs. She seems relaxed, and all she wants to do is sleep. She told me to come home to you children. You know how she says, 'I'll be fine.'" Dat shook his head ruefully.

Then the girls told him about the old green pickup and its occupants, their fear, Lizzie's lie, and the arrowheads.

"Never let rough-looking men like that know you are alone," he said.

"But Lizzie lied."

"I know it isn't right to lie, but what else could

she have done? In a way, it was the right thing to have done, and yet..." Dat just didn't know.

Later that evening Dat sat all alone on the porch for a very long time. Lizzie wondered what he was thinking. The tree frogs' chorus from the creek was deafening as a half-moon appeared in the sky. Lizzie hoped Dat was a strong enough person to make it through the next few weeks without Mam. She hoped she was, too.

Chapter 10

Lizzie was very nervous, sick to her stomach with apprehension. Today was the first day of school in Cameron County. She didn't know what to expect. She wished Mam was here, but she was still recovering in the hospital.

Lizzie had completed eighth grade before they left Jefferson County, and so now she would attend vocational school just one morning a week until May. She needed to hand in her diary where she kept account of the homemaking jobs and farming chores she had done that week. And along with the other vocational "scholars," as the Amish called them, she would study arithmetic, spelling, and German, a few hours each week.

Earlier in the week, Dat had made arrangements for them to travel with an English van driver who also hauled two other Amish families' children to school. Because there weren't enough families in Cameron County to build an Amish school, the few

Amish children that lived in the area attended an Old Order Mennonite school. Lizzie didn't know one thing about these Mennonites. Dat said they drove horses and buggies, but they had some practices that were different from the Amish.

Lizzie tried to remain calm and serene as she wet down her hair and worked at combing it in the new Cameron-County way. After four or five attempts, she decided it was good enough, especially since there wasn't much time to try again. She smoothed her new dark purple dress, pinning her black apron and her covering into place. After one last glance in the mirror, she was ready to go.

"How do I look?" she asked as she stepped into the kitchen.

Emma was at the counter, kneading bread.

"You look fine," she said. "You're hair doesn't even look too bad."

Lizzie tried to smile, but she felt as nervous as Mandy looked. It was also Mandy and Jason's first day at school, and both of them were near tears over breakfast. Outside, Jason made up songs as he ran little circles in the driveway.

"I wish you were coming with us, Emma," Lizzie said.

Emma added some more flour to the bread and began to shape the dough into a loaf. She had finished her vocational class before they left Jefferson County and now worked at home full-time, like other Amish girls her age.

"You'll do fine," she said.

Lizzie nodded. She took a deep breath as a black pickup truck with a flat camper on the back popped over the hill and rolled to a stop at the end of their drive.

A white-haired, balding gentleman jumped out and helped them into the truck. Inside were two boys and two girls. The boys looked so much alike with their very blond hair and blue eyes that Lizzie thought she must be seeing double. They didn't say anything as they watched Lizzie climb into the back of the pickup as gracefully as she could.

"Hi," said the girl with the same blond hair and blue eyes as the twins. "My name is Sara Ruth. These are my brothers, Joe and John."

"I'm Lizzie," she said. "This is my sister, Mandy, and my brother, Jason."

Jason squirmed in his seat, while Mandy smiled.

"And this is my cousin, Sharon," Sara Ruth said.

"Hi," Sharon said quietly.

Sharon wore a navy dress that had little lines in it and lovely sleeves with pleats in the shoulders. Lizzie could hardly wait to ask Mam to make a similar dress for her. Sharon's hair was dark brown and very straight, rolled up neatly along the side of her face. Did her hair look that nice? Lizzie wondered.

The truck rolled to a stop outside of the brick schoolhouse and they all clambered out. Lizzie slipped her hand in Mandy's.

"I hope the Mennonites are half as nice as the Amish are," she whispered.

"Me, too," Mandy said quietly as they followed

Sara Ruth into the cloakroom. Pretty floral sunbonnets hung from hooks around the room, next to narrow-brimmed boys' hats made of black straw.

A large group of girls followed them into the classroom.

"Lizzie, this is Viola, her sister Irma, and Marlene," Sara Ruth said, pulling or pushing each girl forward. Some of the girls giggled and others shrugged as they tried to free themselves from Sara Ruth's grasp, but they all managed to say, "Hello."

Lizzie knew she met Lucy, Etta, and Jean, but she could not keep their names or their faces straight. She thought there were three sisters in the Zimmerman family and two in the Hoover family. One— no, two—with the last name of Martin had eyes as brown as she had ever seen. They had straight brown hair and skin tanned almost the same shade from their long days in the summer sun.

"So! These are the *new* girls!" the Mennonite teacher said, welcoming them in a rush of color and warmth as she came into the room.

"We heard for a while already that you were moving in," she said. "You're not from Lamont, where the rest of the Amish are from, right?"

"N-no, we're from Jefferson County," Lizzie said.

"Same kind of Amish? I mean, is there a difference?" the teacher inquired.

"Yes, there is," Lizzie said, uncertain about how to explain the distinctions between the two Amish groups.

"Really? That's interesting. Did you like it in...
did you say Jefferson County?"

"Oh, yes. We loved it. Well, I did. I...I...we had
lots of cousins and friends there."

"Well, hopefully, you'll find lots more friends
here. We're happy to have you in our school!"

Lizzie didn't know what to say. Mandy smiled
and said, "We're glad to be here."

Lizzie wasn't sure that was quite true. She didn't
know how she'd feel until she had spent the morning in vocational class.

"Time for the bell!" and the new teacher was off
in a whirl of tiny little flowers. "Oh, I didn't even tell
you my name! Esther!" she called over her shoulder
as she disappeared behind the tall white doors.

Esther reappeared promptly, clanging and banging an old hand-held bell. At the sound, boys of all
shapes and sizes charged past her into the school,
dust flying and gravel spitting as they ran. They
milled around the entry, hanging up straw hats,
clomping their feet, and talking loudly. But as soon
as they stepped into the classroom, they quieted
down until every noise faded away and there was
complete silence.

As Teacher Esther read the Bible, Lizzie chewed
her fingernails in her seat at the back of the room.
The Mennonites did dress differently. The boys
wore jeans and plaid shirts, or striped ones, and
their hair was cut short like English boys'. The only
thing that made them look like Mennonites was
their suspenders.

The Mennonite girls were so pretty. They combed their thick, wavy hair back and secured it with clasps, and then wove it into a heavy braid on each side of their heads. What really caught Lizzie's eye was that they were allowed to wear rubber hair bands with brightly colored baubles on the ends, and that they had barrettes in their hair. She would love to look so fancy.

Joe and John sat one row in front of her. The twins were decidedly good-looking. They were a bit small for their age, but they'd probably grow taller soon. Lizzie thought she would probably marry one of them and Mandy would marry the other. Of course, that left Emma out, but these boys were too young for her anyway.

Lizzie was relieved to know there were boys here in Cameron County whom she could marry. Of course, Mam said it was not up to them. They needed to pray every evening and ask God for his will, not their own. That was all very good and right, Lizzie was sure, but it was hard to know exactly what that meant. You couldn't help it if you thought some boys were nice-looking and others weren't.

The way Mam sometimes made it sound, all the handsome boys weren't good husbands—just the homely ones. It caused Lizzie to fall into a great state of sadness most times when Mam gave them that lecture.

"You don't go by looks," she would say, shaking her forefinger at them. "God has a special person for each one of you, so it's very important you don't go by his looks."

Well, Lizzie was too young to take this husband matter very seriously, but she certainly hoped one of these twins would be God's will, as Mam put it. She couldn't wait to talk to Mandy after school to ask her which twin she wanted.

Lizzie leaned back in her chair. Were lovely girls bad wives, too? she wondered as she studied the girl next to her. Viola was strikingly beautiful. She was beautifully tanned and had deep-brown, wavy hair with gold overtones, almost as if sunlight had reached in and dyed some of her hair, just not all of it. Her eyes were slanted and very dark, and she had white teeth that flashed when she laughed.

Marlene sat on the other side of Lizzie. She looked a lot like Viola, suntanned with such dark eyes, except her hair was straight and soft and pulled back into heavy braids that fell below her waist. Lizzie had never seen such pretty girls before. She shifted in her seat, suddenly aware of her skin and how much she weighed and how her dress was made. Why couldn't she be prettier? Each miserable thought settled on her like a huge, wet blanket until she could barely breathe.

Then Lizzie remembered what Aunt Vera had told her when she visited just after they moved to Cameron County. Aunt Vera walked like a duck. She was short and round, with solid little legs on solid little feet that rocked her from side to side when she moved. Her face was round, with big blue eyes and a small nose, and Lizzie had discovered, much to her joy, that Aunt Vera's nostrils looked exactly like her own.

"Aunt Vera!" she said gleefully.

"Now what?"

"Your nostrils look like mine!"

Vera had thrown back her head and laughed her raucous laugh. "Now, mind you, Mousie! You think my nostrils are ugly and you think I'm short and fat and I walk like a duck. You wait! When you're as old as me, you'll be shaped like me. Yessir, you will. Now mind, won't be long!"

How did she know what Lizzie had been thinking?

"No, no, Vera. I think you're just right. You wouldn't be Vera if you didn't walk like you do," Lizzie assured her.

Lizzie sat up straighter. She wouldn't be Lizzie if she didn't look like she did. She would have to "brace up" as Mam said. She tried to think of all her attributes. Brown hair rolled flat in this Cameron-County, slicked-down fashion that she would never get used to. Ordinary eyes, slanted nostrils, flat nose, and teeth that looked like a rabbit's. Her covering didn't fit right; her dress that had seemed so pretty this morning was just downright drab-looking now. She could not think of one good thing about herself.

Fortunately, the bell rang. The classroom quickly emptied outside into the school yard. Lizzie followed the others slowly, blinking as she stepped into the sun.

"Over here, Lizzie," Sara Ruth called. "We're picking teams for baseball."

Lizzie hurried over to the group. Joe and John were leaders of the two teams. They took turns choosing from the group of pupils, picking the big boys first. The first girl picked was Viola, who giggled and batted her eyelashes while John grinned at Joe, or Joe grinned at John. Lizzie had absolutely no idea which boy was which.

So... Viola must be a top ballplayer. Lizzie's heart beat faster as she thought about when she'd be chosen. She knew she could play ball every bit as well as some boys and better than most girls. That was one of the reasons why she got into so much trouble in Jefferson County. She was hot-headed and fiercely aggressive when it came to winning in baseball.

The twins were looking at her and Mandy, trying to decide if they should choose them before some of the smaller children, Lizzie realized. She felt her face heat up and quickly scuffed the toe of her shoe in the dust.

"Lizzie!" one of the twins said.

"Mandy!" the other one echoed.

Viola walked over to John or Joe and asked for his glove, holding her pretty head to one side. A tug of raw jealousy pulled at Lizzie. Oh, so Viola even shared gloves with them.

Her eyes narrowed as she set her chin resolutely. *I may not be as pretty as she is, but I'll show her a thing or two about playing baseball,* Lizzie thought.

When Lizzie's turn came to bat, she was so

nervous, she felt like fainting. She hoped no one could see her heart beating through the fabric of her dress. The blood pounded in her ears and her mouth was dry as sand. She licked her lips nervously, biting down hard on the lower one to steady herself.

The first pitch was too high, but she swung anyway, misguided by nervous energy, sending a foul ball just shy of third base. No one said anything. There were no groans or calls. A strange silence hovered over the ball field. Lizzie was one of the new girls, so everyone had to be nice.

Lizzie had never wanted anything quite as badly as a good solid hit to show all of them what a good ballplayer she was. But she was far too nervous. She knew she had to calm down and relax.

The second pitch she let pass on purpose, taking a few deep breaths to get her bearings. The third pitch came in fast and low. She swung with every bit of strength she could muster.

A solid THUMP! and Lizzie was off. The girls screamed and the boys yelled as loud as they could as she ran for first base. Somewhere out beside the road the boys scrambled in the tall grass, still looking for the ball as she rounded first base and streaked for second.

"Go! Go! Go to third!" Everyone sounded hoarse from yelling. Just as she reached third base, one of the twins caught the ball at the pitcher's mound, and she knew she had to stay. She was panting and her heart was swelling as the third baseman said, "Good hit for a girl!"

Lizzie tried to think of some witty answer, but nothing came. So she just smiled at the boy whose name she didn't even know.

Sharon was up to bat next and made a good solid hit, sending Lizzie to home plate. Her teammates crowded around, asking her if that was how she always hit. Lizzie told them demurely, no, not always. But she knew there was a good chance she probably would quite often.

By the end of the game, Mandy and Lizzie had both established themselves as good baseball players. Mandy was very quick, dashing fearlessly to catch grounders and tagging people out quite easily, amazing even the boys.

It was so exciting and so much fun to be a part of a serious baseball game that Lizzie felt like hopping and skipping the whole way home.

And when Viola told Lizzie that she and Mandy were good for the team, Lizzie forgot all about her jealousy. Touching Viola's sleeve she said, "You are, too. You were picked first."

After school, Lizzie and Mandy walked slowly up the lane towards their house. Lizzie swung her arms and smiled.

"I think I'm going to marry Joe or John," she said.

"Lizzie!" Mandy shrieked.

"I'm serious. They're so cute," Lizzie said happily.

"They would never want us. We're way too...I don't know how to say it, plain, or *fadutsed*, or whatever. We don't near know how to dress and do our hair like Sara Ruth and Sharon."

"We can learn!"

"Don't you know it's just common knowledge among the upper graders that Joe likes Viola and she likes him?" Mandy said, eyeing Lizzie skeptically.

She stopped and looked at Mandy, her mouth open in surprise. "Who said?"

"Sara Ruth."

"They can't like each other—he couldn't date a Mennonite!"

"Lizzie, you're so bold, even *thinking* they would even *notice* us. We're just like...country mice going to the city!"

Lizzie's heart sank along with her happy plans. Well, she would not always be a country mouse. It was a horrible feeling to be left out and way behind everybody else, just because she wasn't as pretty and her dresses were plain. How would she ever marry? There were lots and lots of Violas in the world.

"Don't worry, Lizzie. We're too young. Mam would have a fit if she knew how you talked," Mandy said. "We don't have to worry about such things now!"

Lizzie knew Mandy was right, as she usually was. But no wonder she doesn't worry, Lizzie thought. She's thin and pretty and her complexion is as smooth as silk.

Chapter 11

LATER THAT WEEK THE GIRLS WERE ALLOWED to go with Dat to the hospital in Falling Springs.

Jason and the twins weren't old enough to go, so they stayed with Uncle James and Aunt Becca who lived about five miles away. Aunt Becca drove her horse and buggy over to pick up the younger children and take them home with her. Dat said the way Becca drove her horse, she'd be over in a hurry and be back home just as fast.

Lizzie laughed because she loved the way Aunt Becca drove a horse. Becca's horse was little, with deep lines running down his haunches. Lizzie thought this made it look as if he had lots of loose skin on his behind and his haunches flapped up and down along with the breeching on his harness.

Sometimes when they turned a corner, Lizzie had to bite down on her lower lip and clutch the seat, because it seemed as if they were only on two wheels. When Aunt Becca clucked to her horse after picking up Jason and the twins, she started off so fast that the children's heads flew backward. Gravel scattered beneath the buggy as it rounded the corner past the barnyard. Dat laughed and shook his head.

"There she goes."

Emma laughed with Dat. "How can she stop that horse?" she asked.

"Oh, she'll get him stopped."

Sure enough, Becca tugged the reins just in time and the little horse stopped at the very end of the lane.

After Becca left, the girls only had an hour to get ready to go to the hospital. Emma picked up the twins' toys and straightened the house while Lizzie and Mandy went upstairs.

"Which dress are you wearing?" Lizzie asked.

"Oh, I don't know. I guess it doesn't matter too much."

"I know. But most of our dresses are still all from Jefferson County."

"Guess I'll wear that new lavender one."

"Are you nervous about going to church, Mandy?" Lizzie asked, taking the hairpins out of her hair.

Lizzie could hardly believe that only a few days had passed since they had first arrived in Cameron County and so they hadn't attended church yet.

"Sort of, I guess."

"We probably don't have to go because Mam's sick and can't go with us."

"I hope not."

"We don't know one single person except our Glick relatives."

"I dread it."

"Me, too."

Lizzie yanked at a tangle in her hair. She pulled out the hairbrush and gazed at it. "Look at all this hair! I'll be bald!"

Mandy giggled. "You can lose a bu-unch of hair before you'll be bald."

"Can you roll your hair?" Lizzie asked.

"Not really."

"Do we have to, just to go to the hospital?"

"I don't know."

"I hate to wet my hair down and roll it."

"Ask Emma."

So Lizzie yelled down the stairs, asking Emma if they had to roll their hair.

"Of course you do," came Emma's exasperated reply.

"Why?"

"Because we live here now. That's how we have to do."

"I can't get it right!" Lizzie wailed.

There was no answer, so Lizzie knew Emma wasn't going to extend any mercy to her. She went back to her dresser, peered closely into the mirror, and yanked her hair back as hard as she could. Lifting both arms, she grasped some of the hair growing along her forehead and twisted it back.

A big mound of hair above what she was already twisting poofed up and away from her head. She tried to smooth it back, but lost the whole part she had been holding, so she had to start all over.

She snorted, stamping her foot impatiently.

This was going to be impossible, that was all there was to it. She dashed to the bathroom and wet her hair until water ran off the tip of her nose. Using the palms of her hands to flatten her hair, she ran back to the bedroom, picked up the fine-toothed comb, and raked it along each side of her head.

"Are you done?" Emma asked, popping her head in the door.

"No!"

"Here." Mandy came over and stood in front of Lizzie. She took the comb and used it to push some of Lizzie's wet hair up and away from her forehead. "Now try rolling it."

Lizzie leaned over the dresser, her face inches from the mirror, and gently twisted her hair back. Mandy stood back and watched, her arms crossed.

"Go ahead, laugh. You're going to anyway!" Lizzie snapped.

Mandy turned and hurried out of the room, her shoulders shaking.

Good, she's gone, Lizzie thought as she tilted her head to one side, trying to roll the other side the same way. The sides looked all right, but in the front, at her part, one roll went straight up and the other roll hung down. When she pushed the bobby pin in place, both rolls stood up and away from her head, making her look like a frog.

She sighed, tears close to the surface. The driver

was coming any minute. She pulled her hair back securely and started twisting it into a bob again. She was not, absolutely *not*, going to call for Mandy. Mandy, her younger sister, could roll hair perfectly. Well, not perfectly, but much better than Lizzie could.

She pulled her hair back as tightly as she was able, only to discover that her rolls of hair now lay flat along the side of her head. So that was how it was done! She finished twisting her hair on the back of her head and stuck in hairpins as fast as she could. She grabbed her good covering and flopped it on top of her head, turning to look for a black belt apron.

"Driver's here!" Mandy yelled from the bottom of the stairs.

Lizzie pinned her apron as fast as she could, adjusted her dress, and ran down the steps. Emma stood in the kitchen, carrying a bag with extra clothes for Mam.

"Come, Lizzie," she said. And she sounded so like Mam that it made Lizzie miss Mam unbearably much. She couldn't wait to get to the hospital.

Chapter 12

Dat held the door for the girls as they entered the cool interior of the hospital. The glass doors were huge. Lizzie gazed at the tall ceilings as she followed Emma into the lobby. The vast windows looking out at the pink trees and the warm sunlight brightened the soft carpet.

Dat went to a desk that said "Information," where a small, white-haired woman was adjusting the glasses on her nose.

"Hello," Dat said. "Could you tell me which floor Room 377 is on?"

"The numbers go by the floors; the 300s are on the third," she said.

Dat thanked her and herded the girls toward the elevator past a gift shop with pretty plants, balloons, cards, and flowers making a bright display along the windows. Dat stopped to look at the price of a bouquet of yellow carnations and white daisies.

"Dat, you should get it," Emma said.

"Twelve dollars!"

"So? Mam probably doesn't have any flowers because we don't know our English neighbors like we used to in Jefferson County. Please?"

Dat reached into his pocket for his wallet, one Mam had made for him years ago. He held it sideways, checking to see how much cash he had, then he smiled and lifted the pretty cut-glass vase.

"I'll have to write a check for the driver," he said gruffly, but Lizzie could tell he didn't mind. Dat was like that, she thought.

They found Mam's room on the third floor. Tears sprang suddenly to Lizzie's eyes when she saw Mam. Her face was ashen—even her lips were pale. She looked so thin and so sick, it made Lizzie feel awful.

"How are you feeling?" Dat asked, going to the side of her bed.

"Oh, I had a rough night, but I can tell the antibiotic is working."

She smiled at Dat and then looked at the bouquet in Emma's hand. "Ach my, Emma. Aren't they pretty? You shouldn't have," she said, turning to Dat.

Lizzie and Mandy stood back, almost shyly. Mam didn't seem like their ordinary, everyday Mam, lying in that hospital bed wearing a green hospital gown. That gown was about the ugliest thing Lizzie had ever seen.

"Mandy, come here. Come, Lizzie," Mam said, patting the bed. So they sat sideways on Mam's hospital bed, while Lizzie tried not to cry.

"What were you doing last evening when I was here?" Mam asked, tucking a stray hair behind Mandy's ear.

Mandy told Mam all about the pickup truck and the strange man with tattoos and long hair. Mam shook her head at Dat.

"Ach my, Melvin."

"There wasn't a thing wrong with him. Not a thing," Dat assured her.

"I guess," Mam said. "And I've often told the girls we can't judge a person by his looks, can we? But...I would feel better if you stayed at home as much as you can, Melvin."

"I will," Dat said.

Mam told them the doctor's diagnosis of her condition. She had acute pneumonia, the worst kind. The doctor wanted to keep her in the hospital for another three to four days to see if her cough stabilized. He warned Mam that it would take months to gain back her usual strength and that she should take it easy as much as she could.

Emma plucked at the crisp white sheet covering Mam's legs. Lizzie knew she worried about the farm. The herd of cows Dat was buying would not arrive for a few weeks, so that would give them time to finish cleaning up. There was so much painting to be done, but Dat assured Mam that would have to wait until she felt better.

Mam sighed and turned her head.

"We're making you too tired, talking about all this work, aren't we?" Emma said.

"No, I just wish I wouldn't have to be here in the hospital."

There was silence while Dat gazed out the window. She would help Emma, Lizzie decided, and try not to complain about anything. She wished their house was not so ugly. She knew they had the sloppiest house of anyone in Cameron County, and now they couldn't paint or fix it up for months.

Suppose someone came to visit? She wouldn't even go to the door. It just wasn't right, having Mam in the hospital and they couldn't do a thing to improve their awful house.

"Why can't me and Mandy paint?" she asked.

"Oh, I don't know," Mam said. "You're hardly old enough to do the woodwork. I don't know if you could use a roller on the walls or not. Maybe if Emma did the trimming."

Lizzie's face lit up with enthusiasm. "We can! Me and Mandy can use rollers and Emma can use a brush along the edges!"

"We watched you when you painted the new house!" Mandy chimed in.

That seemed to cheer Mam immensely. She told the girls how to set the roller pans on newspaper, and how much paint was the right amount when they put the rollers in them. She decided they were allowed to do their rooms upstairs, but the woodwork would have to wait. She didn't want the girls working with that high gloss enamel. Besides, they would not be able to do it without making a mess on the walls.

When a nurse came in to take Mam's temperature, Dat said it was time to leave. Visiting hours would soon be over. Mam smiled, even if her eyes were bright with unshed tears. Lizzie thought she must be the bravest person in the whole world right at that moment.

Chapter 13

THAT FIRST SPRING IN CAMERON COUNTY,
Lizzie's life seemed to take on new meaning. Mam
was home from the hospital. And Lizzie loved every
minute of that one day a week when she went to
school. She would get up in the morning, fret and
worry about her looks, her hair, how her dress was
made, how her covering fit, and whether her complexion was normal or if she was breaking out with
those dreaded pimples.

The warm sun and frequent rains meant that their
new garden was full of produce. Lizzie ate crisp, red
radishes and long, thin spring onions that crunched
like a pretzel but tasted even better.

At lunchtime, Dat would spread butter on a thick
slice of homemade bread, sprinkle salt beside his
plate until he had made a little pile, then select a
spring onion. He would dip the onion in the salt,
bite it off and quickly take a bite of the buttered
bread, and then chew the two together.

Lizzie piled four or five spring onions on a piece of bread and folded it over to make a thick onion sandwich. Sometimes she put mayonnaise on both sides of the bread, which was absolutely delicious, but so fattening. Lizzie couldn't always be careful. As hard as she worked here on the farm, she had to eat enough or she'd feel weak and her head would start to hurt. She wasn't exactly thin, but she enjoyed good food so much, she didn't always care if she was as thin as Mandy and Emma.

The morning before Emma's sixteenth birthday, Lizzie was out hanging laundry on the wash line while Mam worked in the garden. Mam was still recovering from her time in the hospital, but she liked to spend sometime outside each day in the garden. The sunshine made her feel better, she said.

"Lizzie, come look at all these peas!" she called.

Lizzie dropped the towel she was holding and headed to the garden. She stopped in one row and reached down, separating a few pea stalks to have a closer look. Sure enough, thousands of pea pods were hanging in thick clusters, all ready for picking.

"There's a bunch of them!" Lizzie said.

Mam rushed into the house and came back with Mandy, Emma, and even Jason, each carrying a bucket or basket.

At first it was fun picking peas. The buckets filled up fast, and they ate many tender green peas straight from the pod. They chattered and laughed and threw peas at each other as they watched little toads and snails crawl through the dirt.

But as the sun rose in the sky, the rows seemed longer and longer. Lizzie stretched and rubbed the small of her back. In the next row, Mandy was sitting on the ground between pea stalks, shelling one pea after another and gobbling them down. She wasn't putting any in her basket.

"Mandy!" Lizzie yelled.

Mandy had a mouthful of peas and didn't answer.

"Stop eating peas and help pick!" Lizzie shouted.

Mandy chewed, swallowed, and turned to glare at Lizzie. "Stop hollering!"

"Well, pick!"

"Pick, pick, pick. Pick, pick, pick. You sound like a chicken."

"That's enough, girls," Mam called. "Finish your rows and then come inside to help me get ready for Emma's birthday party."

The girls nudged Emma and laughed as they rushed to finish their rows. Emma kept her head down as she worked, but Lizzie could tell she was excited, too. It must be just absolutely wonderful to turn 16, Lizzie thought, especially if you looked as slender and pretty as Emma.

When Lizzie and Emma were little girls, they were chubby, actually more than chubby as they got bigger and older. But when Emma turned 13, she stopped eating calorie-laden foods, becoming steadily thinner until she didn't look one bit like Lizzie anymore.

Lizzie had continued to take three sandwiches in her lunch to school, more than the eighth-grade boys took for their lunches, and Emma was terribly embarrassed by this. Lizzie tried to watch what she ate, especially when Mam was around. But it was hard. Often, when Mam was upstairs working and Lizzie had to watch the twins, she ate two whoopie pies.

Once, after Mam had made creamsticks, Lizzie ate four. Creamsticks were homemade doughnuts, but instead of being round with a hole in the middle, they were cut in an oblong shape. After they were deep-fried, Mam cut a long slit in each of their tops, filled them with creamy vanilla icing, and then put golden caramel frosting on the tops. They were the very best thing in the world of desserts, but Mam didn't make them very often because they were so much work, with two different kinds of icing and all.

Lizzie learned quickly that it paid to be careful what she ate around Mam and Emma, but it didn't matter if they were busy and couldn't see her. When things were stressful, nothing made Lizzie feel better about her upside-down world than a good whoopie pie or doughnut. They were so comforting.

The girls rushed to clean the house and prepare Emma's favorite foods for her birthday meal. When the table was set, Emma and Lizzie went out to the woodshed to gather more fuel for the fire.

Emma went straight to the woodpile. Lizzie trailed behind her, admiring Emma's blue dress and neat hair. It wouldn't be long until Emma had a boyfriend, she thought.

✑

The sight of the stacked wood sent Lizzie right back to a long-ago afternoon, when she had played Mrs. Bixler with Emma. "I'm going to see if I can find some wood to make me some high-heeled shoes," Lizzie had told Emma. But Emma ignored her and continued to pick up wood.

"Hello!" Lizzie yelled in what she imagined to be a stylish, grown-up voice. "How are you, Emma?"

Emma turned to look at Lizzie's feet. Sure enough, she had securely tied a block of wood with baler twine to the bottom of each foot.

Emma extended her hand to shake Lizzie's. "Why, come in, Mrs. Bixler! I'm just fine. And where did you get your new high-heeled shoes?"

Lizzie held her head up high, and in a genuine, English-lady imitation said, "Oh, I just bought them at the store!"

Both girls collapsed on the floor in a fit of giggles. When Lizzie hit the floor and her high heels fell apart, they laughed even harder.

Emma sputtered, "L-L-Lizzie—your shoes!"

Lizzie gasped, "Well, they did feel like high heels a little bit." She picked up the blocks of wood and twine, trying to reattach them to her shoes.

She looked at Emma. "There's hardly any use, is there? These aren't really high heels, and I'm not really English." Lizzie squeezed Emma's hand and loved her so much she thought her heart would burst.

Dear, bossy, big sister Emma. And now Emma had turned 16. Tonight the family gathered around the dining room table to celebrate Emma's big birthday. Each person had a lovely glass dish filled with chocolate cake and vanilla ice cream while Emma opened her gifts. The birthday cake had two layers covered with vanilla frosting—everyone's favorite—and they enjoyed every last morsel of it with spoonfuls of creamy vanilla ice cream.

Emma opened the largest package and found a pair of candleholders with blue candles for her bedroom. Another package contained fabric for two new dresses, a robin's-egg blue and a light dusty green material. Emma was quite overwhelmed, and her cheeks flushed a beautiful pink color as she gasped, exclaiming over the pretty fabric.

After they finished celebrating, the girls washed the dishes while Mam bathed the twins. Jason went out with Dat to finish up the chores, making sure the barn doors were closed properly against the approaching chill of the night.

Suddenly Mam appeared at the kitchen door, looking at the girls and listening for a sound she thought she heard.

"Did someone knock?" she asked.

"No," the girls answered.

But now there was a decided knocking on the kitchen door.

"I thought I heard someone," Mam said, hurrying to open it.

"Come on in," she said, stepping back to let a young Amish man into the kitchen.

"Hello. Sorry to bother you so late in the evening," he said, smiling apologetically.

"That's quite all right. It isn't late yet," Mam answered.

"Looks like you have plenty of help," he said, nodding toward the girls who were clustered around the kitchen sink.

"Oh, yes. My girls are growing up so fast I can hardly keep up with them," Mam laughed.

"That's good. We need *mauda* here in Cameron County." Lizzie's heart sank way down, leaving her stomach feeling all hollow and helpless.

Mauda! Oh, no! I'm not going. Emma can. Mam and Dat can't make me be a *maud*. I'm not going to do it. I'll run away, she thought. She had a wild impulse to run upstairs and hide under her bed where no one would be able to find her and make her go be a *maud*, or maid. Sometimes being a *maud* meant staying for weeks at a time in a family's home, which really, Lizzie thought, was much like being a slave.

She had told Emma that one evening when they were discussing the fact that eventually they would probably need to be *mauda*, with so many young families moving into the community who would need help with housecleaning, canning, or assisting when a new baby arrived.

Emma said, no, that a *maud* was not nearly the same. Lizzie argued vehemently, saying it was the exact same thing, except there was no cruel overseer who cracked his whip above your head when you didn't pick cotton fast enough. Emma told her she should be ashamed of herself, that slaves lived in little hovels or cabins with only bare necessities.

"Well, the reason I'm here is...," the Amish man cleared his throat. "My wife needs some help house-cleaning, and I think she wants to paint the kitchen, too."

"Let's see, you're John King, aren't you?" Mam asked.

He nodded.

"Well, I don't see why not. Emma, would you like to go? When is it? Next week?"

"Monday till at least Wednesday. Maybe two of the girls could help with the painting on Wednes-day," John offered.

"Why, yes! Lizzie could go Wednesday, and Emma will go the rest of the time. Will you send a driver on Monday morning?"

Lizzie glared at Mam but said nothing. She hadn't even waited till Emma said yes or no. But, really, what difference would it make whether she did say yes or no? It was all the same. Either they could go willingly or rebelliously. Either way, they had to go.

As soon as John King left, closing the kitchen door behind him, Lizzie put her hands behind her back and said staunchly, "I'm not going."

"Lizzie!"

"I'm scared to paint other people's houses. I'm afraid I'll make streaks."

Mam turned to look at Lizzie.

"Oh yes, Lizzie, you're going," she said. "The Kings will show you what to do."

"Why must I go?" Lizzie wailed, flopping on a kitchen chair, her arms flung across the back in a gesture of rebellion.

Mam took a deep breath.

"Because. When you girls reach a certain age, you need to learn about working outside of our home. You need to earn some money and learn how to obey and do jobs you would ordinarily not experience at home. Besides, it won't hurt you to give up your own will. That's what a lot of your life consists of." Mam paused, seating herself at the kitchen table, gathering Susan in a big hug on her lap. Not Mam's favorite line again, thought Lizzie. It had been hard enough for Lizzie to learn to do her part at home.

"When I was your age, I was almost never at home," Mam was saying. "Either I was cleaning houses or I was caring for elderly people. These are all good experiences for young girls to have before they get married."

"Good for *you*," Lizzie muttered.

Mam chose to ignore that comment, and Mandy blinked her large green eyes in Lizzie's direction. Lizzie caught her gaze, and Mandy blinked again. Lizzie knew she meant she had better watch it.

"I'm kind of excited to go. John's wife, Hannah, always talks to me at church. She's so full of fun, sometimes it seems as if she's my age instead of being a mother with children," Emma said, wiping the counter clean.

"Well, good! Then if you feel that way, we'll just forget about me going. You can paint the kitchen, and I'll stay here and do the work for Mam. Right?" Lizzie looked hopefully in Mam's direction.

Mam shook her head. "You'll go," she said, and she was not smiling.

Chapter 14

So that's how Lizzie found herself at the Kings' new house at the bottom of the mountain, six miles away from her family's farm. Because John had come to get her in his horse and buggy, the drive there was long enough to give her a good chance to think about painting for a very long time.

Emma and Hannah had already spread newspapers on the floor. They had set up a stepladder in the middle of the kitchen and had gallons of paint and fresh new rollers and brushes scattered across the plastic-covered kitchen table.

Hannah greeted Lizzie warmly and explained that she needed to help John in the fields that forenoon so the girls would start painting the kitchen on their own. After Hannah left, Lizzie went upstairs to change into her old dress and tie a bandanna around her head. She clattered back downstairs to find Emma covering the stovetop with an old sheet and then carefully moving everything away that could accidentally be spattered with paint.

"Where's the paint?" Lizzie demanded.

"Lizzie, this isn't our house. You need to be careful," Emma said.

"I know what I'm doing," Lizzie said.

Lizzie picked up a paint can and set it on the table without bothering to put any newspaper underneath it. She pried off the top and started stirring the light green paint so vigorously it sloshed over the side of the can.

"Watch it!" Emma yelled.

She dashed over to grab the wooden paddle from Lizzie's hand.

"What?" Lizzie asked.

"The paint! It's spilling down over the side. I mean it, Lizzie, if you don't slow down and listen to me, I'm not going to help."

"Good, then I'll do it!"

Emma gasped as Lizzie tilted the bucket of paint into the roller pan.

"Not so much! Not so fast!" Emma wailed.

"Oh, calm down," Lizzie said.

Emma sighed. She picked up a tray and brush and put them carefully on a sheet of newspaper that covered the floor. Lizzie slid her roller deeply into her own tray before heading straight for the wall in front of her, a trail of sticky paint dripping behind her.

The kitchen walls and ceiling were old plaster with deep cracks, some broken spots, and peeling paint. Covering them well would be hard work, she knew. She smacked on the paint as if her life depended on it, furiously rolling straight up and down in long, uneven rows.

Emma grabbed an old rag and wiped up the paint Lizzie had dripped on the floor.

"Lizzie, see what you did? Don't fill your roller quite as full next time," she said.

"Okay," Lizzie said cheerfully, continuing her mad rolling.

The two girls worked side by side, covering the walls with new paint.

"How do we do the ceiling?" Emma asked.

"That's easy—with a broom handle stuck in here," Lizzie said airily, pointing to the end of her roller.

Lizzie used the rollers as if she was brandishing a serious weapon and the ugly old plaster was a great enemy she needed to conquer. She dashed back and forth from her paint tray to the wall, spattering paint on the floor, on the table, on anything that was not sufficiently covered. Emma tried in vain to keep all the paint spills under control. She continued to clean up drops of paint while brush-painting the trim.

"I love this color!" Lizzie said.

"It is a nice shade," Emma agreed.

The forenoon passed quickly with Emma chattering happily, going from one subject to another. Lizzie could tell that Emma enjoyed painting. Lizzie hoped that someday soon she would be as confident as Emma was in new situations. It hadn't always been that way. Lizzie remembered when Emma would get scared and would even admit it—like when they were eight and nine and going sledding with the big kids at school.

❦

"Lizzie, don't tell anyone, okay? But..." Emma had lowered her voice, "I am so terribly afraid of going sledding that I...well, Lizzie, don't tell any-one—promise?"

"I promise," Lizzie answered solemnly.

"Cross your heart?" Emma asked worriedly.

"Cross my heart."

"Okay. I was so scared at lunch that when I tried to eat my bologna sandwich, I almost threw up. Really, I had to take a drink and put my sandwich away."

Emma stopped and looked squarely at Lizzie. "And Lizzie, I don't want to go sledding. Don't tell anyone, but I'd almost rather sit at my desk and do my lessons."

Lizzie's eyes squinted as she looked out over the sparkling white hill. She watched as the boys tried to push each other off their sleds while they were flying down at quite an alarming rate. Then she turned to look at Emma, who looked back quite solemnly at Lizzie.

"Emma, that doesn't matter one bit," Lizzie had said staunchly. "I will not tell one single person ever that sled-riding scares you if you don't tell one single

person that I put five whoopie pies in my lunch this
morning."

"Five?" Emma was horrified. "Why five?"

Lizzie looked carefully over her shoulder and
whispered to Emma, "Because. And I'm not even
giving one to the teacher!"

Emma had laughed, throwing back her head,
and Lizzie had smiled, glad that her sister was feeling better. And now here they were together today,
but with Emma stepping out ahead.

The Kings' house was new, built only a few
months earlier. It offered a lovely view of the mountain, which really was only a big hill, but quite a
beautiful one, nevertheless. Lizzie thought she could
have stood at the kitchen window for a very long
time and watched the trees swaying like natural
dancers with the mountain providing the stage.

John King's brother, Elam, lived on the same
farm, with only the large white barn separating the
two houses. His wife, Priscilla, was a small, dark-
haired woman, and she was good friends with Hannah.

Lizzie wondered if she and Emma might marry
brothers and live together on the same farm. That
would be all right as long as Emma and her husband
did the milking. They might share a farm, but her
husband would most definitely *not* be a farmer. Even
to imagine a whole cow stable full of huge black

and white Holsteins was so depressing, she could not think about it too long. Smelly creatures!

Mam always told the girls they must learn to pray for God's will for their lives. Lizzie didn't know if it was alright to ask him to please not make her milk cows, though. There were lots of other ways to make a living that were just fine. Would Joe and John ask her and Emma for dates? She doubted it, but then, you never knew.

"I'm hungry!" Lizzie said.

"It's not even 11 o'clock!" Emma said.

Lizzie glanced out the window and across the front yard toward the team of horses and the wagon moving slowly across the hay field. Hannah was driving the horses while John stood on the back of the wagon, stacking bales of hay.

"Oh, that almost scares me, Emma. I cannot imagine Dat plowing a field with those huge, fearsome-looking workhorses. They're five times as big as Bess and Billy."

"Not that big!" Emma laughed.

But Lizzie found the idea of Dat working as a serious farmer both exciting and scary. How could he handle those large, heavy horses? He was not a big man. It was all too much to think about, Lizzie realized. The only way she could have any peace was to think Dat and Mam must know what they were doing. Everything would turn out alright, especially with Doddy Glick helping Dat to get started.

Lizzie kept rolling paint onto the ceiling. She grimaced as she put one hand up to rub the back of her neck. The ceiling was a lot bigger than it looked. Her arms ached and her lower back hurt, but she wasn't going to complain.

She thought about what kind of horses Dat would buy and if she would ever be allowed to drive them. If Hannah could, then so could she, Lizzie thought. That would be much more of a challenge than anything she had ever experienced before in her whole life.

She was thinking about driving the new workhorses and walking backwards as she painted the ceiling.

THUMP!

Lizzie's foot hit the edge of the roller pan. Warm, sticky paint flowed over her foot, across the newspaper, and onto the tile floor. She dropped her roller and held up her foot. Paint dripped steadily onto the floor.

"Oh, my word!"

"Don't move!" Emma shouted, as she dashed to the back porch for rags.

"I didn't do it on purpose. Maybe you should have offered to do some of the ceiling!" Lizzie wailed.

"Be quiet. Stop your yelling. You weren't watching what you were doing," Emma ground out between clenched teeth as she knelt on the floor and grabbed Lizzie's foot. "Hold still."

Emma muttered and grumbled to herself as she swabbed Lizzie's foot viciously.

"Now go to the bathroom and stick that foot in the bathtub," she instructed.

"Go to the bathroom?" Lizzie shrieked. "How?"

"Hop on one foot, of course," Emma said.

So Lizzie hopped through the living room, tears rolling down her cheeks.

Emma followed her, trying to clean up any paint that fell on the floor.

"Stop your crying, Lizzie, you big baby," she said. "Maybe if you'd grow up once and stop being so... so much in a hurry when you do something, things would go better for you. I didn't say anything on purpose, so we could get along, and look what happened. Nobody can ever tell you one thing, Lizzie Glick, so you're only getting what you deserve."

With that Emma closed the bathroom door. Lizzie sat on the side of the bathtub, letting water run over her foot and crying her heart out. She just wished she could go dig a nice big hole and crawl in it, never to show her face until everyone liked her again.

Emma thought she was goofy and dumb, Lizzie was sure. She had it easy, being so thin and without one blemish anywhere on her face, while Lizzie struggled with awful-looking skin. And she was fat. Well, not really fat anymore, but not as thin as Emma.

The water sloshed over her foot, and tears ran down her cheeks as she squeezed her eyes shut. She pitied herself so much she wondered if this is how you felt right before you died. She hoped God still liked her at least.

Sometimes she was still afraid of God, especially at times like this. She had just wanted to hurry up and get the kitchen painted so Hannah would think she was a hard worker. She hadn't stuck her foot in that pan on purpose. It was probably just God punishing her for some other things she had done wrong. That's always how it was.

After her foot was clean, she wiped her eyes and her nose, smoothed back her hair, and went back out to the kitchen. Emma was on her knees, mopping up paint, her cheeks flushed to a rosy color. Hannah, who must have just come in from the fields, sat beside her rubbing furiously at some other paint spots.

Lizzie just stood there, both hands to her mouth, still not quite able to comprehend what she had done. It was so embarrassing and so awful, watching that green stain spreading across the Kings' linoleum.

"I...I'm really sorry," she managed in a hoarse croak.

"Oh, don't be sorry. It wasn't your fault. It could have happened to anyone," Hannah said.

Lizzie didn't know if she wanted to laugh or cry. She could hardly believe that Hannah wasn't angry at all. Lizzie felt like crying partly because of her kindness. Hannah surely couldn't be as nice as she sounded.

But she was. Hannah laughed as they scraped up the last of the paint, pointing at the nice shade of mint green that her linoleum became. Emma laughed with her, while Lizzie went to the washhouse for some clear naphtha gas. After they applied the naphtha, rubbing at the massive green spot, Lizzie was so terribly relieved to see that the floor wasn't ruined at all that she felt like crying again.

They finished painting the kitchen without any further incidents. Then Hannah made a special meal of delicious cheeseburgers much later than the usual lunch hour. She served tall glasses of Coke with tinkling ice cubes, and lots of ketchup, mayonnaise, tomatoes, onions, and lettuce to put on their sandwiches.

She tried so hard to make Lizzie feel better, to help her forget about spilling the paint, and certainly not to blame herself, that Lizzie decided if she ever got married and had to have a *maud*, she would treat her exactly like Hannah treated her. Of course, she was not going to hire a *maud* unless it was *absolutely* necessary.

Chapter 15

THE ALARM CLOCK ON LIZZIE'S NIGHTSTAND jangled loudly. She groaned and rolled over to turn it off. The hands showed five o'clock. She could hear Dat moving around downstairs in the kitchen.

She swung her legs over the side of the bed and sat there, her elbows on her knees. This just isn't right, she thought. I never in my life had to get up this early. I hate it. She could tell it was going to be a warm, sultry day, as humid as it was already. She yawned and reached for a dress in the closet.

She never brushed her teeth or combed her hair at five o'clock. What was the use? Dat didn't care what she looked like as long as she helped milk.

And another thing—those cows. Cows were the dumbest animals on earth. They smelled bad and she was still afraid of their hooves, those big, dirty, split feet caked with a load of manure that squooshed up between the cracks in the hooves whenever they walked.

The cows had arrived almost two months earlier, but these ignorant, slow learners still did not come in from the pasture early in the morning when it was time to be milked. Usually they were at the farthest end of the pasture, lying down and chewing their cuds.

All they did was chew. You could watch a cow for hours, and she did nothing except chew, her lower lip making half circles all day long. When she did stop the constant movement, a sort of rumble came up from her throat, and she began chewing again in earnest. It was so disgusting.

Down in the kitchen, Dat was heading for the door.

"The grass is soaking wet this morning," he called to her. "You better put on some boots so your legs and feet stay dry."

Lizzie snorted. The hem of her dress always seemed to get soaked, and if she held it up, the dew-soaked grass slapped against her legs and water dripped down into her boots creating bigger problems. Then her bare feet slipped and slid around inside those filthy rubber boots.

This morning she headed to the meadow without any boots. Her skirt trailed behind her in the wet grass as she yelled, "Coom, Sook! Coom, Sook!" her voice scratchy with sleep.

Lizzie wondered why Dat had taught them to yell that when they gathered the cows, especially the "Sook" part. She guessed it was probably a tradition of sorts. Doddy Glick had probably called to his cows the exact same way, and his father before him.

Lizzie's right foot slid into a warm, soft pile of cow manure. She grimaced as she stopped to wipe her foot on the wet grass. It always happened sooner or later as she stomped around in the dark yelling. She had almost gotten used to stepping in cow manure, which meant she had become a full-fledged farm girl. When her foot was clean, she lifted her head, pushed back her tousled hair, and kept on yelling.

No sign of the cows. Lizzie plodded on. Her skirt was wet and snapped against her legs. She winced as a thistle pricked the side of her leg and she stepped into another pile of cow manure.

They had to be around here somewhere, she thought. She had almost reached the edge of the field. Dat would be done with the feeding, wondering where his cows were.

"Coom, Sook!"

Then, quite suddenly, in the half-light of dawn, all sorts of shapes emerged as cows slowly rose from their comfortable positions in the grass. Cows were the most ungraceful animals, Lizzie thought as she watched. When they got up, their hindquarters stuck pointedly into the air for quite a long time until they finally got their front legs unbent and into a standing position. Then they arched their backs, while holding their tails straight out behind in the most ridiculous manner, before starting their slow shuffle to the barn.

"Get! Get! Come on, get going!" Lizzie said,

starting the herd moving toward the barn. A few of the cows glared at her in the most rebellious manner, but she felt a bit of kinship with them. So...get up, cows. I had my alarm clock, and you have me to wake you up, she thought.

Dat met them at the gate, swinging it wide to let the cows through. Typical cows, they began to hurry the minute they smelled their feed.

"Where were you so long?" Dat asked. "It's almost five-thirty."

"The cows were at the other end of the pasture," Lizzie said.

"You're soaked," Dat observed, holding up the gas lantern. "Why don't you wear the barn boots?"

"They don't help anything," Lizzie said.

"They would if you'd wear them."

Lizzie didn't answer. She sloshed into the milkhouse to fill a black rubber bucket with warm, soapy water, yawning as she dropped in a clean cloth.

Dat was whistling, rattling chains as he tied the cows in their stalls. Lizzie wished he wasn't so cheerful in the morning because it only made her tired and grumpy. Absentmindedly, she reached under a cow's udder to wash it clean before a milker was attached. Dat was still whistling, but Lizzie wasn't listening. She was thinking about her last day of vocational class only a week before.

She had been feeling a bit blue as she thought about Joe. He still hardly ever noticed her. He talked to her sometimes about baseball and school subjects, but never for very long. If he didn't notice her more than that, this business of finding a husband was going to be a lot more difficult than she had anticipated.

The last day of school, she was leaning against the old porcelain sink—she could still remember exactly where she was—when Viola and Mandy came charging through the door, arm in arm, giggling and laughing, their eyes shining. Viola was absolutely stunning that day in a dark burgundy-colored dress that set off her long dark braids and tanned skin. Mandy was equally beautiful with her large, expressive eyes and creamy, flawless complexion.

Lizzie had tried to smile at them, but her heart sank steadily as she compared herself to them. She could still feel the panic about being unattractive and, worst of all, absolutely unpopular. She had wanted to go home and talk to Mam or Emma, whoever wasn't busy at the time, and get them to explain this thing about God's will for a husband again. She was never going to get a husband without some help, that was certain.

She stepped into the next stall, bent her head, and was just about to start washing the cow's udders when the cow shifted away from her. This movement was followed by a sharp tugging on her hair. It felt as if every hair on her head was being pulled individually out of her scalp. Was the milking machine sucking up her hair?

"Ouch!" she yelled.

She backed away and turned in time to see the

cow, her neck extended into a long turn, reaching out her tongue towards the top of Lizzie's head. Lizzie jerked back.

That cow thinks my hair is hay! she realized. She brought her fist down on the cow's bony hip, hollering, "Stop that!"

The minute her fist contacted the hip bone, pain exploded through her hand and along her arm, all the way to her elbow. She stepped over the gutter, holding the side of her injured hand, and groaned with pain.

"What in the world is wrong with you, Lizzie?" Dat called.

"Nothing!" Lizzie shot back. She knew her face was red and contorted with the effort to keep from crying.

Lizzie marched into the milkhouse without looking right or left. She went straight to the stainless steel rinse tubs and held her bruised hand under the faucet so the warm, soothing water could wash down over it. She had never disliked anything or anybody as much as she disliked cows.

Any other animal would have been intelligent enough to know her unkempt hair was not hay. Couldn't she smell the difference? Animals were supposed to have a keen sense of smell, weren't they? According to the size of their nostrils, they should be able to smell a bale of hay from a great distance. They had no business slurping at someone's head.

Lizzie hurried back to the cow stable, wiping her

hand on a paper towel. She finished washing udders, carried milk into the milkhouse, and swept the aisle. Dat untied the cows, and, one by one, they backed across the gutter and made their slow, clumsy way out the door.

"Your hand feel better?" Dat asked, as she was sweeping.

"Mm-hmm."

"What happened?"

Lizzie narrowed her eyes. Should she tell him? She shrugged.

"I just hit the cow in the wrong place and hurt my hand."

Dat raised an eyebrow but said nothing as he started sweeping the feed aisle.

"I'm going for breakfast," Lizzie called back as she headed out the door.

"Be right in," Dat answered.

Lizzie slammed the back door a bit harder than necessary. Her future seemed very long and dark if herding cows was her future.

In the house, Mam was frying eggs on the big griddle, her hair combed and her covering positioned neatly on her head. Emma's hair wasn't combed, but she had covered it with a man's handkerchief, which she wore to do barn chores or outside work so her coverings wouldn't get dirty. Emma always wore her dichly or some sort of head scarf if she wasn't wearing her covering, because she was conscientious and a good girl who wanted to do what was right. The girls were taught to cover their heads when they prayed, which included the silent prayer before and after meals.

"All done?" Mam asked, smiling at Lizzie.

"Mm-hmm." Lizzie bent to wash her hands and face at the small sink in the kitchen.

Emma poured orange juice as Mandy came clattering down the stairs, with Jason a few steps behind her.

"Good morning!" Mam sang out.

"Good morning, Mam!" Mandy answered.

"Morning, Mam," Jason echoed, going to stand beside her so she could reach out and put an arm around his shoulders.

"Mandy, would you please make the toast for me?"

"Sure." Mandy hurried to do her bidding, while Lizzie stood at the sink glaring at herself in the mirror. Oh, great, another angry-looking pimple, she thought, dragging a fingernail through it. She winced as the pain moved across her forehead.

"Don't pick your face, Lizzie," Mandy said from her vigil at the oven door.

"I'm not!"

Mandy raised her eyebrows. But Lizzie just smoothed back her hair and sat down at the table. Lizzie couldn't stop a huge, gaping yawn. Tears formed in her eyes, and she blinked back her tiredness.

"Boy, Lizzie, you look as if you're about at the end of your string," Mandy said.

"The word is *rope*, not *string*," Lizzie growled.

"Grouch," Mandy muttered.

"I had to milk, remember?" Lizzie hissed, stifling another yawn as she expertly flipped two fried eggs onto her plate. Mandy was always happy in the morning. She bounced out of bed, humming under her breath as she raced down the stairs to chirp a warm greeting to anyone who was happy enough to answer.

Dat looked closely at Lizzie. He wished she had a better attitude about her new job, but it seemed no matter how hard he tried to make the cow stable a pleasant place, she was always impatient, wanting to be finished with her chores before they had even started. Mandy was exactly the opposite, cheerfully helping and asking questions, learning all she could about the cows, the butterfat content of the milk, or whatever.

"Lizzie, you surprise me," Dat said as he ate a forkful of egg and toast.

"Why?"

"I guess because you were always the tomboy with the ponies and the ridge. But you really resent milking cows."

"Is it any wonder?" Lizzie asked sarcastically.

"Why do you say that?"

"Cows are stupid."

Mam laughed.

"Lizzie, that's not one bit respectful of my profession," Dat said.

Lizzie looked up sharply, almost choking on her bite of egg. "Profession? You mean milking cows is a profession, like teaching or making furniture ... or ... or ... stuff like that?"

"It's a part of farming, a very important part. If it wouldn't be for the milk we're shipping, I don't know how else we'd make a living."

Lizzie had put a spoonful of fried eggs and toast in her mouth so she couldn't answer.

She was so hungry after her morning's work that she ate and ate without even thinking of calories or her weight. She couldn't wait to cut a fresh piece of shoofly pie and pour a mug of steaming hot chocolate over it. Shoofly pie was one of her favorite foods. Mam's shoofly pies were almost as good as Mommy Glick's, with a thick brown sugar and molasses goo on the bottom and a soft crumb cake on top.

When she was finally finished eating, Lizzie pushed back her plate.

"But, Dat, you have to admit it. A cow is not nearly as pleasant as a horse. They swat you in the face with their smelly tails every chance they have. They step on your toes without even thinking about it. They ... they take a *huge* slurp of your hair if they think it's hay!" She started laughing.

"What?" Mandy squealed.

Dat started choking and sputtering, pointing a finger at Lizzie.

"So that...," he coughed, before he resumed speaking, "so that is what happened to your head and your hand this morning, Lizzie!" He laughed so hard Mam raised her eyebrows.

"Oh, my!" Dat sighed. He was still chuckling as he told the others about how Lizzie had hopped around the aisle with a sore hand.

"When I asked her what had happened, she said 'Nothing!' so loudly and so angrily, I *knew* something had happened," he said.

"So...the cow reached back and tugged at your *shtrubbles* with her tongue, thinking it was hay, right?" he asked.

Mandy squealed, holding her hands over her mouth, her eyes wide. Jason guffawed loudly. Mam threw back her head and laughed with Dat.

"Ewww!" Emma said. But she started laughing with everyone else.

The whole table was in such an uproar, Lizzie started laughing as well, because there was nothing to do if everyone else thought it was so funny.

"That will teach you to comb your hair before you go out in the morning!" Dat sputtered, wiping his eyes.

"Oh, my, Lizzie!" Mam gasped.

"Your hair does look a lot like hay!" Jason said. "It always does."

The morning sun shone through the kitchen windows, casting a soft, yellow glow into the kitchen. Lizzie smiled. Everyone thought she was hilarious, and she felt the glow from Dat's eyes. She was so thankful for Mam's health, for Dat's laughter, for this old house which they were continuing to clean up, for Mandy, for dear, proper Emma, and for Jason's curls.

She smiled straight into Jason's eyes and said, "Just be glad my hair doesn't look like yours. Then the cow would probably have eaten my whole head!"

Jason punched Lizzie's arm as Mandy slapped the table and laughed again.

"Alright," Dat said. "Enough now."

Dat was like that, Lizzie thought happily. He was so full of fun and jokes, and then he would remember that he shouldn't be too silly and he would say something serious. But family was such a grand thing, Lizzie thought. Cows and old farmhouse or not, having family around her was one thing that was utterly safe and dependable. Together, she believed they could conquer any troubles they would meet.

Even if life handed them disappointments, like Mam's pneumonia and moving here to the old farm, their loyalty to each other would see them through. Mam would correct her if she said that, insisting that God would stand beside them, which Lizzie knew was true. But the thing was, God seemed so undependable to her. Family you could see and actually touch. God was so far away. He just seemed a bit harder to figure out.

Chapter 16

Emma was the first one to go away to work as a *maud* and stay all week. The man who came to the door looked a bit weary and very anxious to have one of the girls come to help his wife with a new baby and all that goes with it. The family had also just started milking cows, so the man would need help with the milking in the morning and evening, too.

Lizzie held her breath, desperately hoping that Emma would offer to go, and, of course, she did. Emma sat at the table crocheting a blue and white afghan, the crochet hook flashing in the gas lamplight. She looked perfectly calm and poised, her cheeks flushed to a delicate shade of pink.

She looked up and smiled. "Yes, I can come. Monday morning will be fine."

Lizzie actually felt her chest deflating as she let out a whoosh of air. Bless Emma's heart. Lizzie felt like jumping up and down with relief, but she stood

quietly beside the refrigerator, chewing her thumb-
nail to the quick.

≈

How did Emma do it? How did she manage to
always do what Mam wanted? It had been that
way forever, it seemed to Lizzie. It happened even
on days when they were little and some celebrating seemed in order—like the first day of summer
after school was out for the year. Early one spring
morning, Emma had come running down the stairs,
shouting for Lizzie. Sure enough, she had something
bossy to say. Emma told Lizzie loudly that as soon
as Mam was done washing, they had to help mow
the yard, trim around the existing flower beds, and
make new ones.

Lizzie hadn't felt like working in the yard that
day any more then than she did now. Emma just
upset her, always spoiling a perfect day, telling her
what she had to do. So she didn't turn around. She
acted as if she hadn't heard Emma and kept her
back turned.

"Lizzie!" Emma voice rose. Lizzie could tell she
was angry at her. Good for her. Emma could go
mow the yard with Mam and she'd stay in the barn
with Dat and the horses.

"Lizzie!" Emma yelled louder.

Dat stopped combing Dolly's mane. He did not
look very happy as he spun Lizzie around. "Lizzie,
answer your sister when she calls you," he said.

Lizzie looked at the floor, pushing a piece of black leather with one toe as Emma stomped into the barn.

"Dat, you have to make Lizzie listen to me. She's just mad because she has to work. I already swept the floor for Mam and she didn't do a thing," Emma said.

"Lizzie, now go on, and don't be so stubborn," Dat said, giving her a shove. He looked frustrated as he turned back to brush Dolly.

"I don't want to, and I'm not..." Lizzie retorted.

Dat turned very suddenly and loomed over Lizzie. "Don't say it, Lizzie, or I'm going to have to find my paddle. You go right now and be nice. I'm busy here, and Mam needs you to help her. Now go."

Lizzie had burst into howls of rage and disappointment. First of all, Emma was bossy, and now Dat was on Emma's side and was being so unkind. She wailed her way out the door and plopped down hard on the porch step, refusing to budge while she cried loud howls of self-pity.

"Lizzie, if you don't shut up right this minute— oh!" Emma stood by helplessly. When she simply couldn't take Lizzie's crying one more second, she stomped off to the little shed and found the push mower.

Lizzie stopped crying as she watched Emma mow. It looked like fun, and it made the lawn look nice and even in size and color. She sniffed and wiped her eyes and watched Emma some more.

Lizzie wished she were back in school. School was much more fun than this. Emma would boss

her around all summer. Mandy was too little to be
much fun, but Lizzie guessed if Emma was going to
be so grown-up all the time, sweeping floors and
mowing yard, Mandy would have to be her play-
mate. Even Dat was unkind to her today.

Tears welled up in her eyes, because it all hurt
dreadfully. She turned away so Emma couldn't see
and ran to the tool shed. She found Mam's trimming
shears and hurried over to the flower bed farthest
away from Emma.

She clipped halfheartedly at the edge of the flower
bed. A fat brown earthworm wriggled in the grass,
and Lizzie clipped him in two pieces. It served the
slimy old worm right—he had no business crawling
over the grass where she was supposed to trim.

Mam came over and sat down beside Lizzie. The
two parts of the earthworm were wriggling furiously, and Mam could see Lizzie's swollen eyes and
tear-stained face.

"What's wrong with the worm, Lizzie?" she asked.

"I cut him in half."

"On purpose?" Mam asked.

"I don't know."

"Lizzie, why were you crying?" she asked.

"Mam, I–I—" and Lizzie burst into a fresh wave
of weeping. "It's always the same. Emma is so good
and I am so bad. She always makes me do things I
don't want to do, because she likes to sweep and do
things like that. And she makes me so mad I could…
I could kick her. And you like her a lot better than
you like me. Dat does, too."

⁴

Years later, Lizzie sometimes still fought back those feelings of being second best. That evening after the man came looking for a *maud*, Lizzie slipped over to Emma's room and sat down beside her on her bed. She cleared her throat nervously before she said, "Emma?"

Emma looked up from the Bible she was reading and asked serenely, "Hmm?"

"Emma, don't you...? I mean, don't you mind going so far away to those strange people and staying for an entire week?" Lizzie's voice rose to a hysterical yelp.

"I don't know. I'm not exactly looking forward to it, but I feel like it's my duty to go if Mam and Dat think I should."

She closed her Bible and put it carefully in her nightstand drawer, taking out her diary and pen.

Lizzie couldn't believe it. How could she? How could she be so deep-down and honest-to-goodness obedient to Mam's wishes?

"Emma, aren't you one bit angry?" Lizzie asked, watching as Emma opened her diary.

Emma thought, chewing on the tip of her pen.

"No, I guess not. I mean, what good would it do? I have to go and, like Mam said, it will be a good experience, learning to work for other people."

Lizzie took a deep breath, leaned back, and gazed at the ceiling.

"Well, I'm not ever going to do it."

Emma glanced at her sharply. "You shouldn't say that."

"Well, I just did say it. I'm not going to stay for a week, ever. I couldn't take it. Emma, ewww! Are you actually going to get up in the morning and milk? I guarantee you have to get up at 4:30, if not earlier."

Emma didn't answer. She was writing in her neat, slanted handwriting. "Can I read your diary?" Lizzie asked, leaning over to see what she had written.

"No."

"Why not?"

"Because."

Lizzie yawned sleepily, got up, stretched, and said, "Okay. G'night, Emma."

"G'night. Don't worry too much about being a *maud*. You'll be all right when the time comes for you to go."

That was nice of Emma to place so much trust in me, Lizzie thought as she walked down the darkened hall to her room. But she need not worry, because I'm not going. Mam and Dat can't make me.

She guessed she would have to start saying an extra prayer in the evening. Maybe that was why so many scary things happened to Lizzie, because Emma knelt beside her bed faithfully to say her little German prayer, and Lizzie hopped into bed and said it under the warm quilts. And often Lizzie didn't really say her prayers right. She felt silly, or sometimes she felt like God didn't hear her say them. How could he hear it if she just thought her prayer?

And yet she felt silly to say it out loud.

When they were small and Mam helped them say their prayers, she didn't feel silly. Praying had felt just right, because God heard Mam—Lizzie was positive of that. He heard Emma, too, because Emma was a good girl. She was always straightening up the living room or sweeping the kitchen floor, and she loved to wash dishes. Lizzie just didn't feel comfortable with God yet.

The next day, an ordinary-looking postcard arrived in the mail. Mam read the card out loud from her place at the kitchen table. The card came from a Mrs. Mary Beiler whose town Lizzie didn't even recognize. Lizzie sat on the bench along the wall, eating a piece of apple crumb pie with milk before she went to feed the horses and help with the milking. She was perfectly relaxed since she had resolved not to go work as a *maud*.

"So... Mrs. Beiler needs you to help with the fall housecleaning. They just moved, and the house is small, but in need of a good cleaning," Mam said, smiling at Lizzie.

Lizzie blinked, chewing methodically. "Mmm. Mam, this apple pie is the best thing you ever made."

"Didn't you hear me?" Mam asked.

"What?"

"It's your turn to be a real *maud* now."

"That's no problem, Mam. I'm not going."

Mam's mouth dropped open in surprise. What blatant form of rebellion was this? Her cheeks flushed, but she spoke quietly and patiently.

"Why aren't you going?"

"I just decided when Emma went for a week that I could never do that. She's so good, Mam. You know how it is with her. Same as it always was. So I made up my mind that she can be a *maud*, and I'll stay here with you."

Lizzie set down her glass of milk, wiped her mouth with a napkin, and got up to go do chores.

Mam cleared her throat.

"But, Lizzie, both you and Emma can be *mauds*. Mandy can help me here at home. It would certainly not be fair to make Emma work away while you do as you please."

"I don't do as I please. I work at home." Lizzie pulled on her old sweater, preparing to go to the barn. She lifted her nose a few inches as if to remind Mam how pitiful she was, thinking that she would ever work away from home for an entire week.

The screen door was as far as she got.

"Lizzie Glick!" Mam said in a tone of voice that stopped Lizzie in her tracks. Just as luck would have it, Dat stepped up onto the porch at the exact same moment.

"Now what?" he asked, glancing at Lizzie and noticing Mam's heightened color as well.

Lizzie stood stone-still, her shoulders erect, staring out across the brown fields that led to the creek. Mam explained about the postcard from Mrs. Beiler, and Lizzie's arrogant assumption that Emma was the only one who would ever be a *maud*.

Dat sat down.

"Lizzie," he said in a terrible voice.

She tasted defeat, a sickeningly sour, green-apple flavor that would not go away. They were actually going to make her go. Not just Mam, but Dat, too. Dat! Now he was on Mam's side, and those two sticking together meant she had no more of a chance than a chicken feather in a hurricane.

"Let me tell you something, young lady. If you think you're going to tell us what to do, you have another guess coming."

Lizzie whirled around, the sour-tasting defeat bringing tears in its wake.

"I don't want to go!" she cried.

"But you're going," Dat said softening his tone.

"Listen, Lizzie," Mam broke in. "I know it seems cruel to you now, but you have to learn to have a job anyway, from now until you get married. That's what Amish girls do. You may as well give in now, because you're just making it hard on yourself and on us."

"Emma's different than me!" Lizzie wailed, sinking onto the wooden bench, putting her head in her hands.

"That's just an excuse, Lizzie. You can try and grow up and become a bit more like her. I know there's a difference in your natures, but you can't use that as a stepping-stone to just skip out of any situation you don't want to be in," Dat said.

"I don't want to wash other people's dirty laundry and wipe their walls and eat with them and sleep in their beds!"

Mam hid her smile but winked at Dat.

"It's not as bad as you think, Lizzie," she said.

Dat's eyes shone, and he smiled at Mam. "Oh yes, I remember you hanging out wash at Aaron Kanagys. I thought you were the prettiest *maud* I ever saw!"

"Ach, Melvin!" Mam smacked his arm playfully.

That made Lizzie so mad, she literally saw red. How could they be so happy and tease each other when they should pity her? She got up, hurrying around the table in a desperate dash to the stairs, but her sweater button caught on a kitchen chair. She stopped to loosen it, and Dat caught her eye.

"So Mam will write Mrs. Beiler and tell her you'll be ready Monday morning?"

"Well, *I'm* not going to write," Lizzie snapped, turning on her heel and stomping up the steps as loudly as possible.

"Let her go," she heard Dat say, followed by a soft murmur from Mam. She paused at the top of the stairs as Dat said, "She'll get over it."

Lizzie flung herself on her bed. Dat and Mam were cruel. They were mean. She wasn't going to go.

Chapter 17

Emma came home on Saturday, telling all kinds of stories about her week, happier than Lizzie had ever seen her. She hugged the twins and fussed over Jason, telling Mam and Dat how good it was to come home. Lizzie began to suspect that working away couldn't be that bad, or Emma would not be so happy.

So when the driver stopped at the end of the sidewalk on Monday morning, Lizzie grabbed her suitcase and said good-bye to everyone without a trace of anger.

Still, when the driver pulled up to a small white house on the left side of the road, with a huge red barn on the right side and maple trees in the front lawn, Lizzie nearly fainted with nervousness. One of the upstairs windows was flung open, and a slender young housewife looked down at her.

"Well, good morning! You aren't looking for work, are you?" Mary Beiler laughed.

Lizzie looked up and smiled back. She's pretty and neat and so much younger than I thought she'd be, Lizzie thought.

After Mary paid the driver, Lizzie followed her into the kitchen where they sat at the table and talked awhile. She introduced her two young children, a dark-haired, brown-eyed boy named Abner and a sweet little girl named Rhoda.

Lizzie could hardly keep from staring at Rhoda's tiny pink dress. It was the cutest thing she had ever seen. She would make a dress exactly like that for her own little girl one day, she decided.

That afternoon, Lizzie was introduced to the world of Mrs. Mary Beiler's housecleaning expectations. Mary was extremely thorough, much more so than Mam or even Emma. Together they washed walls that were already clean, scrubbed drawers that were already spotless, and washed windows and screens that may have been only a bit dusty. Lizzie learned to use one kind of soap for the furniture and the woodwork, another kind for the walls, and yet another mixture for the linoleum on the floor.

Every quilt, sheet, doily, and rug was whisked off to the kettle house and washed in the wringer washer. Lizzie didn't mind doing the wash if it just meant running it from the wash tub, through the wringer, into the rinse tub, and through the wringer again. But more than that was plainly unnecessary, she thought, though Mam didn't agree. Earlier that week, Mam had frowned when she saw how Lizzie had washed Dat's socks.

"Lizzie, you didn't soak those socks in Clorox water, did you?" she asked.

For one wild moment, Lizzie had a notion to lie and to just say, "Yes." She knew she was supposed to, but she detested the smell of Clorox, and besides, Mam would never know. How could she tell?

"No," Lizzie said.

"You know I don't like yellow socks on the line, Lizzie. Next time you wash, remember to use Clorox."

Lizzie didn't answer. She was too angry. What was the difference? A man's socks were hidden the whole way under his shoes, which came clear up to above his ankles anyway. And his pant legs covered his shoes. Lizzie never saw one peep of Dat's white socks, unless he was ready to take his bath or had just gotten up in the morning. Lizzie never, or hardly ever, saw Dat's socks, so she was positive no one else did. What did it matter if they were soaked in Clorox or not? It was just a bad habit, soaking socks in that awful-smelling stuff.

"Once I'm married, no one is going to tell me to soak my husband's socks. If they aren't white, he will just have to wear them that way."

She had thrown the socks in the washer.

"And another thing, our farm is so old and ugly and sloppy, brown socks on the line would match it just fine," she said, her head held high.

Mam sighed.

"Lizzie, you're going to have to learn," she said. Your attitude is not good, especially about the farm. We'll get this place looking just fine in a few years, you watch."

"And in the meantime, we'll be ashamed every time someone comes to visit," Lizzie burst out.

❧

"Lizzie!" Mrs. Beiler called.

Lizzie jumped.

"What?"

"Do they always call you Lizzie? Doesn't anyone call you 'Liz' or 'Elizabeth?'"

"No."

"Well, you should be called Elizabeth. It's prettier.

"Come on down now. Dinner's ready."

Lizzie was sincerely thankful that it was 12 o'clock and time for lunch. She was almost weak with hunger, since she had been too nervous to eat much breakfast that morning. As she went down the stairs, the delicious smells from the kitchen made her mouth water. Mary Beiler must be a good cook, she thought happily.

"You can wash the children's hands in the bathroom," Mary said. "Abner, go with Liz. She'll wash your 'patties!'"

Liz! Didn't that sound classy! Imagine how nice it would be if everyone called her Liz! That would make it seem as if she was already16 years old.

She turned to Abner, smiling into his dark brown eyes.

"Do you want me to wash your hands?"

Abner placed his hand in hers, melting her heart with his liquid dark eyes.

"Are you our *maud*?" he asked in his slow, proper speech.

"Yes, I am this week."

"Are you going to sleep here?"

"Mm-hmm."

"Good," he drawled, which warmed Lizzie all over again. She hoped with all her heart she could have a little boy that looked and talked like Abner some day.

Lizzie had just sat down at the table when Mary's husband, Jacob, walked into the kitchen. He was big and broad-shouldered with dark curly hair and a slow smile. A tall young man followed him into the kitchen, wearing a short-sleeved white shirt, his face tanned from the sun. Lizzie had never seen anyone whose hair was cut like this young man's. Maybe it was a style she hadn't seen yet because she wasn't running around with the young people.

When he took his place at the end of the table, Lizzie tried not to stare. Yet she had to look sometimes because he was the most handsome person she had ever seen.

"Jacob, this is Lizzie Glick, our new *maud*. Daniel, Lizzie will be here this week," Mary said.

"Hello. So you come from way up at the other end of the county?" Jacob asked.

"I guess," Lizzie managed to croak.

She glanced furtively at Daniel, but he was looking at his plate. He didn't say anything at all, which Lizzie couldn't understand, because surely he would not be embarrassed in front of her. She was only plain Lizzie, with brown hair and clothes that didn't look half as neat as other people's.

"Daniel is my brother," Mary smiled. "He's not quiet usually."

"The cat got his tongue," Jacob teased, and Daniel smiled back.

After they had bowed their heads in silent prayer, they passed dishes of hot, steaming food—fluffy mashed potatoes, thick beef gravy, and succulent young peas in a cream sauce. Applesauce and small red peppers stuffed with cabbage, crisp green pickles, and lots of bread, butter, and jelly completed the meal.

Lizzie tried desperately not to eat too much. She loved Mam's food, but there was also something deliriously wonderful about eating in other people's homes. But today Lizzie didn't eat as much as she would have liked to, mostly because Daniel was sitting so close to her. He was very good-looking, Lizzie decided. She would never, ever have a chance of having him as a boyfriend, and for sure not as a husband. If neither Joe nor John was interested in her, than Daniel wouldn't be either.

She wondered if he had a girlfriend at home. Probably. She would ask Mary if she had enough nerve.

"Does your dad milk cows on your farm?" Jacob asked. Startled, Lizzie dropped her spoon.

"He does now, yes, but I don't know how long yet. They just die."

The men laughed loudly. Oh, dear. Her cheeks felt hot and she blinked self-consciously. Why did she say that? They didn't have to know about their old run-down farm and the fact that so far Dat was not very successful with the cows.

"Why are they dying?" Jacob asked, chuckling.

"I don't know. The vet comes out quite often."

Mary clucked sympathetically. "That can be hard on a pocketbook," she said.

Lizzie had long wondered if Dat knew enough to be a good farmer. When Mandy was little, Dat was a harness-maker. When that business didn't grow fast enough, he started building pallets. So what did he really know about how to run a dairy—with all its expensive equipment, plus animals. What if the crops didn't grow? What if the cows didn't make it?

Lizzie had always been a worrier, all the way back to when she was five and got Snowball the cat and was afraid she'd wander out onto the road and get killed. Lizzie would get up during the night to check that the kitten was still breathing. Now that Lizzie was bigger, she was worrying about bigger things.

Dat had bought their whole herd of 30 Holstein dairy cows from a dealer in Ohio, and they were trying to make a living by milking cows. It still seemed like a risky enterprise, one that often bothered Lizzie as she went about her work. Cows were living creatures who died or got sick, so it all seemed quite unpredictable. She had a hunch that Dat was not thinking carefully enough. He seemed quite positive that the milk would just keep flowing freely and the big stainless steel bulk tank in the milk house would be filled to capacity every time the milk truck rolled in the driveway.

It was the same way with planting corn and making hay. What if it didn't rain? Sometimes it didn't. Or what if it rained when they needed dry weather to cure the hay?

Lizzie took another bite of bread. It was Dat's responsibility, not hers. Everything would be just fine. If only Dat had more experience.

Emma had often told Lizzie that if she prayed more, God could help her not worry so much. Lizzie wasn't too sure he cared enough to quiet her fears. God wasn't as real to her as he was to Emma.

Mary was slicing a chocolate cake and topping each piece with home-canned peaches. Lizzie desperately wanted a large piece of cake soaked with sweet peach juice like she ate at home, but she was too embarrassed to eat that much in front of Daniel. She wasn't exactly thin, but she was trying. She certainly didn't want it to look as if she overate.

Lizzie was relieved when the meal was finally over.

The rest of the day she housecleaned, ironed curtains, and did any job Mary assigned to her. By the end of the day, she was bone-tired and wished she could go home. She missed Mandy and Mam and Dat, their supper table in the old kitchen, and Jason talking with his mouth full. Everything about home seemed so dear and precious. A wave of homesickness enveloped her in a gray mist.

Finally, it was time for Lizzie to take a warm bath and get ready for bed. The bed in the guest room felt strange, so different from her own lumpy mattress with skinny Mandy beside her, reading as Lizzie fell asleep. The sheets were smooth and luxurious, the pillow twice as thick as her old pillow at home. She lay in the dark, thanking God for a room of her own, this nice soft pillow, and the cool sheets. Even if she had to be a *maud*, there were little things along the way to give thanks for.

Mary proved to be a good, kind person to work for. She was very fussy about the way things were to be done. But Lizzie didn't mind. She just remembered to ask when she wasn't sure how to do something. Mary always explained in detail how she wanted jobs to be handled.

The best day was when Mary sent her outside to rake leaves and mow the lawn for the last time before winter set in. Lizzie loved to work outside. She clipped dead plants, hoed flower beds, raked leaves, and pushed the Beilers' new reel mower.

Abner ran alongside the lawn mower, asking a

dozen questions whenever Lizzie stopped. She always took time to answer, loving the way he drawled out his words and rolled his brown eyes for emphasis as he talked.

Toddlers certainly beat babies in Lizzie's estimation. She didn't really like babies that much, especially if they yelled and screamed and drooled on your hand when you held them. In church, each little girl wanted to get someone's baby after services, so they could pretend they were its mother. Lizzie never liked that. Babies were such a mess, and they made Lizzie nervous. She was never sure how to hold a baby. They were too soft and slippery, and Mam said you had to hold their heads carefully. Lizzie was always afraid she had the wrong end up. But a two-year-old was plain-down entertaining. Most of the time.

When Mary came out to bring in the laundry from the line, she threw her hands up in the air and made quite a fuss about everything Lizzie had accomplished.

"It looks like a different yard!" she said.

Amazing how it worked, Lizzie thought. If you made someone else's day brighter, just like magic your own was bright, too. Maybe that was why Emma had been so happy when she came home from being a *maud* for a whole week. She had made other people's lives happier by lifting their workloads.

When the driver came on Saturday afternoon, Lizzie couldn't wait to go home to her family, but she felt almost sorry to leave the Beilers, too. Mary thanked her profusely, handed her a check, and gave her some lavender-scented stationery with matching envelopes.

When Lizzie reached the farm, she flew in the sidewalk, burst through the door, threw her suitcase on the floor, and yelled, "I'm home!"

Everyone made a good and proper fuss, so much, in fact, that Lizzie wondered why she had acted like such a baby to begin with. Being a *maud* had a goodness all its own. The best part, probably, was learning to be a less selfish person.

Chapter 18

Now that Emma was 16, she spent Saturday evenings and Sundays with a group of young people in the neighboring county where there was a larger Amish community. Her new girlfriends invited her to stay at their houses. She was also learning to know many young men. Together they ice-skated, took buggy rides, and gathered for supper crowds and hymn-singings. Emma always came home late Sunday evenings with a driver. Her eyes shone Monday mornings as she told Mam, Lizzie, and Mandy all about her weekend.

Lizzie was thrilled as she listened to Emma. How unbelievably exciting it would be when she turned 16 and went to the neighboring county. She still had to stay at home most of the time, although sometimes she and Mandy were allowed to have fun with their friends from vocational class.

One morning when Emma came down the stairs, her cheeks were flushed with excitement. She looked as if she could absolutely walk on air. In fact, her feet hardly seemed to touch the floor.

"Good morning, Emma!" Mam said, turning to add another egg to the pancake mixture.

"Morning!"

She said it louder than usual, and Mandy turned toward her as she placed the last of the forks beside the plates. Lizzie looked at her, narrowing her eyes.

"Boy, you're happy!" she said.

Morning was not Lizzie's favorite time of day, although for some strange reason, she was *never* very happy it seemed. She was usually fine until Emma or Mandy became too chirpy, too enthused about their day, or just too plain-down good for mornings. Then Lizzie felt grouchier than ever.

Why couldn't they eat breakfast a few hours later? Lizzie wondered. But no, Dat and Mam got everyone up and to the breakfast table before the sun came up. No one was allowed to stay in bed.

"Yes, I guess I am," Emma said, ducking her head shyly, her cheeks absolutely flaming.

"You have a date!" Lizzie burst out.

"Yes, I do!"

Mam dropped her spoon into the pancake batter and gripped the edge of the countertop with one hand. Slowly she turned toward Emma, her mouth open, but no sound came out. She put one hand to her chest and took a deep breath.

"Who?" Lizzie squealed. "Who? Who?"

"Let me guess!" Mandy said, jumping up and down. "David?"

"No."

"Sam?"

"No. Of course not."

"I know. Joshua," Lizzie said.

Emma said nothing, turning away as she tied her bib-apron string.

"It is him, right? Right, Emma? Joshua asked you for a date. This weekend? Is he coming here? Here to our house?" Lizzie asked.

Emma covered her face with her hands and laughed.

"Stop it, Lizzie. One question at a time. Yes, Joshua asked me for a real honest-to-goodness date for next weekend, and yes, he's coming here to pick me up!"

Mam found her voice. "But...but, Emma! You're so young! You just turned 16. Are you sure this is what you want?" she said, rather quietly and a bit weakly for Mam, Lizzie thought.

"I've been 16 for awhile, Mam," Emma replied. And then she said something that Lizzie often thought about afterward, and it never ceased to amaze her.

"Mam, I've known for quite some time exactly who I want. The first time I met him, I knew he was the one I wanted for my husband. It's just so real."

Mam sat down almost as if her knees could no longer support the weight of her body.

"But...but...did you pray about this, Emma?"

"Of course, Mam, many times. Now I feel as if God answered," she said softly.

"Did you ask God for Joshua, Emma? I thought we weren't allowed to do that? Aren't we supposed to ask only for God's will when it comes to finding a husband?" Lizzie asked.

"Now don't start that whole thing," Mandy said as she placed plates on the table.

Lizzie thought about the last day of vocational class, about Mandy and Viola giggling together in the cloakroom.

"Mandy," Lizzie said quietly, standing almost against her.

"Hmm?"

"You know the last day of school?"

"Mm-hmm."

"When I was in the cloakroom, you and Viola came barging in there, your cheeks all red, and giggling together in a corner. What was that all about?" Lizzie felt a thud in the pit of her stomach, already knowing what Mandy would say. She didn't even know why she asked her this question now, but she had to know the answer for sure. She had to know before she could handle another morning in the cow stable.

"What?" Mandy shrugged. "Oh, that!" She turned away to pick up the milk bottle and put it on the table.

"You know what I mean, Mandy. You know, too, why I'm asking. Just tell me the whole truth."

When Mandy finally raised her eyes to Lizzie's, she seemed almost apologetic. "Ach, Lizzie, I can't help it that Joe likes Viola and not you," she burst forth, quite miserably.

"Then he still does," Lizzie said, just as miserably.

"Well, Lizzie!" Mandy said. "What does it matter anyway? We're only schoolgirls who are not nearly old enough to even think about a husband."

"But you know we do! And you know that John likes you, and the only reason you talk like that is to make me feel better. Good, if Joe likes Viola. That's just great! I don't care one bit! I'm never getting married, anyway." Her voice rose to a hysterical screech. "And besides, I'm fat and homely-looking with pimples all over my face, and you're thin and pretty with no pimples!"

There was an awful silence, with Lizzie's outburst hanging in the air like a choking cloud of dust.

"O-oh, Lizzie! You make me so angry! Your favorite cry for attention is telling me how ugly you are. You *know* that's not true. You know, too, that you are not absolutely unattractive. You just...you just wallow around in self-pity like a pig who is *addicted* to its mud hole."

"Mandy, stop it. Now you listen to me. I *would* stop saying those things if you would understand how it feels to be me. Every time I kind of, sort of, you know, not *real* love, but I like someone, they don't like me. The only person who ever liked me was Ivan, and he's my first cousin. So, how, Mandy, tell me how, am I ever going to be able to get a husband? See, you have no idea, because John likes you, for real, and I guarantee he'll end up marrying you. So what do you have to worry about? Nothing!"

Mandy just looked at Lizzie with her big green eyes; then she wiped her face with the hem of her apron.

Dat hurried into the kitchen with Jason right behind him, the cold air whipping past them.

"No girls to help milk this morning?" Dad asked good-naturedly.

"Mandy's turn," Lizzie informed him.

"That's all right. Jase is about as good as you girls. Thirty degrees out there this morning," he said as he hung his coat and hat in the closet.

"More snow?" Mam asked, trying to ease the tension in the room.

"Emma has a date with Joshua King!" Lizzie blurted out.

"What?"

Dat's face broke into a warm smile. "Really?"

"I guess," Emma said, turning toward the stove.

"Well," Dat said, sitting down at his place at the head of the table. "I suppose you are 16 years old, after all, and that's what keeps the world turning," he said, grinning broadly.

"Not exactly," Mam smiled.

"Is he nice?" Dat asked.

"You'll see, Dat. Of course, he's a nice young man. He's...he's the one I thought about for a while."

"Good, Emma! I'm glad you take this seriously," Dat said.

Mam returned to the stove saying happily, "Oh, Emma, we'll have to see what good things we can think of!"

"You mean to bake and cook?" Emma asked, hurrying to help her finish breakfast.

"Why, of course!"

Later, when Lizzie and Mandy were on their way to the barn, Mandy said, "Maybe we need to talk to Mam about all of this."

"No!" Lizzie barked.

"Why not?"

"Well, you know how Mam is. She'll give us this whole row about God's will and I don't understand what she means."

"Lizzie, surely you know there's a higher purpose than just our own selfish wills?"

"Stop acting like a little preacher!"

"Lizzie!"

"Well, you know I don't understand God when he seems so far away."

"I don't always, either."

"Okay, then."

"But we shouldn't feel that way. Mam says God should be more real in our lives."

"Jesus is more real. He's not as big and scary as God is to me."

"That's nice, Lizzie. I suppose it's different for everyone. But I never think too much about a husband, not in a serious kind of way."

Chapter 19

Saturday evening Lizzie sat in Emma's room, watching every move she made. She couldn't believe Emma was going on a real date with a young man Lizzie had never met. Emma combed her hair for the third time, leaning in over her dresser to get a better view of the right side of her head.

"Aren't you nervous?" Lizzie asked for the fifth time.

"Of course, Lizzie. Stop asking me that question or I'm going to scream as loud as I can!" she said.

"Do! I want to hear you," Lizzie laughed.

"It's not funny. Go on out of my room. You're making me nervous for sure. Go on."

"No. I want to watch you get ready."

"All right. But you have to be quiet."

So Lizzie sat silently, her arms wrapped around her knees, watching as Emma finally got her hair combed to her satisfaction. Lizzie sighed with relief. She wasn't too sure about having a date if it made you so nervous. Suppose Emma would just pass out flat on the floor from nerves? Then she'd have to go tell Joshua he couldn't see Emma that evening because she had passed out, and he'd have to turn around and go home again. Wouldn't that be the most embarrassing thing ever? She giggled to herself until Emma frowned.

"What's so funny?" she asked.

Lizzie told her, and Emma laughed and seemed to relax.

"Lizzie, I'm not that nervous."

Lizzie wandered off to find Mandy, and together they sat at the upstairs bathroom window and watched for Joshua and his driver to pull in the lane. They turned out the kerosene light so he couldn't see their silhouettes against the sheer white curtains. Settling themselves comfortably against the wide windowsill, they giggled together in the thick darkness.

Lizzie and Mandy had become good friends as Emma spent more time helping Mam. Mandy was even getting close enough to being Lizzie's size, so that that winter when she started school, she got Lizzie's hand-me-down coat. Mam did have to open some seams and make the coat smaller, because Mandy was really thin compared to Lizzie.

The linings made the girls' coats slippery on the inside. Lizzie loved the feeling of wearing a new coat with a slippery lining inside, because if she held out her arms and turned first one way, then quickly in the opposite direction, her coat swished around her, making her feel like she was being twirled. Emma always told her to stop that, because it looked as if she was dancing. Lizzie couldn't see anything wrong with holding out her arms and twirling around, so she kept going. Mandy just giggled.

Now together they watched headlights coming down the creek road, holding their breaths as each car swerved around the bend in the road but kept on going past the barn.

"Nope, not him," Mandy whispered.

Suddenly the bathroom door was yanked open, and Emma said, "Where is the bathroom light?"

"It's out," Mandy said.

"We blew it out," Lizzie said.

"What are you doing?" Emma asked.

"Watching for Joshua."

"Why in the dark?"

"He'll see us if we let the light on."

"Here come lights!" Mandy yelled.

"In the drive?" Emma asked.

"Yep!"

Emma whirled away with a nervous little yelp and ran into her room while Lizzie and Mandy stayed at the window with its bird's-eye view of the front drive. Headlights turned up the drive, stopping at the sidewalk.

"He's here," Lizzie yelled to Emma. "Go down the stairs!"

"Shhh!" Mandy said, smacking Lizzie's arm hard.

It took forever for the door to open. The interior light went on in the car, but they couldn't see very much of Joshua as he paid his driver. He climbed

out of the car, closed the door, and turned toward
the house, pausing at the end of the sidewalk as his
driver backed the car down the slope.

"Why doesn't Emma go out to him?" Lizzie
hissed.

"Oh, goody, there she goes."

Lizzie was silent, her heart thumping in the quiet
as she imagined how nervous Emma must be.

"He's not very tall," Mandy whispered loudly.

"Taller than Emma," Lizzie whispered back.

"Emma's short."

"I pity him. Now he has to meet Mam and Dat.
I bet he wishes he didn't have a date. Now I bet he
feels like running out the driveway and never coming back."

"Not if he likes Emma enough."

"He's supposed to love her."

"Not yet."

"Oh, yes, he is."

"You don't know."

They held their breaths as they heard low voices
in the living room.

"Should we go down?" Mandy whispered.

"Let's just sit on the stairs for a while and listen.
I feel kind of sorry for Joshua, having to meet the
whole family all in one Saturday evening."

They settled themselves on the lower step, pushing the door open wide enough to allow a bit of
light and noise to enter their hiding place.

❧

With Emma slipping away into her new life, Lizzie was glad that Mandy was still nearby. She shivered as she remembered how close they had come to losing Mandy during the auction when Dat bought their Jefferson County house.

"Where's Mandy?" Mam had suddenly asked in the middle of all of the excitement over their new house.

"Mandy?" Lizzie looked up from the doughnut she was eating. "I don't know, Mam. Emma and I were walking around looking at everything. I thought she was with you or Dat."

"Go look for her," Mam said. "I need to sit down."

Mam sat down weakly on a porch chair, holding Jason. She looked drained and tired after all the suspense of the sale, Lizzie remembered. Emma and Lizzie had pushed through the crowd of men standing in the big open doorway of the barn. She had followed Emma back to the house, and they had looked in every room, calling Mandy's name, more frantic by the minute.

"Mand-dee! Mand-dee!"

They burst back out through the screen door.

"We looked everywhere," Emma told Mam. Lizzie was trying hard not to panic because kidnappers were one of her worst fears. In a crowd this size, and with Mandy being so little and skinny, Lizzie could not bear to think about what might have happened.

Mam got up from her chair.

"Lizzie, we have to find her! Please go get Dat!"

They looked for what felt like hours, but Mandy was nowhere around. Lizzie and Emma were walking slowly back to the house when suddenly Emma stopped.

"I think I see her," Emma said, still looking across the lawn. Lizzie looked, and, sure enough, a small brown head was barely visible out at the end of the lawn. It might be Mandy! They both hurried out across the flat yard, and there she was, her thin little arms wrapped around her knees.

"Mandy!" Lizzie said breathlessly.

"She's here!" Emma called to Mam who started to run towards them.

"What?" Mandy had asked.

"Where were you, Mandy? We couldn't find you," Lizzie said.

"Lizzie, look!" she said, pointing to the yard across the road. Two pure white cats emerged from beneath a flowering bush. They were long-haired, and even their tails were long, thick, and glossy, every strand combed and flowing with the delicate movement of the cats' dainty feet.

"What kind of cat are they?" asked Mandy.

"I don't know. All I ever saw were ordinary barn cats and Snowball. But Snowball looked common compared to those cats," Lizzie said.

On the way home, Mandy would talk of nothing else but the Persian cats which had so dazzled her.

❧

Lizzie reached over and squeezed Mandy's hand. Mandy slapped Lizzie's arm and hissed, "Here they come!" But it was only Emma on her way up the stairs for her coat.

"Wha... Wha... Watch it!" she stammered as she hurriedly yanked open the stair door to find her two sisters huddled directly inside. "What are you two up to?" she asked.

"N...nothing," Lizzie said, trying hard to appear nonchalant.

Emma bent low and said menacingly, "Get up. You act like you're three years old. Go out there and say hello to Joshua and talk to him while I get my coat. Go!"

So Mandy and Lizzie went.

Joshua was standing at the sink, leaning back, his arms crossed, and looking at ease in his strange surroundings. He was of medium height with wavy brown hair and deep-set, blue-green eyes. He was quite good-looking, and when he smiled, he had a wide grin which made Lizzie feel a bit less self-conscious.

"You must be Lizzie and Mandy," he said in a deep voice.

"Mmm-hmm," Lizzie said, lowering her eyes as she bit her lip.

"You must be Joshua," Mandy said, smiling.

Tonight Emma was planning to take Bess the horse and Dat's buggy. She and Joshua would spend the evening with Emma's best friend, Sara, who was dating a young man who had recently moved to Cameron County. He had purchased his own farm and lived there all by himself, so Dat said he must have lots of money for such a young person, as prosperous and well kept as that farm was. Sara was a tall, light-haired girl with large blue eyes, whom Emma was grateful to have as a best friend.

Then there was nothing else to say. The water faucet dripped steadily. Joshua cleared his throat and looked out the kitchen window. Mandy slipped behind the table and sat on the bench. They listened to Emma opening and closing her closet doors upstairs.

Lizzie searched frantically for something to say. Should she ask him how many brothers and sisters he had? Definitely not. That would be too personal. The weather! That was it. If Dat needed something to talk about, it was always the weather. Oh, why didn't that Emma hurry back down from her room? She was probably just checking her covering and her hair again.

"Is it still as cold outside as it was today?" Lizzie blurted out.

"It probably is. It usually turns colder at night," Joshua answered with just a hint of a twinkle in his eye.

"Uh, yeah, I guess so," Lizzie said.

Much to Lizzie's great relief, she heard Emma close her room door and then her light steps raced down the stairs.

She came through the door, her coat slung across her arm, her green eyes sparkling as she crossed the room. Joshua watched Emma, never taking his eyes from her face with such a soft expression in his deep-set eyes that Lizzie felt like an intruder. Emma smiled at him as she stopped to put on her coat, and Joshua stepped forward to hold it for her.

Lizzie was mesmerized. Her very own sister seemed like a sparkling Cinderella and Joshua was her prince. So this was how it was to have your very first date.

"Ready?" Joshua asked.

"Yes. Oh, we need a flashlight to get Bess hitched up," Emma said as she opened the cupboard door.

And then they were gone. Lizzie and Mandy looked at each other for a very long time, saying nothing at all. Mandy pleated the tablecloth with her fingers, and Lizzie sighed as she looked at the kitchen door.

"I'm surprised they didn't leave a solid trail of stardust as they walked out the door," she said.

"They like each other so much it isn't even funny," Mandy said.

But Lizzie couldn't put another thought out of her mind. Sometimes being married seemed like a lot of trouble. Take Mam, for instance, and the fact that she had to move far away from her family when she and Dat got married. Lizzie decided that she was going to be very careful about whom she married, and then they were going to talk a lot before they moved from one settlement to another.

Maybe Mam should have stayed in Ohio to begin with, Lizzie thought. Then she wouldn't have to be so homesick for her relatives. How had Mam and Dat met, and why had they never lived in Ohio where Mam's people were from? How could you love someone enough to move 300 miles away from your parents? Lizzie snorted, thinking that a man would have to be either extremely good-looking or wonderfully kindhearted to get her to move that far away from Mam and Dat. It was just safer not to get married at all.

Suppose you did get married and your husband decided he wanted to move? If you were Amish, you had to go with him wherever he went; it didn't matter if you wanted to or not. If you were English, and you really, really did *not* want to go, you could get a divorce.

Amish people didn't believe in divorce, Mam said. Lizzie wondered why not. Once she had asked Emma what she thought about all of this while they were in the pea patch.

❧

"Emma, would you move to Alaska if your husband wanted you to?" Lizzie asked, opening a pea pod and scraping out the tender green peas.

"I'm not thinking about Alaska!"

"But, Emma, how did Mam and Dat get married?"

"By a *preacher*! Now come on and pick *peas*!"

Emma wanted to be finished as soon as possible.

Lizzie picked another pea and ate it. "No, I mean, how did they meet?"

"Didn't Mam ever tell you? Of course you know, Lizzie," Emma said.

"How?"

"Mam's brother Eli and his wife lived in Jefferson County and needed a *maud*. So Mam came to work for them, and Doddy Glicks lived there, too, so Dat used to go to the singings and Mam did, too, so they started dating."

"That sounds boring," Lizzie said indignantly.

Whack! A pea hit the back of Lizzie's head.

"Stop your talking and pick peas, or I'm telling Mam," Mandy said.

So Lizzie bent her back and picked, her thoughts wandering back to Mam and Dat and moving so far away from your family to live with your husband. It's not like Dat was astonishingly tall or handsome. He was short, actually, although he had very blue eyes and nice, wavy brown hair with a neat beard. He could sing any song you could possibly think of and was very talkative, always entertaining company when they came to visit. Lizzie bet he was fun to have a date with.

She wondered if Mam had been very pretty and slender. Hardly. She had told the girls she was never thin. That was comforting.

❧

Suddenly Mam came bustling out to the kitchen, her cheeks flushed, excitement making her eyes snap. Dat followed her, a big silly grin on his face as he sat at the table. Jason slid in beside Mandy, looking at Lizzie and back again to Mandy.

"Bet you wish you had a boyfriend," he teased.

Dat laughed, slapping the table with his open palm. "Now, Jase!" he said.

Mam opened the refrigerator door, checking to see if her seven-minute frosting had cooled properly. She tasted it, nodded her head, and got the bowl out of the refrigerator so she could ice the big round chocolate cupcakes.

"They might be hungry when they come home," Mam said softly.

"What did you think of Joshua, girls?" Dat asked, as he poured coffee from the pot on the stove.

"He's nice," Mandy answered.

The wind whistled softly around the eaves of the farmhouse as Mam frosted cupcakes and Dat sipped his coffee. It was a cozy, secure feeling, being there in the kitchen with Dat and Mam, both of them smiling contentedly.

Somewhere out in that dark night, Emma and Joshua were traveling steadily down the road, away from them, to spend the evening with Sara and her boyfriend. It was a good feeling to know Emma and Mam and Dat were so happy, but it also stirred up Lizzie's old worries.

Why did changes have to happen? Couldn't Emma just wait awhile before she started dating and stay home with her family on weekends? Lizzie already missed her, mostly because she seemed too grown-up now, too preoccupied whenever Lizzie tried to talk to her. It seemed as if Emma's thoughts were a million miles away, and half the time she didn't even hear Lizzie when she said something.

Lizzie sighed, suddenly feeling very tired and a bit old. "Guess I'll go to bed," she said, getting up and stretching. As she went up the stairs, she heard Dat ask Mam what was wrong with Lizzie, and Jason said that Lizzie wished she had a boyfriend herself.

Not really, Jase, not really, Lizzie thought. Too many changes too fast made Lizzie feel as if she needed Mam for a very long time.

Chapter 20

LIZZIE'S HEART SKIPPED A BEAT WHEN SHE read the postcard from Sara Ruth inviting Mandy and her to attend a skating party.

"Oh, my!" Lizzie breathed as she leaned against the mailbox, reading the postcard. "Oh, my," she repeated, her eyes narrowing as she contemplated the message on the postcard. Mandy would be thrilled to see Joe's brother, John, again. Some of Sara Ruth's cousins from Lamton, a huge Amish settlement 50 miles away, would be there. Joe would be there, and Viola, who was not Amish, would be nowhere around. Sorry, Viola, Lizzie thought.

A grin spread across her face as she tucked a strand of hair nervously behind her ear. She yanked her scarf tightly under her chin, then she burst into a run, racing up the driveway, her breath coming in short hard puffs. The frigid air hurt her lungs, but she didn't care one bit. She was going skating!

"Guess what!" she yelled as she clattered through

the kitchen door.

"Shut the door!" Mam said, as she bent to open the oven door. "I declare it hasn't gone one degree over zero today!"

"Guess what, Mam! Sara Ruth wrote a card saying she's having a skating party! Can we go? Huh? Can we?"

Lizzie bent down beside her mother, peering into her face as Mam squinted, testing a shoofly pie with a toothpick.

"Better not," she muttered to herself as she closed the oven door, straightening her back to look at Lizzie.

"Better not what?" Lizzie asked. What if Mam wouldn't let them go? She wouldn't be so cruel, would she?

Mam threw her pot holders on the countertop and sat down at the kitchen table. She sighed as she gave Lizzie her full attention. "I meant better not take those shooflies out quite yet," she said. "Now what are you so excited about?"

"Sara Ruth wrote and said she's having a skating party," Lizzie said patiently.

"Where?" Mam frowned.

"I guess at her house," Lizzie answered.

"Is the ice thick enough? And how would you go?"

"I bet the ice is a foot thick!"

"I wonder."

Mandy came clattering down the stairs. Lizzie jumped up and grabbed Mandy's shoulders. "Sara Ruth is having a skating party!"

They squealed and hopped and danced across the kitchen until Mam said they had to calm down because the whole house was shaking.

And so, the following Friday evening, Lizzie and Mandy took their baths earlier than usual. Lizzie carefully combed her hair and chose a pale blue dress to wear. She couldn't wait to see her friends from vocational school again.

Dat hitched up Bess and made sure the battery in the buggy was charged so their lights would stay bright on the way home. He also double-checked that the turning signals and the orange blinking rear lights worked as well. He complained a bit about letting the girls drive so far by themselves in the dark, but he was smiling as he told them to be careful.

It was almost six miles to their destination, but it didn't seem far. Bess clopped steadily through the star-strewn evening. The heavy, warm buggy blanket covered their knees, and the steel wheels rattled gently on the macadam. Lizzie and Mandy chattered on about lots of subjects as Bess pulled the buggy up hills and around bends, through little tree-filled hollows and across different roads.

"They have a beautiful farm," Mandy said as they approached the well-lit house.

"I know," Lizzie said. "That's because their house is bigger and better than ours, and it has classy white shutters on it."

"They have more money than we do, don't they?"

"Probably. Yeah, I'm sure they do."

The Kings' red brick house stood like a sturdy

sentinel in the night with warm yellow light radiating from the windows. Isaac King, Sara Ruth's Dat, finished up his evening milking in the glowing barn. He helped Lizzie unhitch Bess beside the big new cow stable with a rounded roof and the two new silos which towered over the other buildings.

Through the darkness, Lizzie could see a bonfire burning down by the pond next to a line of willow trees. On the pond, dark figures dashed across the ice, while others huddled around the bonfire. Lizzie shivered with cold and something almost like fear. For one wild instant, she felt like hitching Bess back up again and heading home as fast as she could.

"M...Mandy!"

"What?"

"Aren't you...I mean...don't you feel afraid, or... shy or anything?"

"Kind of, yes. But we won't for long."

Sara Ruth and Sharon came running towards them, calling their names.

"It's so good to see you again," Sara Ruth gushed as she linked her arms in theirs. "You'll have to meet our cousins. And, oh yes!" She let go of their arms as she skipped forward, then turned to face them as she walked backward. "Do you know that new Beiler family who moved in from Allen County?"

"Who are they?"

"I don't know. Their oldest boy is 16 already. They have a girl about exactly our age named Anna."

"Are they coming tonight?"

"Probably."

They reached the pond where they met Sara Ruth's cousins from Lamton. These girls were perfectly thin and so pretty, Lizzie could only stare at them. They wore pretty colors in the latest style, and their hair was combed so beautifully, Lizzie could only hope to be able to comb herself half as neatly someday.

They look like little dolls, Lizzie thought miserably, feeling very much like the fat little country mouse being shown the trim city mouse. But the cousins, Linda and Louise, smiled so honestly, welcoming them so sincerely, that Lizzie soon forgot about being self-conscious.

Joe and John skated up to the bank, their grins welcoming the girls to the pond.

"Did someone help you put your horse away?" John asked.

"Your dad did."

"Good!"

And they were off, racing across the pond with a few of their smaller cousins.

The girls sat down on the straw bales and pulled on their white socks.

"Do you always wear white socks?" Sharon asked.

"Yes, to go skating."

"That looks nice."

Sara Ruth started giggling, saying she never even thought about wearing white socks to skate. She was going to bring a bunch of the twins' socks down to the pond. Then the girls were off, leaving Lizzie and

Mandy to put on their skates.

They were still struggling to lace up their skates when a dark shadow hovered over them. Lizzie looked up from tying her skates at a tall, thin guy standing beside the fire, holding a pair of black skates.

"Hi," Lizzie offered.

"Hello. Are John and Joe here?"

"They're skating. Oh, there they are."

A grin spread across the boy's face as the twins swooped up on the bank, almost colliding with the youth.

"Stephen!"

"Hey!"

So that was his name—Stephen. Lizzie glanced at him sideways. His hair was way too long in the back, and his bangs almost fell over his eyes. His eyes were big, huge, actually for a boy, and a light baby blue. Long, dark lashes surrounded them, unlike any Lizzie had ever seen. She wondered why he didn't get his hair cut.

Girls swooped down on Lizzie and Mandy like a bunch of blackbirds in the fall. Lizzie couldn't help giggling. Sharon pushed Lizzie over on her hay bale and started pulling on a pair of socks. Stephen stood watching in his eerily quiet way.

"You sound like a bunch of wild geese," he said.

"Where's your sister, Stephen?" Sara Ruth asked.

"Too cold for her."

"You should have brought her. Lizzie and Mandy don't know her yet."

"They'll see her in church."

And with that, Stephen moved off as quietly as he had come. Lizzie burst out, "He's different! He's so quiet, he gives me the creeps."

Lizzie jumped up and skated onto the pond. She threw back her head and laughed. She loved skating with all of her heart, and this was the first ice-skating of the season. She didn't think about boys or fancy girls as she glided across the ice with wings on her skates. She twirled and turned, skated sideways and backward, warming to the thrill of being alive.

Suddenly she heard girls clapping and cheering from the bank. She slid to a stop.

"What?"

"Can you ever skate!" Sara Ruth called.

"Show-off!" Sharon teased.

Lizzie laughed happily as Mandy, who was even more graceful because of her slight form, joined her. They skated together until the boys hooked arms with them, and they all met in the middle of the pond and decided to play Freeze Tag.

This was one of the best nights of Lizzie's whole life. The stars were so close she could almost reach out and grasp one. The air was sparkling cold, burning her nose the way it did when she drank Pepsi and then burped.

Stephen was an extremely fast skater. No one could escape once he decided to pursue them without mercy. Joe chased her a lot during the evening. Maybe he might someday like her without Viola around. Who knew?

Lizzie's heart was light. She was chased and held captive, dipping and swaying, breaking free, being caught again, all under the light of the too-close stars. Before Lizzie had even begun to tire, Sara Ruth announced that her mother would serve an evening snack just as soon as they went to the house. Lizzie wanted this evening to go on forever, this perfectly crisp, thrilling, heartfelt, starry, wonderful evening on the ice.

Inside the house, Mrs. King had all kinds of delicious food for the skaters, which helped ease Lizzie's sense of disappointment about leaving the pond. The dining room table was filled with big thick slices of homemade pizza piled high with cheese and browned ground beef, root beer in glass mugs, crackers, pretzels and potato chips, and warm chocolate chip cookies for dessert.

Sara Ruth beamed, Linda and Louise flitted about like rose-colored parakeets, and Sharon giggled in a corner with Mandy. Stephen was quite shy, staying well away from the bright gas lamp in the kitchen. Lizzie wished her family could have a skating party at their house. They had the creek that was perfect for swimming in the summer, but no pond on the old farm for ice-skating.

When the evening finally ended, they all walked to the barn to hitch up their horses.

"Does the creek ever freeze solid?" Lizzie asked Joe.

"I don't know," he said.

"I doubt it," John echoed.

"Is the water pretty swift? How deep is it?" Stephen asked.

"It depends. Some places it's way deep and quiet, and other places it runs real fast over rocks."

"If it stays this cold, it'll freeze over."

Lizzie and Mandy talked the whole way home. Bess plodded faithfully, her breath coming in hard, round little puffs of steam as she pulled the buggy safely back to their farm.

In their kitchen, a kerosene lamp shone bright. The girls hurried to the warmth of the coal stove, quickly shedding their snow boots, pushing their stocking feet against its glowing warmth.

"Mmmm!" Mandy closed her eyes, enjoying the stove's wonderful heat.

"You home?" Mam tiptoed out from her bedroom, her housecoat clutched in her hands. She smelled of talcum powder just as she had when Lizzie was a little girl.

"Yes, Mam. We're almost frozen."

"I'm glad you're here. I haven't slept yet." She turned to go back to bed, relaxed now that her girls were safely in the house.

"She looks like an angel."

"She smells like one."

Lizzie could hardly bear the feeling of love she felt for Mam. Wasn't it just wonderful that God made soft, warm Mams who smelled so good? Her soft housecoat felt like Lizzie imagined heaven must feel.

Lizzie decided there was no place sweeter than

home, and she wanted to stay there for a very, very long time.

She only blinked at the moonlight once before she fell into a deep, lovely sleep.

Chapter 21

ONE DAY MAM FROWNED WHEN EMMA handed over her paycheck. She had been away for five days, but the money she brought home wasn't much for an entire work week.

"Emma, I don't mean to criticize or complain. I know you work hard, but if I need to think about buying your hope chest and starting to fill it for when you get married, we're going to have to earn more money somewhere. I know these young dairy farmers who you're helping are struggling, and they have to spend a lot on your transportation, too, so it isn't their fault that you aren't earning more. I just wish we could find a better paying job for one of you, at least," she said.

"Mam, I could work in town at a restaurant," Lizzie volunteered.

"I guess not. We're not that desperate," Mam said, shaking her head.

Lizzie knew that was what Mam would say. But

ever since she was a little girl she had wanted to be
a real waitress in a real restaurant.

Her first restaurant meal was etched forever in
her mind. On the second morning of their once-in-
a-lifetime family vacation to Luray Caverns, they
had eaten breakfast in a real restaurant! Lizzie had
never eaten in a restaurant, so she didn't know what
the inside would look like.

There were lots of electric lights, and a shiny
green floor with dark blue lines and streaks running through it. The place was filled with so many
tables and chairs, Lizzie could not imagine how the
waitresses could remember who sat where and what
they wanted to eat. It was all a bit frightening and
confusing, until a smiling lady with a small white
apron came to seat them.

She was so friendly, Lizzie felt much more at
ease, especially when she made a big fuss about the
twins as she helped Mam put them each in a high
chair. Some of the other waitresses had watched
Lizzie and her family as they sat down around the
table. That was one thing about being Amish that
Lizzie did not like—when people unfamiliar with
their plain clothes stared at them. Most people were
just curious about their long dresses and coverings,
but some people were not very polite.

When the kind waitress handed them a large plastic-covered paper, Mam told them it was the menu,

and they should look for food listed under "Breakfast." That breakfast was plain-down unforget-
table. Lizzie didn't think of her weight once, as they
all enjoyed bacon, eggs, and pancakes topped with
huge globs of butter and all the syrup they wanted.
Tall glasses of ice-cold orange juice and crispy toast
that was also saturated with butter made their meal
extra special.

Mam was smiling and saying they had the best
coffee she ever tasted. Dat was smiling at Mam
as they all enjoyed the delicious food. Emma was
fascinated by how fast the waitress poured coffee. She had never seen anything like it, she told
Lizzie.

"You could pour coffee every bit as fast as she
does if that's what you did all day. That doesn't look
as hard as balancing all those trays of food. Did you
see how many plates were on that one tray?" Lizzie
asked.

"Yes. That would be fun," Emma answered.

"I wonder if Amish girls are allowed to be waitresses," Lizzie said.

"No. Certainly not," Emma said.

"We could go English and all work in the same
place," quipped Mandy.

They had giggled together until Mam said they
had to be quiet since they were not being respectful.

❧

Lizzie spun around on her kitchen chair. She had eaten in restaurants only a few times since that first meal, but each time she thought it would be so fancy to wear a small white apron, writing down orders and putting her pen in the pocket of her little white apron.

"But Mam, I would love to work in a restaurant," she said.

"Absolutely not," she said. "No daughter of mine will be prancing around a whole roomful of English men. No good could come of it."

That's how Mam was. She wouldn't think of letting her daughters work at questionable establishments. She was very careful about everything, even the van drivers she chose.

"Lizzie, you shouldn't complain," Emma said. "Mam is only being careful because she cares about us."

Lizzie stuck her nose in the air and made a snorting sound as she left the kitchen. Mam was a bit over-protective.

Lizzie continued to pester Mam about working in a restaurant. But Mam wouldn't agree. Instead, Mam was overjoyed when Darwin Myers, a local Mennonite man, came to the kitchen door a week later.

Mam was washing dishes at the kitchen sink when Darwin stepped up onto the porch. "Oh, I know who that is! I bet he wants some help," she said to Lizzie.

Quickly, Mam dried her hands on her gray work apron and went to open the door. She greeted him warmly, and he asked how they were. They talked about the weather, as people always did, Lizzie mused.

Finally, Darwin got down to business.

"I need someone to help with the egg-grading," he said. My wife does too much of it for her age, and she's not as well as she once was, so would you consider letting one or two of your daughters come work for me? I would need them on Mondays, Wednesdays, and Fridays."

"Oh, yes!" Mam responded eagerly.

So that was that. Lizzie would go, and if he needed more help on summer days, Mandy would also help at the hatchery, whatever that was.

After he left, Lizzie picked up a dish towel and absentmindedly wiped at a dry plate. She always dreaded starting a new job, but she knew she was getting older and everyone had to have a job after they were out of school.

"How many hours do I have to grade eggs in a day?" she asked, turning to look at Mam with what she hoped was a sweet, martyred expression. She thought that if she lifted her eyebrows at just the right angle and made her eyes look as sad as possible, there was a slight chance that Mam would take pity on her and make Emma go.

Mam was busily reading a recipe card, but she

stopped and looked at Lizzie. A smile tugged at the corners of her mouth.

"Didn't he say he'd pick you up at eight o'clock? Then probably until four or five in the evening. Around eight hours."

Lizzie grabbed another plate and wiped it ferociously. Well, that hadn't helped.

"Well, Mam, I think if we need money to fill Emma's hope chest, shouldn't Emma be the one to make the most money?" Lizzie ventured again. She was trying to complain in a very polite way.

Emma sat at the table cutting sheer white fabric that she would make into coverings, whistling under her breath as she worked.

"Lizzie, I do work away most of the time, but someone has to sew our clothes, too. Do you want to stay home and make coverings?" Emma asked.

Lizzie turned her back and didn't answer. She was too old to cry, and she knew it was plain childish to complain.

"Lizzie, you know you're very fast with your hands. You can do anything you try, and rapidly too," Mam said. "That's why grading eggs will be a good job for you. You do your work just like Mommy Glick, so be glad you inherited her talent. I think you will make a very good egg-grader, and a competent one. Emma is much better at doing fine, careful work like sewing our coverings, so I think this is the best arrangement."

Emma started whistling under her breath again as she watched Lizzie. She didn't say anything. She just looked at her.

Lizzie swallowed all the rest of her complaints, because what Mam had said made her feel good. Maybe that was true. She probably would be a good egg-grader. She just wished the first day was over.

Chapter 22

THE NEXT MONDAY MORNING, WHEN DARWIN stopped his car in front of a long, low, silver building, Lizzie's heart sank. The chicken house was a corrugated steel box with huge round fans on each side. An unruly jumble of weeds and briars grew along the building's base, and old chicken coops leaned in an odd pile-up beside the door.

The door itself was wooden with layers of paint peeling off the front. The window was so splattered with fly dirt you could barely see it was a window at all. Cardboard cartons lay strewn beside the chicken coops, and eggshells littered the gravel drive.

When Lizzie opened the car door, a stench filed her nostrils and turned her stomach. Her first thought was to make a wild dash for freedom, but instead she followed Darwin into the hatchery. Inside, a lone yellow light bulb hung from the ceiling, reminding her of a jail cell. The bright green walls were barely visible between the stacks of cardboard boxes and dull metal carts piled high with square gray cardboard trays used to hold eggs. A huge machine stood along one wall, which Lizzie assumed was the grader.

Through a door at the far end of the room Lizzie heard a rustling, cackling sound. Apparently that was where the chickens were housed. A green door burst open, and an older gentleman pushed out a darker green cart, piled high with cardboard trays of white eggs. He wore an old denim coat and denim overalls, and a navy blue hat covered his white hair. His face was still quite handsome, Lizzie thought as his light blue eyes shone and he smiled.

Lizzie smiled back and said, "Hello."

"This is Enos Martin. He gathers the eggs every day and pushes them into the cooler room," Darwin said.

He pointed at another large green door. When Enos opened it, Lizzie saw that it was insulated, like a refrigerator door. The dim interior of the cooler room gave her the creeps. A wet, rattling sound from up high on the wall came from a cooling unit. Water dripped down the walls into a round granite tub. Would it be her job to empty that tub of cold, dirty water? Lizzie wondered. She shivered and wished with all her heart that Emma was here in this new, scary place and that she was still in school with Sara Ruth and Joe and John.

Darwin showed her where to stack the boxes of jumbo eggs, the extra-large, large, medium, and pullet-sized. That's a lot of eggs, Lizzie thought. Oh, I hope I can do it without breaking them. She chewed her lower lip nervously and took a deep breath to steady herself.

Darwin flipped a switch on the wall and the long lights attached to the ceiling flickered on, filling the room with bright, white light so that the area was no longer haunted and shadowy.

Pulling a cart of eggs over to the machine, Darwin flipped switches, opened boxes, and adjusted dials. The whole machine purred, rattled, and hummed into action. He stepped to the right of the machine, motioning to Lizzie to come and watch.

"Come closer so you can see," he said.

Using both hands, he lifted six eggs and quickly laid them on the moving belt. He did it so rapidly and with so much ease, Lizzie almost forgot that he was holding fragile eggs. The eggs rolled across a light so bright that the eggshells appeared transparent. A dark round object appeared inside each one.

"That's the yolk," Darwin said.

"Now watch," he said. "The reason for this bright light is to find any blood inside the egg. If there is any, you'll be able to see it quite easily, and you put that egg on this flat."

Lizzie nodded. So that was what the cardboard containers were called—flats.

Darwin led her down to the left side of the machine where the eggs were already rolling out, washed and dried to a glistening finish. Stepping up to the machine, Darwin showed her how to pack the eggs.

"Now, if you can't keep up, just holler and I'll stop the machine. You probably won't be able to go very quickly at first," he said.

So the egg-grading began in earnest. Lizzie felt as if someone had pushed her off a cliff and she was hanging in midair. It was absolutely terrifying, all those eggs coming down the moving belt and rolling across the shining stainless steel trays. What if she couldn't keep up and all the eggs got stuck in the moving belt, breaking apart with yellow egg yolks dripping all over the floor?

Darwin was calmly dropping eggs on the light, whistling under his breath. Just like Emma, Lizzie thought. At that moment she resented Mam, Emma, the hope chest, Joshua, growing up, and everything else in her life. This was awful. Mam may as well give up, because she would not spend one more day in this stinking, creepy place.

But Lizzie set her jaw and lifted eggs off the belt, trying to put them into the flat with the pointed side down. It was impossible. There was no way she could lift six eggs at a time and then get them into the right position. Her hands moved quickly, but she needed to stop and turn eggs over so often that the trays were soon overflowing. Meanwhile, the flats were filling up. She was supposed to reach over and lift another one on top of the already filled ones. Once there was a stack of six flats, she had to place them into the big brown cardboard box marked "EGGS."

Lizzie struggled to keep her tears from showing

when she finally asked Darwin to stop the machine. He smiled as he came over to help her, but the lump in Lizzie's throat was so big she couldn't respond. What a dreadful job, she thought, pushing a strand of hair away from her face with trembling hands.

After Darwin helped her catch up, he returned to his station, and Lizzie started picking up eggs again. She wondered how she could ever run back to the cooler room, get the cart, push it under a stack of eggs and take them back, all while the eggs kept steadily rolling into the trays. But as the forenoon wore on, she calmed down enough to holler to Darwin whenever the trays got full. He took care of moving the stacks back to the cooler room since it was her first day.

By lunchtime, she was becoming much more accurate at directing six eggs into each cardboard flat, but her back felt as if there was a knife between her shoulder blades. She swung her shoulders, trying to ease the pain. But there was no time to stop and really do anything about it, so she kept going.

At noon, Darwin turned off the egg-grading machine.

"I'm going to the house for lunch," he said. "I'll be back at one."

Oh good, Lizzie thought, I get a whole hour for lunch. Her mouth watered, thinking of the good food she had packed in her insulated lunchbox that morning.

Lizzie washed her hands in the bathroom and went outside to eat her lunch. She found a freshly-mowed strip of grass that stretched beneath a towering oak tree. If only the smell wasn't so bad, my lunch would taste a lot better, she thought as she sat down on the grass.

She opened the lid of her lunchbox and pulled out her plastic container of juice. She took long gulps of the ice-cold drink. She felt so much better as she unwrapped her sandwich made with Mam's homemade bread, sliced turkey, white American cheese, and lettuce. It was so good, she thought, as she munched it down with a handful of crunchy potato chips. She was so hungry that she didn't worry about counting calories at all. After all, you couldn't work if you didn't eat.

Her spirits lifting, Lizzie watched the leaves swaying in the breeze. Trucks and cars sped past on the road below her. She wondered where they were all going. She sat up straight when a truck pulled into the drive leading to the chicken house. She was all alone and quite a distance away from the house and hatchery, she realized.

The truck ground to a stop, and a middle-aged man leaned out the window, looking at her. Lizzie drew her knees up, pulling her skirt and apron down over her shoes, wrapping her hands around her legs. She gazed up at the driver, hoping he was only asking for directions and would soon be on his way.

"Hello," he said, looking down at her while a slow smile spread across his face. His hairline had receded to such a point that his forehead looked huge. When he took off his dark sunglasses, his brown eyes twinkled at her.

Lizzie smiled up at him. He looked quite harmless, she decided, so she took another bite of her chocolate chip cookie.

"Hello," she said.

"So, why is a young thing like you eating her lunch in a place like this?" he asked, all his white teeth showing as his smile widened.

For some reason, Lizzie thought of the wolf in *Little Red Riding Hood.*

"This is my first day grading eggs for Mr. Martin," Lizzie said.

He opened his door and climbed down from the truck. Lizzie blinked, holding her breath as he adjusted his belt and walked over to her. He was very tall, his shoulders bulging beneath his flannel shirt. He put his hands on his hips and stood quietly in front of her. Lizzie took a deep breath.

"You don't suppose he'd give me a job, do you?" he asked, laughing now.

Lizzie didn't know what to say or think about this man. He was not unattractive. Actually, he was rather good-looking in a masculine way, and he certainly was friendly enough. She felt guilty smiling too much, remembering all Mam's warnings about strange men and that you could never tell what their intentions really were.

Lizzie lowered her eyes and said, "I don't know."

Suddenly he sat down on the grass beside her.

"Do you mind if I wait until Darwin is finished with his lunch?" he asked. "I'm here for an order of eggs to take to Harrisburg."

Lizzie snapped the lid on her lunchbox.

"N...no, that's all right," she said, edging away from him.

He turned to look directly at her.

"You don't need to be afraid of me. I'm quite harmless. I have no bad intentions. Darwin knows me really well. I've been buying eggs from him for years."

"Oh," was all Lizzie could think of to say.

"What's your name?" he asked, still watching her.

"L...Lizzie. Or Elizabeth," she added.

"Elizabeth. That's a beautiful name."

Lizzie turned to thank him, but his brown eyes were too disconcerting so she looked down at the grass, a slow blush creeping across her cheeks. Now she was absolutely at a loss. She didn't understand her rapidly beating heart. Was it fear, or just the unusual way he spoke to her? She couldn't remain sitting here beside this man. What would Mam say?

So she tucked back her hair and got to her feet, bending to pick up her lunch.

"I...I have a bit of cleaning to do," she stammered, without meeting his eyes.

"Really? I bet your lunch hour isn't up yet. Why don't you stay here and talk awhile?"

"I really should...shouldn't."

"Are you Mennonite?" he asked suddenly.

"No. I'm...I'm Amish."

"Really?"

There was nothing to say to that, so she stayed

quiet, holding her lunch with both hands, her eyes downcast.

"Let me guess how old you are. Seventeen? Eighteen?"

Lizzie shook her head, a small smile playing around the corners of her mouth.

"I'm 15."

"I don't believe it."

"Yes, I am. I'll be 16 in a few months."

He said nothing, and Lizzie was puzzled, so she looked at him again. His brown eyes were still as unsettling as ever, and she knew that she needed to get away, anywhere, do anything, because something, she didn't know what, made her think of Mam's warnings. A whisper of guilt was beginning to shadow her.

That afternoon, Lizzie's thoughts were completely jumbled as she continued to grade eggs. She couldn't understand them. Her lunch hour had turned into a jigsaw puzzle of questions, but without a design and without many of the pieces.

Lizzie had not really been afraid of the man. Yet, why had she walked away from him? He was very friendly, actually. She felt like she should go home and tell Mam and Emma all about her lunch hour, but she knew she couldn't. How often did he pick up eggs?

She let go of the eggs and raised her cold hands to cool her face. It was just the way he said "Elizabeth." That was all. She needed to go home and tell Mam. She also knew she wouldn't.

Chapter 23

Over the next week, Lizzie learned to love her job at the egg-grading machine. A week after she started working, a young woman named Dora joined her. They split the work, with Lizzie putting all the eggs on cardboard flats, while Dora placed the eggs on the belt.

Dora was older and had never married, perhaps because of her health problems. She was an epileptic and her seizures could occur at any moment. She was soft-spoken and shy when she first met Lizzie, but as the weeks passed and the two of them worked side-by-side at the grading machine, she became friendlier.

Every day at lunch, they sat beneath the oak tree in the soft fragrant grass and shared the food they had packed. Dora's mother made soft, light-as-a-feather dinner rolls, which melted in Lizzie's mouth. Sometimes she also sent chicken salad made with great succulent chunks of white chicken and crispy pieces of celery and onion, mixed with creamy white mayonnaise. Lizzie shared Mam's homemade cupcakes filled with lovely white frosting or her big, round molasses cookies sprinkled with sugar.

They covered many subjects as they ate. Dora even talked about getting married, although shyly and a bit wistfully. Lizzie felt so sorry for her, it actually hurt. Lizzie admitted that she couldn't wait to turn 16 and start dating. But who would ask her?

One afternoon, when the leaves were turning colors and the breeze was a bit chilly, Lizzie and Dora sat by the oak tree with their sweaters wrapped around them as they finished their lunches. Lizzie leaned back against the rough bark of the oak tree and closed her eyes, sighing. Dora turned toward her.

"Lizzie, you better be careful with that Don Albert," she said.

Lizzie's eyes flew open and she sat straight up, staring at Dora, her cheeks flaming. "Dora! I'm not…I'm not…," she stammered.

The eggman's name was Don Albert, and he wasn't married, he had told her. He always stopped to talk to her when he came to pick up the eggs. His attention made her heart flutter each time and the color rise in her cheeks. Lizzie wondered if that was how it felt to have a real boyfriend. Dora always watched him when he talked to Lizzie, her eyebrows drawn down and her mouth unsmiling.

There was no doubt about it, Lizzie was flattered by this handsome stranger's attention. It brought a thread of excitement to her otherwise mundane job. But she kept her feelings to herself, never telling Mam or Emma. She almost confided in Mandy one evening when she was feeling especially guilty. But she convinced herself that there was no harm done as long as she only talked to him and stayed polite and respectful.

"I know. I know exactly what you mean, but I can also tell how glad you are to see him come for eggs on Tuesdays. He's a nice-looking man, and no matter what you think, you are an innocent young girl. If I were you, I would be extremely careful."

"I wasn't even thinking about him. I would never go out with him or try and …flirt with him," Lizzie said.

Dora looked at her steadily, as if she knew more than Lizzie was willing to admit. Finding it hard to meet her gaze, Lizzie lowered her eyes and felt a little cheap and guilty.

"Lizzie, I know you want to be a good Christian, and you haven't met many temptations in the world, as young as you are. But be careful, because you could be playing with fire. Does your mother know about this man who talks to you every week?"

"Of course not!"

"Why not?"

"I…I don't know."

Lizzie twisted her gray apron around and around on her finger. There was no harm in talking to Don. It was only natural to be attracted to a good-looking man who called you Elizabeth and made you feel like a princess. Besides, there was no chance of them getting to know each other better. He was English and she was Amish. Talking with him was just a harmless thrill to lighten up an otherwise ordinary week. She was sure.

The following Friday, Dora felt weak and ill with a headache, and she left work early. Lizzie finished cleaning up the egg-grader by herself. When she was finished, she threw out her bucket of soapy water just as a cool wind blew, tugging at her skirt. She glanced up and saw that the sky was thick with clouds.

She stood for a moment, her blue dress billowing around her legs, searching the rolling gray clouds for the first raindrops. Most of the leaves from the oak tree were already lying in brown heaps at its base, reminding Lizzie that winter was fast approaching. The fresh, autumn breeze felt wonderful after grading eggs all afternoon. She lifted her arms and stretched, glad her work week was over.

Suddenly two large, heavy hands encircled her waist. She yelped with surprise. She tore loose of the hands, whirling around to face her assailant as she stifled a scream. Her eyes were large with fear and apprehension, and she clenched her hands at her throat.

"You!" she burst out.

"Me!" Don Albert said, laughing. "Scared you, didn't I?"

"W...what are you doing here? It's Friday."

"Where's Dora?" he asked, not bothering to answer her question.

"She went home early with a headache."

"Good."

He took a step toward her, and Lizzie backed away. His eyes held hers, but with a strange new light, terrifying her so that she pressed both hands to her mouth. Her breath came in rapid gasps.

"Now, don't act all scared of me. I just came down here to ask you to go to the movies with me. It's Friday night, and I want to be alone with you. Let's go into town and have a good time."

Lizzie shook her head, her hands still pressed to her mouth, her eyes wide, watching him.

"Come on. I will be the perfect gentleman. I just want to get to know you better. Please?"

He spread his hands, and for one moment Lizzie thought how exciting it would be to throw all her fear to the wind and go to town with him. But the next moment, Mam's face and all her admonitions brought her back to her senses.

"No."

"Why?"

"I...I can't. I'm Amish. My parents would never allow it."

"They wouldn't need to know."

Lizzie shook her head, refusing to look at him.

Suddenly, he gripped her shoulders, shaking her gently. "You shouldn't have talked to me for so long and been so happy to see me. I know you were glad. I could tell."

"I'm sorry," Lizzie whispered.

Rain started falling in large splattering drops and

he relaxed his grip diverting his attention. Lizzie wanted to run back into the hatchery, but she was afraid he would follow her. She wouldn't feel safe once they were in the building and out of sight. She had to leave, and she had to leave now.

"It's raining. I have to go get my paycheck down at the house. I...I have to leave now."

She backed away as she spoke, her skirts blowing in the wind and her hair coming loose beneath her navy blue kerchief.

"Wait!" he called, as she turned and started running down the drive. "Come back!"

But Lizzie ran blindly down the lane, rain pelting her face. She never looked back, knowing she couldn't risk that. A sob tore at her throat and the raindrops on her face mixed with her tears, cooling her warm cheeks.

She heard his truck bumping down the lane before he pulled up beside her.

"Elizabeth!" he called, leaning out of the truck window.

Lizzie's pace slowed, and she lifted her face to him.

"Leave me alone," she said.

"Get in. It's raining."

"I can walk."

"No. Get in."

Lizzie stood in the rain.

"Elizabeth, trust me. I'll take you to the house. I promise."

Slowly, Mam's face burning her conscience, Lizzie walked around the truck, opened the door, and slid onto the passenger's seat. He didn't look at her. He sat gripping the steering wheel with both hands, the knuckles of his hands showing white. Finally, he put the truck in gear and drove slowly down the lane and out onto the road. He turned left and then pulled to a stop in front of the Martins' house.

The wipers whispered across the windshield as the rain increased. It pelted the top of the truck and coursed down the windows.

Don Albert did not say one word as he stared straight ahead at the rain. Lizzie gripped the door handle as she opened her mouth to say something, anything to break this awful silence. She cleared her throat.

"I...I have to go."

He turned slowly and reached for her hand.

"Elizabeth, yes, you do have to go, but wait until the rain slows down."

He held her hand until Lizzie pulled it slowly away from his grip.

"So. That's how it is. Amish girls don't go out with ordinary men."

"No."

Suddenly, Lizzie felt horribly ashamed of herself. She had no business harboring flirtatious thoughts, of being glad to see him. It was not right. Oh God, please, please forgive me, she prayed, as tears pricked the corners of her eyes. Just please, God, let me get home safely and talk to Mam and Emma and Mandy.

She had never felt as if she had done something

so horribly wrong as she did at this moment. Little things in her life had never bothered her much, as they had Emma. But sitting here in this stranger's pick-up truck, the rain rushing down its sides, she begged God to forgive her. She felt as low as she could ever remember.

"Good-bye," Don whispered.

Lizzie didn't say anything. She couldn't. There were no words to convey the depth of her shame and misery. She opened the door and slipped out, standing in the rain as he drove away without looking back. Rain fell on her head, running in little rivulets down her cheeks. Guilt mixed with longing, obedience fought with yearning, all in one churning moment of time like the pinwheels Mam used to buy for them at the Ben Franklin store. When she blew on them as hard as she could, the two different colors became one constant whir of blended color. But as soon as she stopped, the colors separated and became distinct again.

"Lizzie! Get in out of the rain!" Darwin called from the house. Lizzie snapped to attention.

"Oh, yes, I will," she said running up onto the porch.

"You look like you've seen a ghost. Either that, or been scared out of your wits. How did you get to the house?" Darwin asked, peering into her pale, wet face.

"I...I walked," Lizzie said, unable to meet his eyes. "I...I mean, partways."

Luckily, Darwin left it at that as he helped her

into the house. He picked up her paycheck from the kitchen table and handed it to her.

"You will need a ride home, won't you?"

"I suppose."

"I'll see if Carol can take you."

Lizzie sat down at the kitchen table. The warmth of the room suddenly made her very, very tired. She crossed her arms tightly, pulling her sweater closely around her shoulders as she waited for Carol.

In the car, Carol kept up a running conversation, talking on and on about the flock of ducks she raised by the creek. She loved to see the white Muscovy ducks paddling along the water's edge, she told Lizzie, as they hungrily fed on the abundant watercress that lined its banks.

Lizzie answered in monosyllables, never quite sure what the conversation was about, her mind repeatedly drifting back to the events of this long, rainy, mixed-up day. She felt worse than she had ever felt in her whole life. As Carol talked about church and their need for a stronger youth group, Lizzie planned her way out of this miserable, alone feeling.

She would tell Mandy what happened as soon as she had a chance. She would help Mam as much as she possibly could. She would set the table, play with the twins, Susan and KatieAnn, and agree to help with whatever task Mam assigned her.

Then when supper was over, she would start at the very beginning and tell Mandy every detail of her…what would she call it? It certainly was not a friendship, and "flirtation" sounded too plain bad and disobedient. Well, she wouldn't call it anything at all. She would just tell Mandy. Mandy was so wise and attentive to all Lizzie's fuss about everything, always taking Lizzie quite seriously.

Lizzie was so deep in thought that when Carol pulled up to the sidewalk in front of Lizzie's house, Lizzie actually had to shake her head a bit to clear it.

"I'll see you on Wednesday," Carol said.

"Oh... oh, yes, of course," she stammered.

"Good-bye," Carol said.

"Bye," Lizzie answered, turning to walk up to the porch, certain of her plan that would not fail.

Chapter 24

After dinner, Lizzie went up to her room. She found her Bible in her nightstand drawer and carried it with her as she climbed into bed. She propped up both pillows and leaned back against the headboard. She bent her head over her Bible in her lap.

Very little about the Bible made sense to Lizzie. Plus reading it was usually inconvenient. Even on gorgeous Sundays when their church district wasn't meeting, Dat insisted on taking time to study the Bible.

Once when Lizzie was little and the leaves were orange and red, Dat said to Mam, "Let's hitch up Bess and go to the mountain today."

"We could," Mam agreed and smiled at Dat.

"Good. After dishes and a Bible story, I'll hitch up the buggy and you can pack a lunch."

"We don't have to have a Bible story," Lizzie said.

"Oh, yes," Dat told her. "Every Sunday."

While Mam gathered the dirty breakfast dishes and put away the leftovers, Dat sat on the couch and read the story of the lost sheep. Emma sat beside Dat and listened attentively, but Lizzie wasn't interested in that little sheep story.

So what if he didn't make it into the pen with the others? He could stay out on the mountain till the next morning, when the shepherd drove his sheep back down that way. Lizzie thought the shepherd wouldn't have had to light his lantern and go look for the sheep in the dark. That was a lot scarier than waiting till morning. The shepherd was lucky he didn't get eaten by a bear, walking around the mountain yelling for one sheep.

Lizzie remembered Dat telling Emma to always remember to be a good little girl and do as Mam said. Lizzie had picked at a scab on her knee and wished he'd be quiet now. She just wanted to go for a ride in the mountains.

But now Lizzie was reading her Bible intently because she wanted to be good again.

Mandy opened the bedroom door. Lizzie didn't look up so Mandy cleared her throat, but that failed to get Lizzie's attention. Finally, it was too much for Mandy, and she plopped down on the bed beside

Lizzie. "Why are you reading your Bible?"

"What's wrong with that?"

"Nothing, Lizzie, of course not. If it was Emma, I'd think it was good and natural, but to see you reading it so seriously is kind of a surprise. Did you have a bad dream?"

Lizzie put down the Bible and turned to swing her feet off the side of the bed. She lowered her head and whispered, "I wish it would all have been a bad dream."

Mandy gasped audibly. "Lizzie, what in the world?"

Lizzie sighed and ran her hand through her already tousled hair. "Mandy, you have to promise, cross-your-heart-promise, not to tell Mam or Emma, or I won't tell you."

"I promise," Mandy said. She placed her hand on her heart as she leaned forward.

"Okay," Lizzie began. "You know how dreadfully dull that egg-grading job is? I hate it so much. I would never, ever go near that smelly place if it wasn't for Dat and Mam."

"Ye-e-ss," Mandy said slowly, kind of as if she was carefully walking on thin ice, knowing it could break at any moment.

"Well, it's all right, I guess. The job itself, I mean. It's just that this very...well, kind of very handsome, but not very, *very* good-looking man started coming to the chicken house to pick up an order of eggs to take to Harrisburg every week."

"Go on," Mandy said, her fingers plucking nervously at the tufted chenille bedspread.

So Lizzie launched into the whole exciting, miserably tormenting story, trying to make it appear innocent, but also trying to honestly relate the parts that pricked her conscience.

Mandy listened attentively. She nodded her head wisely, her green eyes a portrait of her inner feelings—fear, suspicion, surprise, and, as Lizzie's story spun to an end, disbelief.

"Lizzie, I cannot believe how dumb you are," Mandy said when Lizzie finished.

"Why did you say that, Mandy? Why?" Lizzie wailed.

"Because!" Mandy shrieked.

"Not so loud!" Lizzie hissed.

Mandy lowered her voice and bent her head so close to Lizzie that she cringed.

"You are old enough to know better. How could you? How could you even dare to get in his pickup truck? Lizzie, can't you see? He could have driven off with you, and none of us would ever have seen you again. It happens all the time."

"Not Don Albert. Mandy, you don't understand. He's nice. He was serious. He liked me."

Mandy snorted.

"He did!" Lizzie cried.

"As long as you're going to stick to that part of your story and refuse to admit that you did anything dumb, I'm going to tell Mam."

And before Lizzie had a chance, Mandy was up and running down the stairway.

"No-no, no!" Lizzie called.

There was no use. Mandy was already clattering down the stairs. Lizzie flung herself on the bed and stuck her fingers in her ears. She was in a barrel of trouble now. Even the Bible did not give her too much hope. She felt like a real sinner. She would have to pray for a very long time, which she planned to do, as soon as she survived Mam's wrath. Probably, with Mandy telling everyone her secrets, Dat would get involved, too. Maybe even Doddy and Mommy Glick and all the preachers in Cameron County.

Chapter 25

SURE ENOUGH, MANDY STOOD AT THE BOTTOM of the steps calling her name. Lizzie went downstairs without answering. She felt like a prisoner being led to her fate, alone and condemned because of what had occurred.

Mam, Emma, and Mandy sat around the kitchen table. Dat was in the blue platform rocker reading a farm magazine. Surely Dat didn't have to hear this, she thought fiercely. He was acting more and more suspicious of her ever since she started combing her hair a little more fancy. Lizzie sat down without lifting her eyes.

"So, Lizzie, what happened? I could tell the minute you walked in the door that you were not your usual happy self," Mam said, not unkindly.

Lizzie glanced nervously in Dat's direction. She swallowed the lump in her throat and knotted her hands in her lap. Slowly, resolutely, she retold the events of the past few months. She did not leave out any details or skip over anything that had led to that afternoon.

She felt as if she was hacking her way through dense underbrush, and that the further she came through it, the closer the soft, yellow light of a relieved conscience warmed her. She couldn't believe how good it felt to be free of her hidden feelings in just in a few moments' time. For so long she had tried in vain to decide what was wrong and what was right. Sitting here at the kitchen table with her family, Lizzie knew. She knew so suddenly and with such clarity that the huge backpack of guilt, which had tugged her strength away, was suddenly lifted off her shoulders. She felt as light and airy as a feather floating on a breeze.

Mam was silent as Lizzie finished her story. She shook her head slowly. "Lizzie, it just makes me weak in the knees, the danger you could have been in," she said quietly.

"That's what Mandy claimed, same as you. But the part you don't understand, Mam, is that Don is very nice. He never would do anything dishonorable. I mean, the thing that actually scares me most is how much I wanted to go with him."

Mam stared at Lizzie. Dat put down his paper and looked at her as if he were seeing her for the first time. Emma's jaw dropped, and her mouth formed a perfect O. Mandy gawked at her as if she had gone completely crazy.

"Lizzie!" she gasped.

"Oh, my!" Mam said.

Dat stared sternly at her, his eyebrows drawn down over his blue eyes. "What did you just say?" he asked.

Then Mam found her voice. "Lizzie, let me tell you something. I believe that the real danger in this situation is not the kind all of us are thinking about. It is a far more exciting danger, isn't it?"

Lizzie nodded, her eyes lighting up with the knowledge that Mam really did understand. She knew!

"Yes, I mean... Mam, I want you to know that if it hadn't been for your face and my remembering you, I probably would not have realized that something was wrong. My feelings of *wanting* to go with him were very strong."

Mam bit her lip as quick tears sprang to her eyes. "Oh, Lizzie," was all she could say.

Suddenly, Dat sat up straight, put away his magazine, and, directing his voice to Lizzie, said quite harshly, "You're just a flirt, Lizzie."

Lizzie looked away, biting her lip.

"I don't ever want to hear anything of this sort again. You're only 15 years old. How do you plan to behave when you're 16, if you're already acting like this with an English man?"

Dat's words hurt as badly as if he had spanked her. Lizzie's face reddened, and she slid down in her chair, trying to become as small as possible. Every word was true, but Dat's harsh, biting tone produced a rebellion in her which reared its ugly head, blotting out the light of Lizzie's clear conscience.

"I wasn't doing *anything* wrong!"

"No, Lizzie, probably it didn't appear as if you were," Mam cut in. "That's the scariest part of raising all my daughters. You girls are not unattractive, and there are many pitfalls out there for innocent young girls. You knew there was something wrong going on, Lizzie, or you would have come home in the evening and told us all about this man coming for eggs. Why didn't you?"

Lizzie blinked, her face reddened again, and she stammered, "I...I guess I knew you wouldn't like me to...to...look forward to seeing him."

"So you knew then already that it wasn't 100 percent harmless?"

"Yes, I suppose so."

Mam sighed again. "Let me tell you something. When I was a young girl, I worked as a *maud* and became a bit too familiar with some of the family's hired hands. To make a long story short, I got involved in a frightening situation. You girls must learn that there is a line, sometimes a very thin line, separating friendliness from flirtation. There is nothing wrong with friendliness. But if you become too familiar, even nervous or thrilled about seeing a young man— or an older one, for that matter—you've already crossed over that line of safety." Mam laughed a bit, before she said, "Actually, it would really be nice if there was a piece of plastic tape surrounding you all the time, so you could clearly see that line."

Dat was nodding his head, agreeing with everything Mam said. "So, you see, Lizzie, it would probably be best if you wouldn't work there any-more," Dat finished for Mam.

Lizzie was incredulous. Not grade eggs! That seemed like a dream come true until she thought of the fact that she needed to be working somewhere, and then grading eggs didn't seem quite that awful.

"We'll see," Mam said.

"Does this...this man still come for a load of eggs every week?" Dat asked.

"I guess. I mean, I don't know why he wouldn't," Lizzie said.

Dat gazed at her with a serious look in his blue eyes. "No, I think you had better find another job, Lizzie. The way it sounds to me, I see no wisdom or common sense in having you continue at that place."

Mam nodded her head in agreement.

Emma and Mandy watched Lizzie, their eyes large and staring and each of their faces set in a seri-ous expression. Lizzie wondered if this was what it felt like when a criminal appeared before a judge to be handed her sentence. Everyone looked like unblinking owls, watching every emotion and inner feeling portrayed on Lizzie's face.

Quite suddenly, she knew she didn't detest her job. It wasn't nearly as bad as working away from home as a *maud* when you got so homesick that you had to try not to burst into tears at a strange, new supper table.

"But, Mam!" Lizzie protested.

"No, Lizzie, don't even try. There's just no sense

in letting you go back. I'll call Darwin this evening yet."

When Dat picked up his magazine and resumed reading, Lizzie knew without a doubt that her sentence had been handed down. A mixture of rebellion and resentment coursed through her, and she picked at the tablecloth with her thumb and forefinger, her eyes downcast. There was nothing more to say.

She sighed, stood up, and headed toward the stairs and her room. She needed time to think about the whole situation alone, away from all of them, even Mandy. As she went up the steps, low voices resumed in the kitchen, and she knew that they were talking about her again. Let them, she thought angrily. I'm always the one to get into trouble, and even Mandy is always on Mam's good side. They just don't like me.

Within her, self-pity fought with the warm brightness of a cleared conscience. Lizzie closed the door to her room quite firmly. She knew one thing. She wanted to go back and grade eggs again, not so that she could see Don Albert again. Well, not totally anyway. Instead, she was afraid of the unknown, of the new job which she knew could be a whole lot worse.

Sure enough, that evening Mam walked over to the neighbors and made the phone call to Darwin and Carol. They were very kind and understanding about the situation. In their conversation, Mam learned about a very good, new opportunity for Lizzie. Darwin and Carol's son, Lawrence, and his wife had just had a new baby. They lived almost 20 miles away on a farm close to Dunnville and needed someone to help with their other small children, the laundry, and the housework.

Mam thought it was perfect, a job for Lizzie that would take her away from the egg-grading plant.

The following morning Mam watched Lizzie a bit warily as she came down the stairs, unkempt and the last one to appear, as always. Mam hardly knew how to approach her about this new job offer, knowing she was still smarting from the previous evening's conversation.

Through breakfast, Mam said nothing while Dat cheerfully described the milkman's account of the weather prediction. They were going to have record snowfalls this year.

"It's going to snow in a few weeks, I bet," he finished, as he buttered his toast generously.

Lizzie watched with narrowed eyes, irritated this morning because he used so much butter. How could they all be chatting away happily as if nothing in the whole world had happened the evening before? Didn't they know she was extremely apprehensive about her future and fighting back some rebellion about having to quit grading eggs?

"Lizzie, pass the jelly."

Lizzie didn't hear Emma, so she asked again.

"Lizzie!"

"What? You don't need to yell at me," Lizzie retorted sourly.

So Mam kept the news of the upcoming job to herself until the dishes were washed and Dat had gone to the barn. She was wise enough to know she could not successfully approach Lizzie at the breakfast table when she was in such a stormy mood.

After the girls were chattering among themselves, Mam told Lizzie about Darwin's proposal that she work for their son in Dunnville.

Lizzie dropped her mouth open in disbelief. She stared at Mam without saying a word.

"Well?" Mam finished.

"Darwin's son? They're Mennonites and use electricity, don't they? Well, you know that I don't know the first *thing* about sweepers and automatic washers and dryers and ... and ... *toasters*!" she wailed.

Mandy burst out laughing and Emma promptly joined in. Mam hid her smile as she assured Lizzie that she was able to learn how to use electric appliances and that she was sure Darwin's daughter-in-law would willingly teach her.

Lizzie sagged on the bench and leaned against the kitchen wall, her arms crossed defiantly in front of herself.

"Emma can go!" she burst out.

"No, Lizzie, Emma cannot go. You can," Mam said.

"I'd rather grade eggs!"

"No, you're not going back there, Lizzie. We can't trust you after the things you told us last evening."

Lizzie was so angry she could not speak. The lump in her throat threatened to choke her as she bit her lip, glaring at Mam.

"You know that this new job can't be any worse than staying an entire week in Amish homes," Emma volunteered, trying to cheer Lizzie.

"You like to work away!" Lizzie spat out vehemently.

"Now girls, that's enough. I worked in English homes at your age, Lizzie, and it's not going to hurt you a bit. And yes, you'll be staying for a week at a time, sleeping there overnight, so you'll need a suitcase," Mam said firmly.

"But...but...it's my birthday, Mam! I'll be 16! Surely when your daughters turn 16, they should be treated at least a bit special, shouldn't they?"

"We'll have a birthday cake when you come back on the weekend," Mam assured her. "Plus we'll have all your presents, just like we did for Emma."

Lizzie clamped her mouth shut and said nothing. Maybe if everyone was so mean to her, she'd just become English.

"I think I'll leave the Amish," Lizzie ventured out loud.

Emma and Mandy stared at her. Mam frowned.

"Lizzie, now grow up and act your age," Mam said. "That kind of talk is exactly why we can't trust you to grade eggs for Darwin anymore."

"I'll be so old and tired when I get back, I'll never get a boyfriend," Lizzie said, trying not to laugh.

"Well, then, I guess you'll be an old maid," Mam said.

For a moment, Lizzie indulged herself, imagining how it would feel to be English. She had taken these mind excursions every since she was a little girl. They had started when she had sneaked a moment by the magazine racks at the grocery store while Mam shopped.

She loved to look at all the fashionable girls on those glossy pages. They were so fascinating, with long, shining blond hair and wearing all kinds of beautiful clothes. How would it be to look like that? She had always longed for high-heeled shoes after all. But she knew there was no way she could be like the women in the magazine.

She was Amish, and Amish people dressed plain. She had been content most of the time to dress in the clothes Mam made, pin her covering on, and go. She was starting to understand that there was a lot more to life than trying to get Mam to buy her a pair of high heels or even seeing Don Albert.

Being Amish kind of settled things. The English world was beyond her reach. That was just how life was if you were Amish, and Lizzie was pretty sure that she really didn't want to be anything else. She loved her secure circle of family and friends. And how could she ever hurt Mam and Dat by telling them she was going to leave the church? She wouldn't know how to be English now even if she tried.

Chapter 26

THE WEATHER TURNED PREDICTABLY COLDER with gray skies and a biting wind as Lizzie carried her suitcase to Darwin's car a few days later.

She had used up all her protests, including the one about a snowstorm keeping her stranded in Dunnville. There was absolutely no use. Mam smiled at her lovingly, telling her to keep her chin up when she left, which did very little to help her depressing thoughts.

The farther they traveled, the more Lizzie fought her anxiety. It seemed to take forever, through the large town where Mam had lain in the hospital with pneumonia, onto a big three-lane highway, past industrial sites and places of business, until the countryside turned into an agricultural area with large red barns, neat white houses, and tall blue silos. Seeing that hospital only heightened Lizzie's anxiety on this harsh morning—and she couldn't shake the uncertainty that suddenly filled her. The last time she had been in this town, Mam was very sick.

But soon they were winding their way through the countryside again. At a crossroads, Darwin slowed the car and turned onto a winding gravel road. They snaked between hills and woods, twisting and turning until it seemed as if they had entered another world. The fields were brown and bare with only the stubbles of the corn crop showing, along with dead grasses flattened by the icy rains of autumn.

As they turned right and started the steep ascent up a winding dirt driveway, Lizzie clutched the door handle until her knuckles turned white. A large, rambling old farmhouse stood at the top of a hill with a huge barn and outbuildings opposite it. The whole farm looked as if was run by a very busy person trying to do all the work by himself.

"You are about to meet young parents who need some help right now," Darwin remarked. He turned to look at Lizzie whose eyes were wide with consternation.

"I hope you can feel at home here," he added.

Lizzie took a deep breath, mostly to summon all the courage she could. "I...I'm sure I'll be fine," she said without much conviction.

Darwin led her down the sidewalk to the front door, streaked with mud from the farmer's boots. The entry was cluttered with children's clothes, boots and shoes, boxes, and newspapers, with a smell which belonged to all farmers' clothes. Darwin opened the kitchen door, and Lizzie walked into a large white room with bright lights illuminating every object. She saw dishes waiting to be done, a table holding the remains of the evening meal, and clutter everywhere.

Darwin heard the delightful squeals of his grand-children in the living room. He headed for that side of the house. Lizzie didn't know what she should do, so she stood rooted to the kitchen linoleum, blinking in the strange, brilliant lights, and wishing with all her heart that she could go home to Mam and Dat.

"Lizzie, come meet Amanda," Darwin called, already seated on the recliner with a toddler on each knee.

Lizzie set down her suitcase and walked across the carpeted area. Amanda smiled up at Lizzie from her comfortable position on the sofa and extended her hand. "So you're Lizzie! My, I'm so glad to have someone come to help out. You'll have to excuse everything, because it's just a grand mess."

Her tinkling laughter captivated Lizzie, and she smiled back, immediately feeling relaxed. Amanda was small and round. She had beautifully thick, wavy, dark hair combed loosely over her head, with a small Mennonite covering pinned on the back. Her complexion was flawless. Her small upturned nose made her look like she was 16.

Lizzie told her that things really didn't look that bad, explaining how much work was involved when the twins were born.

"You have twin sisters? Oh, I would so love to

have a pair of twins someday."

Lizzie stiffened slightly, going a little queasy in her stomach as she thought about any babies, but especially two at once. Lizzie still didn't like babies. But that would appall Amanda. Emma didn't understand Lizzie's feelings about babies either. She loved to sew, whistling under her breath, which indicated that she loved what she was doing. And anywhere there were babies, Emma was watching the mothers, hoping for a chance to hold one.

Lizzie figured that she didn't like babies because she had been around them too much when she was younger. After all, Jason was still a baby when the twins, KatieAnn and Susan, were born. Emma and Mandy had been much more excited about the new babies than she was, Lizzie remembered.

"Are we really going to have another one? Jason is still a baby, sort of. And besides, he's finally cute, and now we don't have to have more, do we?" Lizzie had asked.

"Lizzie, you just aren't normal! Why don't you like babies more? You should be ashamed of yourself," Emma said.

"I guess," Lizzie said slowly.

"You could grow up and be glad. It's a blessing to have children," Emma told her.

Lizzie sighed as Amanda showed her around the kitchen. Maybe she wasn't normal, like Emma said. Oh, she knew she was normal as far as her brain working well because schoolwork was not hard for her. But maybe she wasn't normal where babies were concerned. That was something new to worry about, seeing that Emma seriously thought so.

But sometimes babies screamed for a very long time, their faces looking awfully contorted. Some babies opened their mouths so wide you could easily see their tonsils, all bright red and looking like kidney beans. Babies were just not something Lizzie was very happy to think about.

But she had learned to hold a baby and figure out which end was up. Emma was a much better helper, because Lizzie got tired of babies quickly. But Mam told her she did well and that she would be a good mother someday, which made Lizzie feel considerably better about babies in general. Well, now Amanda needed her. Maybe she'd discover that babies and toddlers weren't nearly as annoying as she used to think they were.

Chapter 27

Amanda's children looked just as charming as their mother. Two boys with reddish brown hair and large brown eyes full of mischief bounced around on Darwin's lap. And littlest of all was a wee child of about two with a riot of reddish curls all over her head, a face peppered with tiny little freckles, and huge blue eyes. She was so tiny and looked so fragile that she reminded Lizzie of a porcelain doll. She hid behind the recliner, and when she thought she wasn't being noticed, peeped out at Lizzie. She resembled a rabbit, blinking her eyes without moving otherwise.

Amanda watched and smiled at Lizzie. "They'll be a handful for you. The oldest one is Timmy, then Martin, and the little girl is Bethany."

What an adorable name for an adorable child, Lizzie thought. Her ruffled dress had lavender daisies strewn into the fabric, which now, Lizzie thought, made her seem like a fairy.

Suddenly, Lawrence appeared. A husky farmer, he wore a red bill cap with a seed corn logo on it, muddy jeans, and a green work jacket. He smiled appreciatively at Lizzie and invited her to make herself at home, just as Amanda had done.

After peeping at Rosanne, the tiny newborn, Lizzie followed Amanda upstairs. Amanda showed Lizzie where she would sleep and apologized for the fact that she had to go through the children's room to get to her own.

The upstairs was freezing cold, but Lizzie was quite accustomed to a drafty old farmhouse, so it didn't bother her much at all.

She was just grateful to have a room of her own, even if it was cold. The tall, dark four-poster bed had a clean white quilt on it, and plenty of thick pillows made it look very comfortable. She hung her dresses in the closet and unpacked her suitcase as Amanda returned to the children.

Lizzie took only a moment to part the white curtains and gaze out at the barren, lonely-looking fields. Her longing to be at home with her family only deepened, but she resolutely turned and, with a deep breath, made her way downstairs and to her duties.

She rolled up her sleeves, washed dishes, emptied garbage, burned trash, swept, dusted, scrubbed floors, and prepared meals. The hardest part was making meals, because Mam did almost all of the cooking at home. Amanda helped her get each meal started, but then Lizzie was on her own to figure out how to fix everything and get all the food on the table at once and on time.

The kitchen had never been Lizzie's favorite place, except for eating, of course. Lizzie would need every ounce of resolve today. At home, they mashed potatoes by hand, plunging a sturdy hand-held masher into a steaming stainless-steel kettle filled with soft-boiled potatoes. But Amanda brought out a strange contraption that she plugged into an electrical outlet. She pressed a button and the beaters began to spin at an alarming speed.

"Here, use the mixer to mash the potatoes. It's so much easier," she said, heading into the living room as the baby's shrill cry sounded through the house.

Carefully, Lizzie held the mixer in what she hoped was the right position and pressed the button. Instantly her hand vibrated and chunks of soft, hot potato flew out of the bowl, landing with soft, sodden plops at her feet. Lizzie quickly bent to pick them up, hurriedly rinsing the globs of potatoes under running water before returning them to the bowl. Grimly, she repositioned the mixer, pressed the button, and tried again. This time the potatoes hit the back of the countertop and slid behind the glass canister set.

Her face turning red, and her mouth tight, Lizzie returned the steaming potatoes to the bowl, held the mixer as straight as possible, and pressed the button only halfway. She was rewarded by the beater starting more slowly. The potatoes began to mash, and then all at once, the thing stopped.

Oh, dear, Lizzie thought wildly. Now I've clogged everything up. She pressed the button as hard as she could and was horrified to hear a high, thin whine. The potatoes flew first around the bowl, and then out onto the countertop, onto Lizzie's shoes, and onto her apron. Some even landed in the sink.

She was almost in tears when she heard Amanda's giggle directly behind her.

"The mixer giving you a hard time?" she asked as she patted her baby's little bottom, a diaper draped across her shoulder.

Lizzie turned sheepishly, her face red with embarrassment. "I just can't seem to get the right speed," she said nervously.

"It takes some getting used to," Amanda said easily and handed the baby to Lizzie. With a skill born of practice, she pressed the button lightly, finding the proper speed. The potatoes whirred into a fluffy mass. She added salt and butter and a small amount of milk at regular intervals until the mashed potatoes were finished.

With Amanda's easygoing, good-natured attitude, Lizzie learned to relax, ask questions, and take her time discovering the whole world of electricity. Toasters, blenders, automatic washers, dryers, and even the steam iron, which she used to iron Bethany's small ruffled dresses, were all new and strange to her.

Every evening she was bone-weary, grateful for a good hot bath and her warm bed with the heavy quilts which kept her snug and warm through the long winter nights. The children's chatter kept her awake a few nights, but not for long, she was so tired.

Lizzie's sixteenth birthday fell on Thursday of her week at Lawrence and Amanda's. She woke up feeling much the same as always, although she knew she was crossing a big threshold into a new chapter of her life. Turning 16 was a long-awaited moment. Now she could be with the youth every Sunday. She could even start dating. How thrilling to wake up on a Thursday morning and realize that she had become a young woman.

Lizzie sat up in bed and stretched, wondering if Mam and Emma were remembering her birthday, and if they had gifts ready to wrap for her. She missed Mandy terribly, and the thought of being with her whole family made her giddy with anticipation.

Only two more days and I'll be going home, she smiled. Home had never seemed more dear to her than at this moment. She had often been away from home, but never over a birthday, and certainly never for her sixteenth.

Lizzie dutifully went about each task, whistling lightly under her breath as she hurried along. Two more days, two more days, she hummed in rhythm to her movements. The children could sense her lively mood and teased her playfully. They kept getting in her way and being generally annoying with little mishaps that wore on her patience.

Later that afternoon the door burst open and Lawrence stepped into the kitchen, shaking his hands and blowing on them to warm up. His cap was pulled low over his forehead, his collar was turned up, and his ears were red from the cold.

"We better get ready!" he announced in his usual enthused manner. "Feed man says there's about two feet of snow on the way with high winds."

Lizzie dropped the towel she was folding and opened her eyes wide in absolute disbelief. How could he come in like that, as if this was the most exciting event of the year? Didn't he know how desperately she wanted to go home?

Lizzie's mouth turned dry with fear and anxiety. She walked quickly to the kitchen window, parting the ruffled white curtains to survey the sky anxiously. Oh, mercy! The sky was a flat, leaden gray with not a glimmer of sunshine or any puffy clouds to dispel her fears.

Amanda talked animatedly with Lawrence as the children skipped and sang about the coming snow.

Lizzie fought back her fear, trying to hide her feelings from the family. No one even noticed her, so she went on folding towels, trying to conjure up enough courage to mention the fact that she would like to go home sometime before the storm hit.

She opened her mouth a few times, glancing edgily in the direction of the living room where Lawrence and Amanda stood talking, only to lose her nerve and resume her towel-folding. Her confidence melted like an ice cube in hot water. They talked so long that she panicked, certain that they had forgotten she existed, let alone even thought about taking her home.

Lizzie set her mouth determinedly, waiting for a lull in the conversation. "Do...do you suppose you could take me home before the storm arrives?" she asked loudly. I said it too loudly, she thought. Now they won't take me home for sure.

Lawrence looked at her, considering her request before shaking his head. He raised his eyebrows at Amanda and said, "We really need you until Saturday afternoon. No use worrying about getting home before the storm gets here."

So that was that. Lizzie spent a long evening trying not to think dismal thoughts. She wished with all her heart Lawrence would change his mind after the snow began to fall in earnest, but she knew there wasn't much hope. She wondered if it was all right to ask God to wait to let it snow until she got home.

That evening she knelt beside her bed, her knees on the braided rug and her bare feet on the cold wooden bedroom floor. Lizzie prayed as urgently as she had ever prayed in her young life. She felt like Emma, but she was so desperate to be with her family, that this time she wasn't self-conscious about being on her knees. She begged God to get her home safely, and please, please not to make her stay for another week without seeing Dat, Mam, Emma, and Mandy.

But who knew if praying really made a difference? Emma believed it did. She always had, even when they were still poor and Dat wanted to move to the worst ramshackle farm ever. Back then, Lizzie had tried to pray for help even though she was barely 10. How could God resist a 10-year-old's prayers?

She remembered lying awake, listening to Mam and Dat talk way into the night. Dat's voice would rise, followed by a soft murmur from Mam, until her voice would yank Lizzie to reality again as she talked fast and loud, almost as if she could cry at any moment. It had been quite an ordeal, listening to their conversation. Dat had bought an expensive piece of equipment from a salesman, which Mam felt they could not afford. Lizzie knew they were poor, but she didn't know it was as bad as Mam said.

The thing that struck terror in Lizzie's heart, that caused her to lie awake deep into the warm night, was when Mam said she just didn't see how they could hang on any longer. Dat had answered Mam in the most awful, loud voice, stomped across the living room, and went out on the porch, the door slamming behind him. Lizzie thought she would surely die when she heard Mam crying softly, sighing, and blowing her nose. She thought of crawling out of bed to get on her knees to ask God to please come help them all. Dat and Mam didn't know what to do because they had so many bills and no money.

But that would have made her feel too dumb, so she didn't. She did turn on her back and clasp her hands over her chest and think a loud thought to God, asking him to help Dat and Mam. Later she thought maybe Jesus would have heard her better, because he was much smaller and not nearly as fierce-looking. He didn't look one bit scary, except he wore a long, white dress, which was very strange. So Lizzie thought the same thought, except this time she directed it to Jesus.

She felt strangely quiet and not so scared after that. Maybe it was because the light went out in the living room, and Dat and Mam went to bed. Or maybe it was really that God had heard her, or Jesus. She was pretty sure that one of them had because she felt so much better.

The next morning when they were getting dressed, Lizzie had turned to Emma.

"Emma, did you go to sleep early last night? I mean, as soon as we went to bed?" Lizzie asked hesitantly.

"Why?"

"Did you hear Mam and Dat argue last night?"

"Were they arguing?"

"Well, yes, Emma. Really bad. Mam was crying. Emma, we're so poor that we can barely hang on here, whatever that means."

Emma sighed.

"Emma, who hears prayers the best, God or Jesus?" Lizzie asked, very suddenly.

"They both do the same," Emma said firmly.

"How do you know?"

"Oh, I just know."

"Does God hear it better if you go on your knees or not?"

"You have to ask Mam that. You should pray on your knees, though. I mean, everyone does in church," Emma had said.

✢

Now here she was, on her knees with Lawrence and Amanda's children giggling and jumping on the bed in the adjoining room. But Lizzie barely heard them, she was so engrossed in wondering if God was hearing her prayer and would answer somehow. She certainly knew from experience that you couldn't just pray for a million dollars, or to be really thin, and have God promptly answer your prayer, even if you got on your knees in the middle of a freezing cold, upstairs bedroom.

But she had a faint glimmer of hope that maybe, just maybe, this request was not too selfish or ridiculous. She hadn't really stated specifically or exactly how she wanted to get home, or how much she wanted it not to snow. She didn't understand very well how God thought, but then, she wasn't sure she was supposed to. Mam said God was her Master, so she guessed that explained a lot.

The following morning the cold tingled Lizzie's nose until she snapped awake, alert in an instant, the knowledge of her predicament crowding out the warm fuzzy comfort of sleep.

She leaped to her feet, throwing back the heavy covers, and tiptoed to the window. Sure enough, exactly as she had feared, tiny pellets of wind-driven snow whirled past the old farmhouse, covering the fields, roads, and everything in their path.

Her heart sank as she put both hands to her mouth and thought another silent prayer. Please, God, just get me home. I don't want to stay here on Sunday. She wondered how many days it would take to dig out from two feet of snow. Why did God allow this snowstorm? Didn't he know she was stuck in Dunnville? Did he even care?

Biting her lip, she grimly resolved to take the day with whatever it brought and to do the best she could. She could not be a big 16-year-old baby, crying because she had to stay a few extra days.

It was a long day. The children were more noisy and active than usual, making Lizzie extremely tense and nervous. There was not one single lull in the storm all day. Every time Lizzie looked out the window, the same swirling whiteness beneath a grayish sky loomed overhead.

Lawrence and Amanda loved the snow, teasing Lizzie relentlessly about staying over on Sunday. They thought the snow was fun and exciting, so Lizzie tried to hide her feelings of desperation. Oh, how she longed to go home!

Chapter 28

THE FOLLOWING MORNING THE SNOW MEA-
sured almost 20 inches deep. Snowplows inched
their way along the township roads. Lawrence
announced at breakfast that he couldn't risk taking
Lizzie home that day since it was still snowing.

Without thinking or even caring, but desperately
longing to be at home, Lizzie blurted out, "Well, I
want to go home very badly. I miss my family, so
maybe if you won't take me, you could think of
someone who will."

Lawrence looked startled at her unexpected outburst. Amanda was immediately sympathetic when
she saw how upset and close to tears Lizzie was.
"Why, of course, Lawrence, your brother Philip
would enjoy the challenge of driving in this snow,
wouldn't he?"

Lizzie blinked back tears of genuine relief and
gratitude. She felt like jumping up and hugging
Amanda, wanting to shout and leap high enough to

touch the ceiling in her pure, unrestrained joy. When Lawrence went to the telephone, then turned to tell her that Philip would be there at one o'clock that afternoon, she thanked him with her whole heart.

Lawrence pushed the snow off the steep driveway with his tractor and at a few minutes past one, sure enough—oh, unbelievable sight—a four-wheel-drive pickup came bouncing up to the house. There were wings on Lizzie's feet as she sprang to the truck, waving good-bye to Amanda and the children. Then she was on her way through a white, white world as pure and crystal-clear as her joy. She was going home! Philip was a good driver, so Lizzie wasn't afraid. But she did keep pushing her feet against the carpeted floor, trying in spite of herself to make the truck go faster.

When he turned onto their road, Philip looked over and said, "You won't get there any faster leaning forward like that."

Lizzie laughed, sat back, and tried to relax. Then— oh, happy day—she was running up the sidewalk, up the porch steps, and through the kitchen door, dropping her suitcase and greeting everyone at once.

The house smelled wonderful. Mam's Saturday baking was cooling on the countertop—apple and blueberry pies with crumb toppings, a fresh batch of cupcakes with caramel frosting, and, her favorite, molasses cookies.

Emma was cleaning the upstairs, but she came running to meet Lizzie. Everyone talked at once, and no one listened to what anyone else was saying.

The evening wrapped around Lizzie's heart like a soft warm blanket, etching itself forever in golden letters in her memory. Welcoming love enveloped her, soft and secure, topped off with all kinds of pretty things wrapped in beautiful birthday paper and finished with bows on top.

Emma gave her soft, rippled, robin's-egg blue dress material and a small chest to keep her little treasures safe. Mam and Dat gave her a piece of navy blue fabric and two beautiful pillar candles with artificial flower rings to arrange around their bases. Mandy's present was a new scarf and gloves with a white bandanna to wear when she went skating. Jason even gave her a small package containing two pairs of warm, woolly knee socks. The twins helped Lizzie open her packages while Dat looked on, his blue eyes beaming at her.

When Mam served the birthday cake and ice cream and everyone sang, "Happy Birthday," Lizzie's eyes shone with happiness and some other emotion that seemed to make her eyes produce tears. She wondered if it was possible to be so genuinely happy that you cried for no reason at all.

Chapter 29

After her birthday, Lizzie went back to spend one more week with the family in Dunnville. And then she stayed home for a week so she could have intensive lessons in learning to make her own dresses, capes, and aprons. It was time, now that was 16.

Emma was already sewing most everything, including coverings for the whole family, which at 17 years of age was no easy feat. She was naturally an accomplished seamstress, taking her time and measuring carefully, while constantly whistling under her breath. She was never happier than when she sat at the sewing machine after she had finished all the cleaning. It was her reward. That was just how Emma was.

Lizzie used to envy Emma's ability to sew, embroider, and crochet, but she never had the patience to sit still with hand-sewing like Emma did. It wasn't that she hadn't tried, especially embroidering. Mam loved to buy cute iron-on transfers of little houses or animals for the girls to cross-stitch. Even Mandy sat patiently still as she learned how to tie a knot at the end of thread, how to thread a needle, and how to separate the strands of embroidery floss. But Lizzie got tired very quickly.

Lizzie knew that this time Mam wouldn't let her escape sewing lessons, even though she had so long dreaded and detested every part of it. Lizzie had tried many times to use their treadle sewing machine, halfheartedly teaching herself until the fabric got all bunched up on the wrong side of the presser foot. Lizzie's left-handedness was a real hurdle. The seam she was trying to sew should have been to the right, while the large piece of fabric she was sewing should have been to the left on the sewing machine's flat surface.

But for Lizzie, everything was exactly opposite. She needed to stuff all the fabric under the machine itself, which meant she couldn't see well. Inevitably, she sewed the seam crooked. Of course she disliked any sewing project. And until she was 16, she refused to trouble herself with the thought that someday she would need to learn how to sew. Unfortunately, Lizzie often thought, you couldn't just walk into a store and buy Amish women's clothes.

The happiness she felt from having completed two weeks in Dunnville spread its warm glow through her heart for quite a while. She was so glad to be at home and so happy to sleep with Mandy in their bed. They giggled and read books by the light

of the kerosene lamp, which they perched precari-
ously over their mattress. Sometimes they tiptoed
to the kitchen for bologna and cheese sandwiches,
along with some lemonade, taking the goodies back
to their room for a late-night picnic on the floor.

These days Lizzie was happy to hang out the
family's laundry, even whistling under her breath
sometimes, which actually alarmed her. Had she
picked up Emma's annoying habit without even
trying? She worked as fast as she possibly could
because the frigid air soon numbed her fingers. She
rapidly picked up the clothes and clipped them onto
the wash line with wooden clothespins.

Then she scuttled back to the protection of the
old washhouse, which wasn't much, but the hot
water felt good to her hands as she lifted the clothing
out of the washer tub and put the soaking laundry
through the wringer piece by piece. The air motor
hummed at her feet. As steam rose to envelop her
face, her soft whistle turned full-fledged and shrill.
It was wonderful to be home and using Mam's
wringer washer in the tumbledown old washhouse.
She must be growing up, she realized. She used to
despise Monday mornings.

She had first learned to do the family wash when
she was 10 and Emma was 11. First they had sorted
mountains of laundry from a big plastic hamper
packed full of dirty clothes. A hose hung in the white

Maytag wringer washer with steaming hot water pouring out of it. They had pushed the granite rinse tub up against the washer, ready to fill it with rinse water.

The washing machine was powered by a small gas engine, which Dat would start for them when they were ready. They were too small either to fill the engine with gasoline or to try to start it. Lizzie always made sure she was close when Dat poured gasoline into the engine because she loved the smell of it.

Everything seemed to be going fine the first time Lizzie and Emma did the washing on their own, until Emma suddenly howled in despair. She had reached into the fast-moving water, only to grab a big blob of tightly knotted diapers. Water sloshed over the side of the washing machine as she dropped the knotted clump back in.

"Lizzie!" Emma yelled at the top of her voice so her sister could hear her over the "putta-putta-putt" of the gas engine. "Go get Mam!"

Lizzie cast one wild-eyed look at the water slopping out of the washer and dashed madly out the door and up the steps to the kitchen. She burst into the house, shouting, "Mam!"

Mam looked up from cleaning the stovetop, an alarmed expression on her face. "Lizzie, whatever is wrong with you?" she asked, turning pale.

"Come quick! Water is slopping out over the sides of the washing machine and the diapers are so wrapped up in each other that they're as hard as a stick," Lizzie panted.

Mam followed her down the stairs, scolding as she went. "Lizzie, you have to stop leaving the diapers in so long. I have often told Emma that. What were you doing?"

They came to the washhouse where Emma stood wringing her hands, despair on her face. She looked relieved to see Mam and burst out, "Mam, the diapers are knotted so tight it isn't even funny!"

Mam pinched her mouth, pulled up her sleeve with one hand, and plunged the other into the washer. She came up with a mass of very white, very knotted diapers, which she proceeded to pull apart with strong hands, objecting loudly as she did so.

"Emma, where were you and Lizzie? You know you can't let these diapers wash for so long! Ach, I should just wash by myself, I guess. You girls mustn't be old enough yet." Mam twisted and pulled on the hard knot of diapers, dropping them back into the swirling, sudsy water as she loosened each one. Emma stood beside her, watching with a bewildered expression.

"Well, Mam, I can't understand why they knotted like that. Me and Lizzie were just sitting on the steps talking for a little while."

"Just be careful. You have to mind your business when you wash." Mam wiped her hands on her apron, watching as Emma put the diapers through the wringer, which pressed out the water from the diapers and then deposited them into the blue rinse water.

Mam turned to go but paused again to watch

Emma rinsing them. "Be sure and rinse them thoroughly. The last time you washed, the diapers were as stiff as a board."

That did it. Lizzie decided she didn't like Mam that morning. Who felt like washing now? Maybe the last time the diapers were stiff and not rinsed very well, but they weren't as stiff as a board. Mam stretched stuff. Lizzie supposed that's where she got it. At least Emma claimed Lizzie did, too—stretch the truth that is, not rinse the diapers.

These days, Lizzie didn't mind doing the laundry as much, even when it was bitterly cold. She lugged the wicker clothes basket filled with wet clothes out to the wash line and then used wooden clothes pins to hang the snowy white, sweet-smelling shirts. They blew straight out and away from her on the sharp winter breeze, flapping quietly as Emma hung each one up.

Things were better at home since Lizzie returned from Dunnville. No one mentioned Don Albert anymore. Lizzie thought about him less, too, now that she was 16 and would soon be running around with Emma on the weekends.

After she had hung the final load of laundry on the line, she swept the last of the water across the old wooden floor, washing out the wringer washer and rinse tubs well. Banging the wooden washhouse door, she ran down the steps and dashed into the kitchen, drawn by the rich aroma of freshly baked molasses cookies.

Ever since Lizzie was a small child, Mam's molasses cookies were her favorite. Mam made them large and perfectly round, not too high but not flat, with little ditches across the top that she sprinkled with sugar. The cookies were perfect for dunking in hot chocolate. You could soak them real well without having them crumble and fall apart. And these didn't sink to the bottom like some did while you raced to the kitchen cabinet drawer for a spoon to save your drowning cookie. When that happened, the worst part was having ruined a perfectly good cup of hot chocolate. It never tasted quite the same when drowned cookie crumbs floated across its surface.

Mam smiled at Lizzie as she came into the kitchen. "All done?" she asked. "Did the wash freeze as fast as you hung it out?"

"Not really," Lizzie answered. "Mmm, these look good. May I make hot chocolate?"

"Go ahead," Mam said, turning to flip more freshly baked cookies expertly.

Emma joined them for a cup of cocoa, and the conversation turned to Lizzie's sewing.

"Oh, I dread it," Lizzie groaned. "Why can't Emma just sew my dresses like she does my coverings? I hate to sew and I can't do it."

"You have to learn, Lizzie," Emma said. "Who will sew for you after you get married?" she asked, her eyes wide and incredulous.

"You can!" Lizzie laughed.

"Oh, no. I won't have time on my old farm with all my children," Emma said, chuckling.

"Oh, Emma! You'll never change. I hope you do marry Joshua and spend all the rest of your days on his old pig and cow farm. You will live there until you're old and fat and wrinkly."

Emma threw back her head and roared. "And you'll probably be my next-door neighbor on another old pig and cow farm!"

"Oh, no, I won't! I will not marry anyone who milks cows, it doesn't matter how nice-looking, kind, or wonderful a person he is," Lizzie shot back.

"Now, now," Mam laughed. "Exactly what you vow and declare you will never do is usually what you end up doing."

"Not me," Lizzie stated firmly.

"Lizzie, you better start thinking about a husband. Four more days and it's your very first weekend to go with me to Allen County. Ephraim Yoders are having the supper for all the youth. Imagine that! Everything is planned already! I'm so excited to be able to take my younger sister along."

Lizzie smiled at Emma appreciatively. "Do you really feel that way?"

"Why, of course, Lizzie."

In that moment, Lizzie realized how good a sister Emma had become to her. Emma helped her style her dresses, she was teaching her how to sew and how to make her coverings fit well, and now she was actually looking forward to taking her along on Sunday evening. Emma was a dear a lot of the time, no doubt about it. She seemed less bossy and more generous and unselfish than ever, devoting her time and energy to helping Lizzie successfully join the young people's social events.

"Lizzie…" Mam began a bit hesitantly.

"Hmmm?"

"I worry about you starting to run around."

"Why?" Lizzie turned to Mam, her anticipation still brightly evident.

"I just do. I suppose that incident with that… that English man, whatever his name was, just put a fear in me. You're not very…how can I say it? You need to be very careful, Lizzie. Remember how we talked about the thin line between friendliness and flirtation?"

Lizzie sighed and rolled her eyes to the ceiling. "Mam, here we go again. Aren't we allowed to flirt a little after we're 16? I bet you did."

Mam pursed her lips as she told Lizzie in no uncertain terms that finding a husband was not about flirting with handsome boys or thinking the decision was entirely up to her or depended on her appearance. Neither, she said, did fanciness and style have anything to do with it. Lizzie should learn to pray sincerely for God's will in her life with a humble spirit, Mam said emphatically, so that God could lead her to the right man.

Lizzie wasn't against praying. She had just never been sure how to do it right. Ever. She had always put her patties down, as Amish children were taught to do. At mealtime, Amish people never prayed out loud like English people did, so Lizzie always felt especially ill at ease when she heard someone praying aloud.

Concentrating seemed to be Lizzie's problem. Dat told them to thank the Lord for their food and to look down at their plates as they prayed. Lizzie often forgot to pray because she was peeping at someone or thinking other thoughts. She didn't know why, but it seemed she could never stop her mind and pray a long prayer during patties down. She tried hard though. Emma dropped her head far and moved her lips as she said her silent prayer. Lizzie often watched her sideways, fascinated by her goodness.

Chapter 30

Aₛ Mᴀᴍ ᴛᴀʟᴋᴇᴅ ᴇᴀʀɴᴇꜱᴛʟʏ, Lɪᴢᴢɪᴇ'ꜱ ꜱᴘɪʀɪᴛꜱ fell into a downward spiral. She wished it would all make more sense. "Well, Mam, you know I don't understand what you mean. If I comb my hair flat as a pancake and make my dresses as long as yours and sit on a chair with my hands folded my first weekend, no boy is ever going to look at me, you know that. That's what you mean by being humble, isn't it?"

Emma burst out laughing and Mam joined her helplessly. As Emma showed Lizzie a dress pattern that she recommended and Lizzie picked the fabric for her first "running-around" dress, Mam resumed the conversation. She first tried to explain to Lizzie how important it was to obey God's will, which basically, for a young person, meant letting her conscience guide her and trying to do what was right in all matters.

Every so often, Mam and Dat got all worked up about the girls' spiritual lives.

That whole year after Emma turned 16 and Lizzie's 16th birthday approached, the girls were learning how to live a new life, trying to live the way that Jesus taught. They learned the rules of the church, and they promised to obey and help build the church.

Mam even had tears, talking to them about all of this. Lizzie could tell that Emma took it very, very seriously. But the whole business depressed Lizzie to the point of tears. This would not be fun. They had to be so careful. What if they said or did one thing wrong ever again in their lives? And if they grew into old people, imagine the hopelessness of their situation, unless they all stayed at home and read their Bibles almost continuously.

Mam read her Bible a lot, urging the girls to as well. Emma read her Bible every evening before she blew out her kerosene lamp, but half the time Lizzie wasn't sure where her Bible was. Mam would have a fit if she knew.

Lizzie never told anyone, but the Bible scared her a lot. It just seemed too holy, too righteous, and too impossible to follow. She often wished she wouldn't feel that way, wondering if she was normal. Emma said the Bible comforted her, which went beyond Lizzie's understanding. That made her feel so guilty that she could never, ever tell Emma how she felt about all the talk about spiritual things.

As Mam launched into one of her speeches that just gave Lizzie the blues, Lizzie quietly slipped out of the room and went up to her bedroom.

She heard steps coming up the stairway, so she quickly closed her door. Nobody had to know where she was.

"Lizzie, are you in there?" Mandy called.

No answer.

"Lizzie?"

She still didn't answer.

The steps turned, the sound ebbing away before starting down the stairs. Good, Lizzie thought. Mandy can go play with Jason.

Lizzie rolled over, searching for a book to read. She had read them all so many times she hardly knew what to read anymore. If only Mam could spot more mystery books, but they were getting harder to find. Lizzie just loved those books about teenagers not much older than she and Emma solving exciting mysteries, some of them even a bit dangerous. They were all interesting, good, clean books that Mam approved of. They weren't allowed to read just anything.

❧

The last book she read was about a huge colony of bats living in a cave—vampire bats. If one of them bit a horse or a human being, the bats gave them a disease called rabies, which caused you to lose your mind and die a slow, painful death.

After Lizzie finished that book, she wouldn't go outside after dark. There was an electric pole light at the corner of their yard, which was actually the neighbors'. Every night in the summertime, a cloud of insects whirled around the light. Bats often swooped in among them. Dat told Lizzie they didn't have rabies; well, only rarely. Bats also have radar that warns them of an approaching object, which makes them steer clear of people.

Lizzie told Dat that vampire bats are thirsty for blood; in fact, they'll sit on horses and drink their blood. Mam said she should quit reading those mysteries if she was going to be afraid of bats. Besides, very likely none of what they had in them was true.

Lizzie's Uncle Marvin had often told her about the time a bat flew into Aunt Rachel's room and sat in her hair. Rachel screamed and screamed, picking up the horrible creature and throwing it against the wall with all her strength, where it slid to the floor, quite dead. The bat was probably rabid, or why would it have become tangled in Rachel's hair? Evidently its radar wasn't working, which meant it had already lost its mind. So Lizzie remained unconvinced of Dat's reassurances, refusing to go out at night for a very long time.

She found her *Tom Sawyer* book, but she had read it so many times that it was boring now. She kept looking. *My Friend Flicka.* Oh, that was a different one. She had only skipped through it before. So happy to have something to read, Lizzie rearranged the pillows, flipped on her back, opened the book, and started in. She was soon transported to a horse ranch in the West, where she worked alongside a family who owned a great herd of horses and cattle.

All at once she became aware of her name being called quite anxiously. It sounded as if it came from outside in the yard. She listened a while but didn't answer. Then she heard someone at the foot of the stairs.

"I *did* look up there!"

"Well, where could she be? Lizzie!"

It was Mam, and her voice sounded as if she was close to tears. For an instant, Lizzie felt like remaining quiet, but her conscience made her do what was right. Putting her book aside, she yelled, "What?"

"Where *were* you?" Mam asked weakly. Lizzie could hear the great relief in her voice. "We looked all over the place for you."

"I was up here."

"Then you didn't answer when I called you the first time," Mandy said.

Lizzie didn't say anything.

"Come on down now, Lizzie. We're having a snack," Mam said.

Lizzie sat up, fixed her hair and covering a bit, and checked her face in the mirror before starting downstairs. She was so pleased that Mam was worried. That was so good for her, because now she would be more careful about what she said and would like her every bit as much as Emma.

Dat and Jason were making popcorn. Lizzie was

instantly hungry. Mam had made a pitcher of ice-cold chocolate milk and put out pumpkin whoopie pies and blueberry pie. Lizzie sat in a chair, smiling at Emma, feeling quite pleased because everyone had been worried.

"Where were you, Lizzie?" Mam asked.

"In my room."

"What were you doing?"

"Reading."

"Didn't you hear us looking for you?"

"Hm-mm."

"I bet you did," Emma said.

"No, not until someone was calling for me in the yard." She unwrapped a pumpkin whoopie pie and took a huge, soft bite. The icing stuck to her cheek, and she wiped it away with her hand. Mmmm. Mam made the best whoopie pies.

The popcorn was ready, and Dat poured it into a huge, stainless-steel bowl, adding salt and melted butter. Everyone took a colorful plastic dish and dug into the bowl, shaking them down, piling more on top to make their dishes heaping full.

This was one of Lizzie's favorite snacks. Buttery, salty popcorn, washed down with cold chocolate milk. Amazing how you could have a whole mouthful of popcorn and the minute the chocolate milk hit it, the popcorn all dissolved and went to nothing. Kool-Aid, iced tea, or water did the exact same thing. She supposed that if they were English and drank Pepsi, it would dissolve popcorn, too. That was because popcorn was mostly air.

"Where's church next time?" Emma asked around a mouthful of popcorn.

"At Levi Kanagy's," Mam said.

See? There Emma talked with her mouth heaping full and Mam did not say one word about it, Lizzie observed to herself.

"I wonder," Emma said, clearly thinking about the main subjects of conversation for the last few weeks, "if everybody's sins are all forgiven when they're baptized, what happens when they sin again?"

"That's a good question, Emma," Dat said. "Actually, that's when the power of Jesus' blood goes into effect. After you profess to believe in Jesus, you become one of God's children, and your sins are forgiven when you repent and pray to be forgiven. That happens over and over again as we go through life."

Okay, Lizzie thought. Well, that makes everything seem much more possible. It didn't seem quite as dangerous to join church if you had a chance of making some mistakes afterward.

Lizzie wished they'd simply stop talking about all this serious stuff. Everything had been strict enough around the house lately. It just gave her the blues. She didn't know why things had to change so much when you got older.

"You girls probably think Mam and I have become a bit hard on you recently. We don't mean to be, but watching the youth join church this summer, and seeing how fast you're growing up, kind of puts fear into us. We want to do all we can to help you girls be the mature young women you should be as you join the youth and go to singings on Sunday evenings." Dat said this so soberly, it sounded as if there were tears in his voice.

That was nice, what Dat said, Lizzie decided. She believed him, and she felt like trying hard to please Dat and Mam in everything. But that was enough now.

Chapter 31

Lizzie's intensive sewing lessons continued during the week after her birthday. One morning, after the breakfast dishes were done, Lizzie and
Emma spread out dress fabric on the kitchen table
while Mam baked cookies

"It's not straight," Lizzie wailed, as she started to
cut into the fabric.

"Hold your scissors upside down, Lizzie. You're
left-handed."

"Ow! Ouch. That doesn't work either. It cuts
right into the soft part of my thumb."

"Well, it's one way or another, Lizzie," Emma
said measuredly.

"Mam!" Lizzie screeched.

"What?"

"Didn't anyone ever invent scissors for left-
handed people?"

Mam dried her hands on a dish towel and went
to see what Lizzie was yelling about. After watching

her attempts, which were more like chewing the fabric than making a clean, slicing cut, she nodded.

"I see what you mean. Yes, I'm sure we can find a left-handed scissors for you at a fabric shop somewhere. Next time we go shopping we'll look for one."

So with a black cloud of impatience and frustration already forming over Lizzie's head, sewing at the machine went quickly from struggle to disaster.

"Not so fast, Lizzie!"

"Yes, you have to zigzag the seams. If you don't, they'll ravel apart, leaving long strands of thread dangling. Lizzie, you have to!"

Mam winced when she heard the chair thump on the floor, and Lizzie came charging toward the counter. Her hair stood out wildly every which way, her covering was crooked, and bits of fabric stuck to her bib apron.

"Mam, why do I have to zigzag? That's the dumbest thing I ever heard of. The fabric is already sewed tight with a straight stitch twice, so why do I still have to zigzag? I'm not going to." And with that, she flounced back to the sewing machine, leaving a trail of loose threads floating behind her.

Emma's patience was already stretched to the limit, so when Lizzie came huffing back, she put her hands on her hips and announced quite firmly, "If you don't do it right, I'm not going to help you anymore."

"But that's so stupid!"

"Do you want to have sloppy-looking pieces of

thread sticking out of your neckline or from under your cape on your very first weekend?" Emma shouted.

Lizzie narrowed her eyes, considering. "No-o-o."

"Okay, then settle down and watch me turn this knob. You have to stay on the *edge* of the fabric. You can't just zigzag anywhere you feel like."

Lizzie's sigh of resignation assured Mam that she was well on the way to learning how to sew, so she relaxed as she started a batch of homemade bread. Susan and KatieAnn pushed their chairs up to the kitchen cabinets. Mam let them stir the yeast into the water, her heart melting as it always did when they wanted to be her helpers.

The treadle on the sewing machine thumped fairly rhythmically without too much noise between the two girls until Emma showed up at Mam's elbow, looking peeved.

"Mam," she whispered, "Lizzie's dress is going to be way too fancy. She cut her sleeves so wide, she can hardly gather all the fabric neatly at the bottom of the sleeve."

Mam's heart sank as she looked at Emma. Dat was already asking Mam why she allowed Lizzie to comb her hair so stylishly. She was increasingly in that difficult position between Lizzie's strong will and Dat's fear of what other people would say about his stylish daughter.

Mam strode purposefully over to the sewing machine. "Lizzie," she said quietly, peering over her shoulder at the alarming length of fancy ruffles which Lizzie was arranging along the bottom of the sleeve.

Lizzie jumped nervously. She had thought it was Emma coming to watch her make the sleeves. "What?"

"You can't have so many ruffles, Lizzie. That's just not allowed. Emma's dresses aren't cut or gathered like that. You're going to have to take some fabric out. Dat will have a fit. It simply looks too fancy."

"Emma's dresses have exactly this many gathers," Lizzie snorted defiantly.

"No, Lizzie, they don't. And if that's how you're going to be, you may as well close the sewing machine right now and wear a dress that you already have for your first weekend in Allen County."

Lizzie set her jaw in a firm line and held her shoulders stiffly as she sat gazing out the window without moving a muscle.

"It's up to you," Mam said, turning to go back to her bread.

Tears welled in Lizzie's eyes as the battle between giving in and having her own way raged. Why did Mam have to have all these plain ideals for her daughters? And Dat was worse yet.

Well, they would soon find out that she was not nearly as good and well behaved as Emma. Why would she be? She never was when they were little girls. And besides, Mam didn't understand how important it was that she was right up there, dressed like all the other girls, especially since she always felt a bit different, coming from Jefferson County and living on this ugly old farm. Why, the barn wasn't even painted, and they weren't nearly as classy as almost everyone else in their church district.

She knew, too, that her fight to look good would be a long battle. She didn't necessarily want to outdo the other girls. She just wanted to look pretty and be noticed as someone who was tastefully fancy. Was that so terribly wrong?

It made Lizzie sad, though, to think of hurting Mam and Dat. For a moment, she looked at Mam and thought about all she had to overcome, living on this terrible run-down farm. She had recently asked Mam, "Do you like it here now? I mean, better than you did that first year?"

Mam had gazed across the living room, seeing nothing as she struggled for the right answer. "Yes, Lizzie, I do," she said quietly, but there was a sigh in her voice, a kind of hollow undertone that wouldn't quite go away when she tried to use words to cover it.

Lizzie couldn't help wondering if Mam believed it was God's will for them to move here. Not only were they trying to make a livable farm and home on this heap of a place, but Dat's and Mam's daughters had to travel to another county for friends, both girls and boys.

She wanted to ask Mam how God's will could work if there were no Amish boys to marry in Cameron County and very few in Allen County. How will Mandy and I manage to get married if there aren't boys?

"Mam," she said when she got her nerve back.

"Hmm?"

"What does 'God's will' mean?"

"It just means he will be able to guide our lives."

"Oh."

"He has a perfect plan for each of you, and if we pray and seek that will, everything will work out."

"How do you know what it is?"

Mam paused. "You don't always. Although, I suppose if we made more of a sacrifice, instead of seeking our own selfish desires, we could tell so much better."

Lizzie's mind conjured up Abraham sacrificing a lamb in the Old Testament. Now that was confusing.

"What do you mean, 'sacrifice'?"

"It's hard to explain, Lizzie. I guess the more we learn to give up our own selfish desires, the easier it is to discern and be content with God's will."

"What do you mean, we have to listen for God's will for a husband? I mean, this is getting serious. I'm 16, and I still don't understand."

Mam put down her sewing and searched Lizzie's face. "Lizzie, if you read your Bible more, and tried to be more mature about your faith, you wouldn't be so confused."

Lizzie's face felt warm and she said quietly, "Right now, I don't know where my Bible is."

"Lizzie, I do not believe it!" Mam was shocked, as Lizzie knew she would be.

So Mam talked, explaining to her how she would understand more fully as the years went by. She had nothing to worry about because God knew her heart and would help her through every situation as life went on. It was all very comforting that day, sitting in the gaslit living room, with the rain and the dark, scudding clouds.

Lizzie's heart felt lighter and quite unafraid as Mam talked. She still did not understand everything, although she was comforted when Mam said that finding the right husband was not a hit-or-miss kind of thing. Apparently it wasn't like Lizzie thought. Mam said that if you prayed honestly, God would direct you to the right husband, although somehow it was still your own choice. *Of course* you could marry someone that you wanted to! she said.

Lizzie walked slowly into the living room, trying to make sense of that slim ray of light that had pierced her soul as Mam talked about finding a husband. She picked up the sleeve with all the gathers, then looked out the window and down across the fields that led to the creek. Her shoulders slumped as she slowly, slowly let out some of the gathers, the battle within far from resolved.

She threw down the sleeve when the thread snapped and yelled at the top of her voice, a sound mostly driven by frustration at her sewing and her own personal battle. "Emma!"

"Coming," Emma said, dashing to her rescue.

As the afternoon wore on, Lizzie finally realized that it was perfectly possible for her to make a dress. It wouldn't have happened without plenty of help from Emma, but she began to see how the pieces fit together. Everything made more sense than ever before.

When she pulled the new dress over her head, letting the soft blue folds of the skirt hang almost to the floor before Emma pinned the hem, she was so happy she felt like a princess. Whirling her way from the kitchen to the living room, she lifted her arms and told Emma she was Cinderella.

Emma grinned wryly. "Well, you're not exactly Cinderella, scrubbing floors as your sisters while away the hours in luxury."

Emma's own patience had nearly run out. Now here was Lizzie, the cause of a whole afternoon of stress, suddenly happy as a lark, showing off, in Emma's opinion, her still too-fancy sleeves. But Emma said nothing as Lizzie climbed up on a chair so Emma could pin up the hem.

"Shorter, Emma," Lizzie commanded.

"Lizzie, your dresses are short enough. No."

"I'm 16 now!"

"So?"

"Mam!"

Mam walked over, assessing the new outfit as Lizzie stood on top of the chair. In Mam's view, the sleeves still looked a bit too fancy. She narrowed her eyes as Lizzie asked if she could have her dresses a bit shorter now because she was 16.

"Why would you want to, Lizzie? Your dresses are too short as it is."

"They are not, Mam. They hang almost to my ankles."

"Stop it. No."

Mam turned to go back to her baking, and Emma pinned the hem securely. Lizzie hopped off the chair and glared at her.

"So, if I don't get a boyfriend by the time I'm 25, it's all your fault, Emma. Yours and Mam's."

"Stop being so childish. Joshua says that's about the last thing he notices about me."

"What?"

"The style of my clothes. Boys don't always think about such things. They think more about a pleasing personality."

"Joshua isn't the only boy in the world. Some boys notice how you look. I'll never be asked out on a date, as long as that dress is."

Mandy abruptly changed the atmosphere when she walked into the house from her day's work at the hatchery. She took one look at Lizzie's lovely new blue dress and shrieked her admiration.

"Li-izzie, you look so nice! You are so lucky to be 16! Mam, I want a dress exactly like that when I turn 16!"

Emma exhaled in relief as a big smile appeared on Lizzie's face and she said, "You think so, Mandy? Isn't it too long?"

"No-o. Not a bit. It makes your gray eyes look blue, Lizzie!"

"I made this dress all by myself, Mandy!"

"Did you really?"

"Yep!"

Mam and Emma exchanged knowing glances. Emma wondered later if Cinderella would be back.

Chapter 32

Uncle Marvin was Dat's youngest brother and only a year older than Emma. He had started accompanying Emma on the drive to the young people's gatherings in Allen County a few weeks earlier. Marvin paid half the amount the driver charged them, which helped cut down on expenses for Dat and Mam.

Dat's youngest sister, Elsie, was 16, too, but she had already joined another group of young people in a larger community about 90 miles away. She had found friends there who were more conservative like she was. She was still a dear aunt whom Lizzie and Emma were very fond of, but during their years of being with the youth, Elsie went her separate way on the weekends.

Not Marvin. He joined Emma most weekends and she loved his companionship, each of them sharing their own thoughts and opinions on many subjects as they traveled to and from Allen County, where there was a larger settlement of Amish. Marvin had always said what he thought to Emma and Lizzie without inhibition. In fact, he had recently told Lizzie in no uncertain terms what he thought about her looks, her behavior, her attitude. In a way, Marvin was like her older brother. He cared deeply about her and wanted her to mature and find good friends.

One afternoon, he stopped at their farm to make plans with Emma for the coming weekend.

"Are you excited to come with us to Allen County?" he asked Lizzie as he sat at the table eating a whoopie pie.

Lizzie nodded as she watched Marvin eat. She had already had a whoopie pie that forenoon, but she wanted another one.

Marvin brushed the crumbs off his hands as he leaned back in his chair.

"Lizzie, I know you hope to meet some boys during these weekends in Allen County," he said. "But I have to be honest. Boys will think you're a lot prettier if you lost more weight. You're still a bit on the heavy side."

Lizzie was appalled. She didn't think she was one bit fat anymore. Well, she knew she wasn't skinny and rail-thin like some girls, but she didn't feel heavy at all. Marvin's comments stung, but Lizzie liked that he was honest. She believed he wanted the best for her.

That night at dinner, Mam was busy filling everyone's plate with steaming chicken stew. Large chunks of chicken, white cubes of soft potatoes, orange carrots, peas, and slivers of onion and celery floated in a thick, creamy sauce. Specks of black pepper and little pieces of dark green parsley dotted the broth. Best of all, Lizzie thought, were the mounds of fluffy white dumplings on top. Mam plopped half of one on each plate, and then spooned gravy over it. Cold macaroni salad and thick slices of homemade bread with butter and peach jam completed their meal.

Everything tasted wonderful, even the macaroni salad. Emma didn't eat very much anymore, picking daintily at her dumpling with her fork. She didn't eat any macaroni salad at all, saying it was too fattening with all that mayonnaise. Lizzie took a huge bite of dumpling and gravy, chewed thoroughly, and looked at Emma with narrowed eyes.

"Mayonnaise isn't fattening."

"It is."

"No, I know it isn't."

"Lizzie!"

"It isn't." Lizzie scooped a large spoonful of macaroni salad onto her plate, her second helping, before taking a large bite.

"Lizzie, mayonnaise is one of the most fattening things you can eat," Dat said.

"Who said?"

"I don't know. I guess everybody just knows—it's quite a common fact."

Mandy jumped up, opened the pantry door, and

came back with a jar of mayonnaise. "One hundred calories for one tablespoon!" she announced. "See?"

"If you're on a strict diet, you are allowed 1,000 calories. So imagine! One-tenth of those are used up by putting mayonnaise on your sandwich," Dat said.

"I'm not on a diet!" Lizzie said loudly.

"No doubt," Emma muttered.

"Mam, Emma is being mean," Lizzie said.

"Emma," Mam said.

So Lizzie ate a large piece of pumpkin pie for dessert, free of guilt, because it seemed as if Mam was on her side. That one piece was not quite enough for her, so when they were clearing the table, Lizzie ate another piece, only smaller, when Emma wasn't looking. That left kind of a yucky sweet taste in her mouth, so when she took the pie back to the pantry, she got a handful of stick pretzels from the jar. Emma came into the kitchen just as Lizzie grabbed another handful of pretzels.

"Lizzie," she said. "Are you still eating?"

Lizzie turned and ran out of the room. She felt miserably full. It just wasn't fair. Look at Mandy. She naturally didn't like to eat a lot. She certainly did not like creme-filled doughnuts. The filling made her gag, she said. Lizzie loved those doughnuts, easily wolfing down two of them at a time, the last bite tasting every bit as wonderful as the first. Lizzie threw herself on the couch, crying, sniffing loudly, snorting, and blowing her nose in a crumpled paper towel she had found on the floor.

"You just like Mandy better. You're both so much thinner and prettier than me," she sobbed when Emma followed her into the room.

"Eww! Lizzie, don't use that dirty paper towel!"

"I will if I want to."

Emma shrugged her shoulders, watching Lizzie crying on the sofa. Suddenly, Emma could stand it no longer. She sat down beside Lizzie, touched her knee and said, "Lizzie, listen to me."

"What?"

"Why do you have this thing about nobody liking you? That gets really old. You claim Mam likes me better than you, and now you're saying Mandy and I stick together. You know that's not true. It's always you and Mandy doing things together, not me. Now you even sleep with her in the same bedroom, and I'm always by myself. You know I like you just the same as I always have. Mam gets impatient with you sometimes, but Lizzie, she has reason to. All you do is..." Emma hesitated, because she couldn't say what needed to be said.

"Eat! Just say it, Emma. I'm fat and lazy. Go ahead, say it!" Lizzie burst out.

"No, seriously, Lizzie, I honestly don't think you like yourself right now—that's why you feel as if no one else likes you. Your weight does bother you, only you won't admit it."

"I'm not that fat, Emma."

"But you are."

Lizzie looked steadily at Emma. Emma looked steadily back.

"See, Lizzie, Mam doesn't mean to be unkind. She's so busy with the twins right now and wrapped up in her own little world. So why don't you and I write each other a diet every day? You write what I can eat, and I'll write what you can eat! That would be fun! Do you want to?"

There was a long pause. "Hm-mm."

"You know what, Lizzie? You're just not yourself anymore. You're not even *happy*!"

"Are you allowed to have *any* mayonnaise on a diet? Emma, I mean this—seriously—I can't eat sandwiches without it."

"No, Lizzie, you can have mayonnaise. But instead of eating three sandwiches at lunch, try taking one. You can have all the mayonnaise you want on one sandwich."

Lizzie thought about this long and hard. Emma watched anxiously as Lizzie blinked, chewed her lower lip, and stuck a straight pin in and out of her dress.

"Lizzie, don't."

"What?"

"Don't jag yourself with that pin."

"I have a rash from doing it."

"Let me see."

Lizzie showed her.

"Lizzie!"

"I guess it's a nervous habit."

"Why are you nervous?"

"I dunno."

They sat in silence before Lizzie said. "Okay,

Emma, you may write me a diet for tomorrow, and I'll write you one. Only don't make it too strict, or I won't stay on it anyway."

"I won't, Lizzie. This is going to be fun!" Emma beamed.

Lizzie didn't say anything. After a while she said, "I'm only 16, Emma."

"Sixteen is old."

"Is it?"

"Yes, it is. You're getting older." Emma nodded her head wisely.

Lizzie sighed. But secretly, she was pleased. How nice of Emma to worry about her. She really did care. Suddenly she leaned over, put her arm around Emma's shoulder, and squeezed. "Thanks, Emma."

"Now you can never say I don't like you, Lizzie. I do."

The first morning of Lizzie's diet, she stepped on the scales for the first time without hanging onto the bathroom sink. She had learned long ago that if you crept onto the scales a bit slowly while you held onto the bathroom sink, you didn't weigh quite as much.

She knew she weighed a lot. Way too much for a girl in her mid-teens. She stepped off the scales. Why? How in the world could she weigh so much? She needed to lose at least 25 pounds. No one had noticed anything different that morning. Lizzie ate a bowl of Cheerios and a piece of toast with butter.

But she drank only a small glass of orange juice instead of a large one. Later, when Lizzie packed her lunch, she took only half a sandwich.

"Lizzie, are you sick?" Mam asked.

"Why?"

"Half a sandwich? You?"

"I'm going to lose weight."

"You are?"

"Good for you!" Mandy had said.

"You can do it," Emma encouraged her.

All those words helped so much, Lizzie could hardly believe it.

That evening at supper, Dat had asked Lizzie why she was eating less.

"I'm not hungry," she said.

"You must be sick then," Dat said, taking a big spoonful of macaroni and cheese.

Lizzie swallowed, watching him lift a steaming forkful to his mouth, shaking his head because it burned his tongue. She could eat the whole dish of macaroni all by herself, she was so hungry. For a moment, she felt like crying, but the thought of her weight and the size of her waistline filled her with determination. She would go through with it.

And she did. The first few days were the hardest, but slowly the weight came off, until one Saturday morning she stood on the scales and weighed exactly 25 pounds less.

She was so thrilled she put her hands to her face and shrieked. Emma and Mandy came running into the bathroom.

"Look! Oh, Emma, look at the scales!" Lizzie had gasped.

"One hundred thirty!" Emma said. "You did it!"

Mandy clapped Lizzie's shoulder. "You really did!"

Mam smiled broadly.

"Well done, Lizzie," she said. "But you know, Lizzie, you'll need to be careful from now on. They say it's harder to keep it off than it is to take it off."

"I know," Lizzie said. "I realize I can't eat everything I want to, probably never in my whole life."

Chapter 33

THEY HAD A FULL CARLOAD THAT FIRST
Sunday afternoon Lizzie went to Allen County—
Emma's friend Sara and her boyfriend, Uncle Marvin, Emma, and Lizzie. Lizzie had never been to
Allen County, so she got caught up in looking at
the homes and roads and scenery around this Amish
community. There were fewer hills than in Cameron
County, and so the roads were wider and straighter,
with only gradual slopes instead of long, steep hills.

When they passed a little white schoolhouse,
Lizzie knew they had reached the heart of the community. They went by a few Amish farms and then
turned into a straight driveway that led to a white
two-story house, a red barn, and a bunch of scattered outbuildings.

The youth were already gathering for supper. The
hymn-singing which followed would be at a different home, the same place where church services had
been held earlier that day.

Marvin talked to the driver about where and when to pick all of them up that night. And then they all headed for the house. Lizzie had one moment of wild panic as she tried to walk gracefully in her long-awaited high heels. They actually weren't that high, just high enough for her to feel very much like a young woman and maybe even just a bit fancy. She panicked briefly as she tried to walk smoothly and assuredly on the crooked cement-slab sidewalk. It was certainly much more difficult than when she practiced with the shoes in her bedroom.

Lizzie was plain-down proud of her shoes. Mam had been a real dear and agreed that she could have them when Lizzie found them at the shoe store in town. The heels were not as high as English women wore, and they tied over the top of her feet with black shoelaces, which made Mam feel comfortable about Lizzie having them. Dat frowned when she showed them to him, but he frowned a lot since the girls were running around.

He was just on edge about his daughters joining the youth at suppers and singings and doing things with their friends on weekends. Dat had been raised quite conservatively as far as clothes and certain social events were concerned. In fact, his dad, Doddy Glick, didn't like to see the young people wear anything fancy. Emma and Lizzie thought that Dat was too much like his father.

Dat objected to the way Lizzie combed her hair, he sighed if her dress was too short, and he made her change stockings if he thought they were too transparent. She felt rebellious sometimes, but when Mam agreed with Dat, there was nothing to do but surrender to Dat's wishes, go back upstairs and redo her hair, change stockings, or try to fix whatever his gripe was at the moment.

A lot of their girlfriends' parents had the same concerns, so they soon decided that Mam and Dat were as fair as most other Amish parents. Emma said they were concerned that if their children didn't keep the *Ordnung* and rules, who would continue to build the church? Lizzie understood that, she really did, but she battled constantly for her own way. She didn't dwell on these tensions all the time; she just liked to look nice. She imagined copying all kinds of fancy things she saw other people doing, even when she was a little girl.

One summer, Mam and the children decided to take the train to Ohio to visit Doddy and Mommy Miller, Mam's parents. Lizzie was all excited because, as she explained to Emma, "When you ride on a train, you can see all the English people and their fancy shoes, and the big tall buildings in the cities that the train passes through."

"Lizzie," Emma said, quite seriously.

"What?"

"You shouldn't be quite so wild in your mind. Why do you have to look at all the fancy shoes, anyway?" Emma asked her.

"Oh, they just look pretty. Especially the white ones with high heels. If I'd be English, that is exactly what I would wear. They make a nice clicking noise, too," Lizzie said.

Emma said nothing, so Lizzie folded her hands in her lap and thought Emma agreed with her. She looked down at her own navy-colored sneakers that had a white sole on them, and thought she had nice shoes for an Amish girl. She was happy with her new lavender-colored dress with a black apron. She liked being Amish—she just liked to watch fancy ladies with high heels. Emma didn't seem to understand that.

All these years later, her high heels helped tremendously to make her feel more accepted by the young people. They bolstered her self-esteem. Still, this is not going to be easy, she thought, as Emma began introducing Lizzie to the girls her age.

There was a thin, dark-haired girl named Barbara, almost exactly Lizzie's age, who was dating a young man from Lamton County. She also met Mary, who had a round face, narrow, almond-shaped eyes, and very black hair. She was quite talkative and accentuated her sentences with lots of eyebrow-lifting and hand motions. She and Barbara were quite warm, so Lizzie soon felt a bit more at ease, although she still depended on her high heels for self-assurance.

When it was time to eat supper, Lizzie's heart did

an absolute flip-flop. She was almost overwhelmed with a sickening sensation in her stomach as she thought about filing into that kitchen full of boys and parents. Barbara and Mary didn't seem to mind at all. Lizzie sincerely hoped they didn't notice the color draining from her face.

When she passed the little kitchen mirror, she made a desperate attempt to check herself, hoping she didn't appear nearly as agitated as she felt.

Her covering was straight—a nice covering and it fit well, thanks to Emma. Her hair was still combed neatly, although not as fancy as she would have liked, thanks to Dat. She had successfully hidden her pimples with Clearasil. She was biting her lips. Have to stop that; looks too nervous, she reminded herself.

She stepped off to the side and lifted the top of her blue cape, checking the pin in front to make sure it was straight. She couldn't see her black apron or shoes in the mirror, but she felt quite confident that her shoes looked snappy. She wondered if boys noticed shoes.

Now there was nothing to do but face the whole kitchen full of people. Lizzie was aware of a line of young men heaping their plates with mounds of food. A few of them cast cautious glances her way. Emma and her friend Sara had already filled their plates and were talking and laughing with the long line of boys.

Surprisingly, Lizzie wasn't hungry or even very interested in what was in the large roasters and stainless steel pots and pans on the long table. She just knew that she made it through the line, filled her plate without spilling it, and ate as if she was in a trance.

Running around and going to a strange community, meeting new girls and feeling so afraid was not one bit fun, she decided. Next to her, Barbara and Mary started laughing and giggling together, then suddenly, without asking Lizzie to join them, got up and dashed into the kettle house.

She sat alone, her empty plate in her lap, not knowing which would be the least conspicuous—to remain there saying nothing or to get up and hurry out to the washhouse after Barbara and Mary. Just when she felt like a true misfit, a young man tripped over her foot.

"Whoa there! Sorry!" he said, turning to look at Lizzie as she quickly pulled both feet back under her chair where they probably should have been in the first place.

"That's okay," Lizzie mumbled.

He took his plate to the table, then turned and came back to sit beside her. Lizzie didn't know if she should be pleased or embarrassed, but his friendly smile put her at ease.

"So…you're Emma's little sister?"

"Mmm-hmm."

"Sixteen years old already?"

"My first weekend."

She dared to look at him. His eyes were as dark as Mary's, his skin even darker than hers. A shock of jet-black hair made him look mysterious, Lizzie thought.

"What's your name?" he asked.

"Lizzie. But I wish I was called Elizabeth, because that's my real name," Lizzie said hurriedly.

"Nothing wrong with 'Lizzie.'"

"It's not very classy."

He laughed unexpectedly, showing a row of very straight white teeth. "What would be classier?"

"Liz. Or Elizabeth."

"Well, Liz, Elizabeth, Lizzie, whatever. Do you play Ping-Pong?"

"Ping-Pong? I used to, but since we moved, we have no place to put the table, so I'm sure I'm quite rusty."

"Come on. There's a bunch playing in the basement."

❧

Lizzie loved Ping-Pong. She was still amazed that years earlier Mam had actually gotten them a Ping-Pong table for their basement. This was not at all like Mam.

One day when Mam was reading the newspaper, she suddenly said, "Girls, listen to this: 'Ping-Pong table. In very good condition. One hundred dollars or best offer.'"

Lizzie had looked up. "What's a Ping-Pong table?"

"Surely you know, Lizzie."

"No."

"Well, it's high time you girls learned. I'll call this number and offer them $75."

"Aren't you going to ask Dat?" asked Emma, looking up from her crocheting.

"Oh, he won't mind. He loves to play Ping-Pong." And with that, Mam was off, hurrying down the driveway and across the street to the neighbors' phone.

"Boy!" Emma said, dryly.

"I'll say," Lizzie agreed.

"She really must want that Ping-Pong table." Emma resumed her crocheting, her needle flashing in the glow of the gas lamp.

In no time at all, Mam hurried back up the steps and into the kitchen, waving the paper with the telephone number on it. "We got it! They'll deliver it this evening! Net, paddles, and all! This will be a big surprise for Dat!"

When Dat came home for supper, Mam was flushed and beaming. She could never keep a secret very long, so before the girls had a chance to say anything, Mam blurted out, "Melvin, guess what?"

Dat was washing up in the bathroom, but he peeped above the blue towel he was using to dry his face and said, "Now what?"

"We're getting a Ping-Pong table tonight!"

"Hah-ah!" Dat said, in disbelief.

"Oh, yes! They're delivering it from close to Marion for $75. It was advertised in the local paper for a hundred!"

Mam turned to the table with a steaming bowl of

chicken stew and dumplings, while Emma poured water into the plastic drinking glasses.

"Wonder if it's any good?" Dat asked.

"We'll see. I'll beat you good and proper, Melvin!" Mam said, her eyes twinkling.

"If I remember right, Annie, I skunked you last time we played!" Dat told her, laughing.

'Skunked?' Lizzie thought. This had to be some childish game they were all worked up about. Dat and Mam sure were acting dumb about it. 'Skunked'?

"What do you mean, 'skunked'?" she burst out.

"Oh, that's a term you use when one person has 11 points and the other has only one or two," Mam said.

"So…Dat was a lot better than you, right?" Lizzie asked.

"Oh, that just happened once or so. He didn't beat me like that all the time," Mam assured her.

Here in the middle of the youth in this basement, Lizzie was transported to that earlier evening. They had all sat down for supper then, and put patties down or folded their hands on their laps as they bowed their heads in silent prayer. Lizzie was so busy thinking about Ping-Pong, she didn't remember to give thanks. When Dat lifted his head she said quickly, "Is it hard to learn?"

"I'm afraid you forgot to say your prayer, Lizzie," Dat said soberly.

"She always forgets. She told me once," Emma sniffed.

"Emma, I do not!"

After dinner, they hadn't yet finished with the dishes when a pickup truck drove up the driveway and stopped. A dark green table with white lines around its edges and another white line straight up the middle stood propped on the back of the truck.

"It's here!" Lizzie yelled.

Dat and Mam bustled out the door, down the steps, and helped unload the huge table.   After Dat wrote a check and thanked the English man who brought the table, he showed the girls how to hold the paddle properly. It was not at all as Lizzie had imagined. You had to hold the round, rubbery part in, and the wooden handle out.

Lizzie and Mandy tried to bat the little white plastic ball back and forth, but they hardly ever got it right. Usually the ball didn't go close to where they wanted it to be, and they bent over laughing again and again. They thought they would never learn.

But when Dat and Mam started to play, Lizzie couldn't believe it. They hit the ball back and forth, almost faster than her eyes could follow. It flew low over the net, always hitting the table before Dat or Mam slammed it straight back. Lizzie wasn't surprised that Dat could do this. He was a man and good at lots of physical things. But Mam! Lizzie was astounded. Mam's eyes sparkled, her arms flew fast, and her hand gripped the Ping-Pong paddle until her knuckles turned white. She pinched her mouth with determination, sort of like when she was upset. She moved faster than Lizzie had ever seen her, with her feet almost dancing to keep up with Dat's furious pace.

Just when Lizzie was positive she could no longer take the suspense, Mam yelled, "Melvin!"

Dat yelled, too, and slapped his knee in triumph. He had hit the ball to the very corner of Mam's side of the table. The ball had gone down over, but first it touched the table lightly, meaning it was Dat's point. If the ball had cleared the table, it would have been Mam's point.

Dat certainly did not skunk Mam that game, because Mam won, 21 points to Dat's 18. Mam's cheeks were red, and she was laughing as she ran over to open a window, saying it was much too warm in the basement. Jason clapped his hands and squealed with excitement as he grabbed Mam's paddle and ran off with it. She caught him, pretending to smack his little pants' seat with it.

They played three games before Mam gasped and said that was it, she was too tired for one more game. Dat had laughed, begging her to play one more, but she said it was high time to put Jason to bed.

Lizzie hadn't played Ping-Pong regularly, so her confidence was a little shaky as she followed the guy down the steps. She smiled, remembering how happy Dat and Mam had looked that evening when they played together. Maybe someday someone would look at her that way.

In the basement, gas lanterns glowed bright and a woodstove in the corner warmed the room. At card tables groups of boys and girls played games, and a lively game of Ping-Pong was underway in one corner. Instead of only two players, there were four, which caused a lot more excitement, frustration, and yelling. When one young man became agitated, he stomped his foot and threw his paddle across the table.

Lizzie turned to look at her newfound friend and found him looking at her, laughing. His smile was so infectious, Lizzie laughed back quite unashamedly until she realized she didn't even know his name.

"You didn't tell me your name or who you are," she said, wondering if that was too bold.

"Didn't I? Guess I forgot or just took for granted you'd know. I'm Mary's brother, Amos."

Instantly, Lizzie saw that he and Mary both had striking dark skin and eyes. When the Ping-Pong game was over, Amos asked her to be his partner and play against Marvin and a girl Lizzie didn't know.

Lizzie hung back, her heart banging against her ribs, not sure she could play well enough to be in a game with four people. She glanced at Amos who gave her a reassuring smile.

"I...I'm not very good," she said.

"Sure you are," Marvin said loudly. "You used to be when you lived in Jefferson County."

Lizzie's face colored and she shot him a "Be quiet" look. He didn't have to say that so loudly in front of everyone in the whole basement.

Marvin's eyebrows spiked, and he said, "What?"

"Oh nothing. Come on, let's play!"

The game started in earnest. Amos proved to be a capable player. He was quick, so Lizzie came to depend on him when an opposing shot was too fast or hard for her to reach. When the opposing players scored nine points to their 10, Lizzie was breathlessly laughing, no longer paralyzed by shyness. She was having so much fun she quite forgot her misery of only an hour ago.

They played two sets, and Lizzie did not want the game to end.

But Amos threw his Ping-Pong paddle down, ran his fingers through his hair, and said, "It's too hot in here! Let's go for a walk!"

Lizzie didn't know what to do. Was he talking to her or Marvin? She couldn't go on a walk with him alone on her very first weekend. That would not be proper at all, she knew that, and she could just hear Mam and Emma on Monday morning if that happened.

But she wanted to go for a walk with Amos. He was fun to be around and quite nice- looking, but... she shouldn't, not her first weekend of running around.

Marvin found his coat and asked Lizzie why she didn't go get hers. "You and Ruthie can go with us."

Lizzie smiled shyly at the strange girl who evidently was named Ruthie. "You want to go?"

"Do you?"

Lizzie cast a sideways glance at Amos who was looking at her, waiting to see what she'd say. "Yes. If you do."

"All right. My coat's upstairs."

Lizzie ran up the stairs with Ruthie, and they looked straight into each other's eyes, smiling happily. No matter if they didn't know each other before this, they were going for a walk with the boys! Ruthie's eyes sparkled as she tied her covering strings more tightly, checking her face in the mirror. "I'm Ruthie Stoltzfus, and I heard that Emma had a sister who would soon be 16. So you're the one!" she said, smiling at Lizzie.

"I am, yes!"

They laughed together as they dashed down the stairs.

Outside, the air was brisk and cold, although most of the snow had already melted. Lizzie pulled her scarf closer and shivered as they set a brisk pace out through the driveway.

They talked about all kinds of things with Marvin leading the conversation, as he usually did. Lizzie saw a few more Amish houses and learned about the community. She also heard about Amos' home, where he lived, and how many were in his family. Ruthie lived only a few miles away and had four sisters.

Lizzie looked at Marvin and smiled. He smiled back as if to say, Isn't this just the most fun ever? Her heart swelled with genuine fondness and admiration for her uncle. Dear Marvin. Even now, at this absolutely important time in her life, good old Marvin was enjoying it along with her, just as had happened many times in their childhoods.

The hymn-singing was taking place a few miles away. Ruthie told Lizzie that when a boy took you to the singing, or when he asked you to go along with him, it was because he liked your company. It wasn't like a real date, not even the start of one, but it was exciting to see who asked you to ride along in his buggy. Sometimes a group of girls asked a guy to take them along to the singing in his buggy, which was all right, too. Ruthie giggled a little when she told Lizzie that it was a really great thing if someone asked you to go along.

Lizzie chewed on her lower lip, nervously eyeing the boys getting ready to go out and hitch up their horses. She saw Joshua ask Emma if she was ready to go, and Emma nodded her head, smiling at him. It would be so safe and secure to have a boyfriend, Lizzie thought.

"Ruthie, what about our walk? That didn't mean anything, did it?" Lizzie asked a bit hesitantly.

"No. We were just cooling off after playing Ping-Pong."

Lizzie nodded. But she couldn't help but be disappointed that Marvin and Amos didn't ask them to ride with them to the singing.

Barbara and Mary caught up with the two girls,

inviting Lizzie and Ruthie to ride along with them and Barbara's brother.

The ride to the singing was the wildest buggy ride Lizzie had ever experienced. She was so glad she was in the back seat and that it was dark. Barbara's brother drove so fast that she was immensely relieved she couldn't see the landscape flying past from where she sat.

More teams of horses tore along, both in front of and behind them. One by one, they overtook the buggy Lizzie was in, streaking past them as if they were hardly moving. Lizzie hid her face, hung on, and hoped there was no vehicle approaching from the opposite direction.

She was sure that they turned into the driveway on two wheels, the horse leaning at a 45-degree angle, but she didn't say anything because she was too new to squeal or state her opinions.

Chapter 34

THE YOUTH ALL FILED INTO THE LIVING ROOM of the large house where a long narrow table had been put together. It was made of church benches set on small wooden extenders to form a table top. Other wooden church benches were set on either side, and hymnbooks were piled in the center of the table. The boys sat on one side; the girls on the other.

Emma and Sara started the first song, an old German hymn Lizzie had often sung in school. She knew the words well and loved to sing, especially with a whole group of people. On this very first weekend she discovered the utter beauty of joining the young people's hymn-singings on Sunday evenings.

She was singing heartily when she looked up and saw Marvin and Amos come in and sit down on the boys' side of the table, followed immediately by two girls whom Lizzie did not know.

She blinked her eyes nervously, hastily looking at the words in the hymnbook. So that was how it was, huh? You could go for a walk with a good-looking young man, and it amounted to nothing.

Already, only a few hours later, he had asked another girl to go along to the singing with him. Lizzie felt absolutely dejected, her future of running around as insurmountable as Mt. Everest. She would have to have a serious talk with Emma.

She noticed Ruthie watching her anxiously, so she knew she had to paste a smile on her face and start to sing again. But all she could think about was Uncle Marvin having the nerve to do this to Ruthie and her.

She was not only planning a serious talk with Emma about how she managed to go for a walk with Joshua *and* ride to the singing with him. She had also decided to give Marvin a good scolding on the way home.

৵

Lizzie felt almost as confused as she did one morning a few years earlier. As they got ready for school, Emma gave her another lecture about how she should look and behave at school. She wasn't even a teenager yet, but if she listened to Emma, it sounded like she was now too old to horse around with the boys. Let Emma be sedate and domestic, Lizzie decided. But she wasn't going to stop having fun.

Lizzie finished combing her hair in silence that day. Emma pinned on her apron, asking Lizzie to straighten it in the back. There was a small piece of cloth sewn to the waist of their dresses, called a lebbley, and their black aprons had to be spaced evenly on each side, according to Amish custom.

"Yesterday your apron was so crooked I couldn't even see your lebbley, Lizzie," Emma informed her.

"So?"

"Well, you could let me straighten it for you."

"I can do it myself. Besides, I don't even care much what I look like. Around here, nobody really cares much about clothes. It's relaxed," Lizzie said, sniffing.

"I agree," Emma assured her. "But you looked so sloppy yesterday in school, I was almost embarrassed. Your hair looked a fright. I mean, I don't want to be unkind, Lizzie, but you should hold still and be a bit more quiet. We're not exactly little girls anymore!"

Lizzie narrowed her eyes at Emma. She had a straight pin in her mouth, because she was pinning her black school apron, so she didn't say anything immediately.

"Emma, we're not old yet. I don't want to have to grow up right now and start worrying about what I look like. There's too much to do yet, like playing baseball and going sledding and skating," Lizzie said, holding a straight pin to the lamp to see why it wouldn't pierce the fabric of her black belt apron.

Emma sighed, turning to hang up her flannel nightgown. She shook her head. There was no use trying to persuade Lizzie to act a bit more grown up. Lizzie assumed she was fine exactly the way she was, although Emma thought she was too noisy in school, often speaking her mind quite loudly and at the wrong time.

As they splashed through the slush on their way to school, Emma hung back a bit because Lizzie was stomping her boots in the shallow ditch beside the road. Bits of slush and water flew in every direction, splattering anyone close to her.

"Stop it, Lizzie," Sadie Mae said. "You got my socks wet."

Lizzie laughed and skipped ahead, trying to catch up with Ivan and Ray. They were talking, never noticing Lizzie's approach. Emma watched as Lizzie sneaked up behind them and then stomped her boot in the slush, splattering their pant legs with cold, wet snow.

"Hey!" Ivan yelled.

"Cut it out!" Ray growled.

Lizzie stomped again, splattering more cold, wet snow across their legs. Ray put down his lunchbox, picked up a handful of wet snow, grabbed Lizzie by the shoulders, and rubbed the snow in her face. Lizzie shrieked and tore out of his grasp, stopping to shake the water off her face. It ran down her chin and soaked her coat. She rubbed a coat sleeve across her face in an effort to dry it. Her face was red as a beet, her bonnet pushed to the back of her head, her hair a disheveled mess, and the day hadn't even begun.

"Lizzie!" Emma scolded.

"What?"

"Behave yourself."

Sadie Mae was scowling at her and Emma looked embarrassed. Mandy walked quietly behind them, but her eyes were at least twinkling.

"That makes Ivan and Ray mad if you splash slush on them," Sadie Mae told her sourly.

Lizzie felt terrible. No one smiled—not even Mandy—so she figured that wasn't a good thing to have done this morning. She pinched her mouth shut and fell behind everyone else. That was just the trouble with getting older, she thought bitterly. There were always these unspoken guidelines about what was nice behavior and what wasn't. Who was to say what was grown up and what was childish? Emma? Emma couldn't always be there with Lizzie to remind her to behave herself her whole life long. And that Sadie Mae had nerve, telling her that Ivan and Ray didn't like slush splashed on them. How did she know? Everybody was mean this morning. Even Mandy was sober and serious.

Now, Lizzie sat at her first singing, wondering again if she had missed some important rule of behavior. She guessed she'd have to ask Emma.

Chapter 35

Spring arrived, along with warm, mellow sunshine and buds bursting from the maple trees in the yard. Even the old walnut tree beside the sidewalk began to shine with a look of light green mist. Thousands of tiny green buds were erupting from its dark branches.

The swollen creek churned on its relentless way to the river, muddy brown from all the April showers. Little green shoots emerged from the moist brown earth under its blanket of wet, decaying leaves which had mulched the baby sprouts to new growth.

Dat was working the horses hard, preparing the soil for another crop. Clyde was back in the harness, still bouncing around as if he had springs in his legs. But the spirited horse was learning to buckle down and behave long enough to pull his share of the plow.

Mam's energy level was almost back to normal a year after her bout of pneumonia, which comforted and relieved Lizzie and Emma. She asked Dat to bring a few wheelbarrow loads of manure into the yard so she could start a new flower garden. And she asked the girls to help her in the evening with laying out a huge new rock garden on an unhandy slope between the house and barn where no grass could grow decently.

New Amish families were moving into the community this spring. When the Glick family went to church, they often met new girls and parents with small children whom they had never seen before.

Each weekend Lizzie went with Emma and Marvin to Allen County, which she looked forward to each and every other day of the week. Running around was even more fun now that warmer weather had arrived, because there was so much more to do. Lizzie thought that baseball games, volleyball, croquet, and just going for drives to different picnic areas or lakes with a group of young people were the funnest things in the entire world.

She became good friends with Barbara and Mary and often spent Saturday nights with them. One weekend blended into the next until Lizzie's world was filled with warm golden sunshine and so much to do and think about that time flew by like the spring breezes.

She still liked Amos, and she was never quite as thrilled as when he asked her to go for a buggy ride with him. Those times felt like romance to Lizzie, if not true love, although she didn't know what the difference was between the two, or how you could know whether your feelings were right or not.

She liked everyone, and all the boys were her friends. But somehow, it seemed a little different whenever Amos was around. It was almost as if the group of youth was not quite complete until he arrived. And as soon as Lizzie knew he was there, she was not completely happy until he had noticed her and said hello.

There seemed to be lots of talk about Emma getting married in the fall. Actually, it was only teasing among Mam and the girls because Emma was still too young. She would be only 18 by November. Lizzie knew how Emma felt, though. She had secretly told Lizzie that she would love to get married in the fall and move to Joshua's parents' farm in Allen County.

The old place had a huge brick house with an L-shaped porch, a barn, and lots of sheds and outbuildings. It was the home Emma had always dreamed of, and there were stars in her eyes as she folded towels and sheets and placed them in the cedar hope chest that had her initials on the front.

Lizzie did not want to get married so young. She discovered that soon after she turned 16. Running around was much too exciting to think of settling down on an old farm with a husband and nothing to look forward to except cooking and cleaning for the rest of your life.

Mandy heartily agreed with Lizzie when they talked about the possibility of Emma getting married so young. Mandy nodded soberly though, when

Lizzie said that Emma had always been different as far as working in the house with Mam, and that she really enjoyed all kinds of domestic duties at a very young age.

"Hey, look at Clyde!" Mandy yelled.

Lizzie was in the garden pulling weeds with Mandy. She looked up, shading her eyes with one hand in the morning sunlight. Mandy pointed toward the big brown horse pulling the plow in the old hayfield.

"What's wrong?"

"See how he can barely settle himself down long enough to stay in line and pull his share with the others? He's always prancing or stepping sideways or shaking his head up and down. I guess he's just too full of himself to act decent when he's hitched up!"

Lizzie continued to watch as Dat plowed the hay stubble. He had already plowed enough so that the girls could see a thin line of dark brown, overturned earth following the curve of their gently rolling land. When Dat and the team of horses returned from the far end of the field, they came close enough for the girls to hear the clank of the plow and the squeaking of the leather harnesses.

Mandy shook her head in her wise way, clicking her tongue. "Clyde's never going to last in this heat!" she said.

Lizzie stood, watching anxiously as Dat turned the team of horses at the end of the furrow. What at first seemed to be an impossible turn became a picture of perfect motion, as Dat called and each horse stepped tightly to the right. It seemed to Lizzie as if they all knew exactly what was expected of them, and they executed the short turn with no effort at all.

Except Clyde. He hopped about three times too often, tossing his head before Dat yelled at him. Lizzie looked at Mandy and they both smiled, knowing how impatient Dat was with Clyde.

As the team pulled the plow up over the slope, making the brown strip wider, the girls bent down and resumed their tedious job of weeding. The sun was very warm, reminding them of the hot summer days ahead.

"Wish we could go down to the creek and cool off," Lizzie said.

She plopped down between the rows of corn.

"Watch out! Lizzie, you sat on some cornstalks," Mandy said.

Lizzie didn't move. Who cared about a few measly little cornstalks? Nine chances out of 10, they wouldn't make it anyway, so what was wrong with sitting on a few?

"Wish we could go down to the creek," she said again.

"Wishing won't get you anywhere. Come on, Lizzie. Help with these weeds."

Lizzie turned and pulled absentmindedly at a few weeds.

This garden is way too big," she said.

"We need a big garden now. We're poor farmers," Mandy said, tossing a handful of weeds into her white plastic bucket.

Lizzie selected a wide piece of grass, stretched it expertly between her forefinger and the base of her thumb, and, lifting it to her mouth, she blew as hard as she could. A shrill explosion of sound followed. Mandy ignored her.

"That was a good one," Lizzie said.

She got no response so Lizzie watched Mandy pulling weeds. She was mad now, Lizzie could tell by the way Mandy jerked on the weeds and hurled them into her bucket. Mandy was so thin, Lizzie thought. These kinds of clothes made her look good, she decided, because the black bib aprons fit her perfectly. She was wearing a dark blue dress with its sleeves made in a looser fashion, which only accentuated her slimness and made her face even prettier.

Lizzie scrambled to her feet, pulled her bucket over, and began pulling weeds in earnest.

"Mandy, did you really, really mind going to church here the first Sunday we went?" Lizzie asked.

"I don't know. Not really, I guess. I mean, Elsie and Aunt Becca and Mommy Glick were there. But it wasn't exactly *fun*, if that's what you mean, with all those strange people staring at us."

"They probably didn't really mean to stare, Mandy."

"I know, but...it felt as if they were all looking at us."

Lizzie walked down the row of corn, lifting her bucket of weeds and tossing them across the fence into the pasture. On her way back, she said to Mandy, "It's because our clothes don't look right."

"What do you mean?" Mandy asked.

"I'll tell you the truth, Mandy. I feel so self-conscious and ugly since we live here. Our coverings haven't been made nearly as neat as everybody else's."

"I know. But you know why? Emma said it's because Mam comes from Ohio, and she doesn't really know how to make neat coverings for young girls. She never did. So Emma told me that's why she's learned to make them. Otherwise, we'd never look any better. She didn't want to insult Mam by saying hers aren't neat enough. They are alright for mothers and little girls."

"Emma can sew anything she tries," Lizzie said.

"I know. Did you see her make bib aprons? They're just as neat as a pin."

"I'm so relieved she's making our coverings now. I was so tired of being embarrassed. I just want to look nice."

Lizzie and Mandy took turns using the hoe to unearth the small weeds as they talked on. Birds circled overhead, calling while they flew into the old walnut tree at the end of the sidewalk. The diesel was droning in the distance as Mam filled the clothesline with load after load of clean laundry.

A desperate cry sliced through their conversation. Mandy dropped the hoe, and she and Lizzie turned to see Dat standing at the corner of the partially plowed field, waving his straw hat frantically.

"Something's wrong!" Lizzie gasped.

"C'mon!" Mandy called, already running across the garden. Together they raced over the tilled plot and out the lane to reach the hayfield. Breathless, they arrived and discovered immediately what was wrong. Clyde was down.

It seemed as if time stood still, immobile as a huge concrete slab. Lizzie stood looking at the beautiful horse who tried desperately to get up from the ground, who wanted just to keep going. She didn't want to look at this fallen creature. It was so awful and so pitiful all at the same time that she could not take her eyes away.

Dat was panting, his eyes wild with fear and worry.

"You need to help me a minute. Lizzie, I'll hold up his head. You try and loosen some of the snaps that keep him attached to the team. I don't know if we can. Mandy, you might have to run to the barn for my leather shears. If nothing else works, we may have to cut the harness. Let's try and get him up one more time."

Lizzie worked to free Clyde, but she couldn't. Finally, Dat turned toward Clyde, lifting at the bit of his bridle. "Come on, boy, come on. Get up! Get up, now!"

Clyde tried valiantly. His eyes opened until the whites of his eyes showed the whole way around, and he struggled repeatedly to get his forelegs underneath himself for better balance.

Dat urged him on continuously, while Lizzie

clutched her hands to her chest, bit her lips, and choked back agonizing sobs. What caused him to go down? She was afraid she knew why, but she wasn't sure she could face the answer.

Dat kept talking to Clyde, trying to get him to stand up. The rest of the horses stood by patiently, tossing their manes as if they knew something was wrong. Clouds floated overhead as the sun beat mercilessly down on poor, struggling Clyde.

Finally, Clyde heaved once more with tremendous strength and managed to stand on all four legs. He was shaking violently, sweat dripping from his stomach and running down his legs in rivulets, pooling underneath him.

"Quick, Lizzie, help me unhitch him!"

Lizzie hurried to unsnap the traces that attached him, while Dat loosened reins and chains and took off Clyde's cumbersome collar.

"He's loose," Lizzie said, her voice shaking.

"Come, boy," Dat said gently, as he led him beneath the shade of a small locust tree. Clyde took a few faltering steps to the spot where Dat wanted him, away from the sun's relentless heat.

There Clyde stood, his head hanging down as far as it would go as he heaved great, unbelievable breaths. His chest and sides rose and fell, rose and fell, in an almost hypnotic rhythm. Lizzie clenched her hands in despair. She could not believe the amount of perspiration draining from this massive animal.

"Dat!" Lizzie cried. "Isn't there something we can do?"

Dat shook his head as the trembling of Clyde's limbs increased. He shook like an aspen leaf in a summer thunderstorm, almost as if his legs had a power all their own. His nostrils flared in and out as he breathed in small, gasping, sucking sounds.

"Lizzie, I don't think so. I don't know. I should have been more careful. It's not even noon yet, and he just became overheated, I guess."

"Can you call a veterinarian?"

"I suppose I should. If you'll stay here, I can go, but honestly, Lizzie, I'm afraid he won't make it."

"Why does he tremble like that?"

Dat lowered his head as he turned to walk down the field lane to use the neighbor's phone. Lizzie called after him.

"Dat, could we try and cool him down with water?"

"Let me talk to the vet first," Dat said.

Meanwhile, Mandy had run to the house, looking for Mam, but she couldn't find her. Now Mandy came flying along the field lane, her skirts billowing around her knees, her face pale with fright. She slid to a stop when she saw Clyde standing under the locust tree.

"He's up!" she cried.

"Yes, but Dat doesn't think he's going to live much longer," Lizzie said.

They stood side by side, their nearness giving strength to each other. Lizzie was grateful she did not have to stand out there all alone with this suffering, broken horse. Tears pricked her eyes as she watched Clyde struggling to breathe. Poor, poor boy, she thought.

Then he folded, his limbs buckling, until he slowly sank to the ground. Lizzie cried and reached toward him, helpless, unable to do anything. Mandy stepped back, wrapping her arms around her own waist.

Clyde rolled over once, his legs stretched out, and, for one heart-stopping moment, Lizzie thought he had died. But his side rose and fell, his breathing accompanied by a deep grunting sound.

"He's never going to make it!" Mandy whispered.

And then Lizzie decided to pray. Whether God heard her or not, and even if he seemed far away, she needed to call on him right now and ask him to do something. They could not afford to lose this good, strong workhorse—God would surely know that. So she prayed, turning away from Mandy and toward the remaining team of horses who still waited quietly at the field's edge.

God, you are going to have to look down here and help us. Please let Clyde live because we really need him. Whatever your will is, I guess, but please, please, please let Clyde make it, she prayed.

"Lizzie!"

Lizzie turned to see what Mandy wanted.

"Look, I think he died!"

She turned and saw that his sides were no longer heaving quite as heavily, but he was definitely still breathing on his own. "No, Mandy, he's just quieting down."

It seemed like hours until they heard Dat return. He was half-running, half-walking, his hair and beard blowing back in the breeze. He was panting as he reached them.

"Is he dead?"

"No, he's still breathing," Mandy said.

"He is, isn't he?" Dat said, bending down to peer into Clyde's frightened eyes. "Well that's something."

He straightened up.

"The vet will be here soon," he said.

"What can they do for him?" Lizzie asked.

"I don't know. I really don't. I just feel awful about this. I'm so ashamed to even have the vet look at him. He'll think I'm some horseman, working my horses until they die of exhaustion."

"Dat, you didn't. You *didn't*," Lizzie said. She felt like hugging Dat, she pitied him so much, but she didn't, because that was just how their family was. They never hugged, because it would be too embarrassing for a grown girl to hug her father. But she wanted to anyway.

A white pickup truck came bouncing in the lane, a cloud of dust rolling behind it. The driver slammed on the brakes and hopped out. He ran to the side of the truck, quickly stepped into a pair of clean, white coveralls, and then ran to kneel beside Clyde.

"Beautiful animal," he said quietly, touching, kneading, taking the horse's temperature, shaking his head, and muttering to himself. He ran back to the truck, asking Dat to come help him. Lizzie and

Mandy watched wide-eyed as they prepared a huge plastic bag of solution. There was a small plastic line attached, which looked very much like the I-V line Mam had around her wrist when she had pneumonia.

"Mandy! Mandy!" Lizzie breathed excitedly. "I guarantee he's going to make it now. They're going to put all that stuff in him."

They watched breathlessly as the vet attached the plastic line to a long, sterile needle which glinted in the sun. The vet jammed the needle into Clyde's shoulder muscle as Dat held onto the huge plastic bag. Clyde never moved or winced, so for a heart-stopping moment, Lizzie thought again that he had died.

There was silence then, everyone barely daring to breathe, as the life-giving solution trickled directly into the horse's veins. The locust tree's leaves swirled in the hot breeze as a horse snorted behind them, the chain on his collar clanking against the jockey stick.

Dat turned toward the waiting team as the vet watched the I-V fluid dripping into the horse. A grasshopper leaped past Clyde, and Lizzie wondered if God cared about the little grasshopper as much as he did about Clyde. Probably not.

Lizzie jumped when the vet lifted his arm and whooped. Dat grinned.

"Looks like he's gonna make it!" the vet said. Sure enough, Clyde's gasping, grunting breaths were slowing down now to an almost normal rhythm.

The perspiration still ran down the sides of his stomach, but his trembling was visibly subsiding as Clyde relaxed.

Dat explained to the vet what had happened. The vet nodded as Dat described in detail how Clyde worried himself, prancing and tossing his head while the other horses conserved their energy for their work.

"He won't be worth too much for the rest of the summer, at least for a couple of months," the vet said when Dat finished.

Lizzie and Mandy heard Mam calling for them in the garden, so they told Dat they had to go. The girls walked slowly down the lane, troubled about Clyde. And Dat. When they reached the garden they told Mam and Jason and Emma what had happened.

"Surely God was with them when Clyde didn't die," Mam said.

Lizzie said nothing then, but later that evening she asked Emma if it was possible that Clyde lived because she had begged God that he would.

"Why, of course, Lizzie," Emma said.

"You think so?"

"I'm sure God heard you."

Every time Lizzie watched Clyde contentedly grazing in the pasture, his beautiful copper-brown color glinting in the sun, tossing his magnificent head until his black mane rippled, Lizzie thought about God. He was probably kinder than she had thought, she realized.

Chapter 36

THAT WEEKEND, DAT BUILT A NICE CHICKEN coop for Mam. It was a tiny wooden building with a tin roof and plenty of windows to let the sun in on winter days. Along one wall was a row of tin nests, or boxes, with wooden perches along the front where the chickens sat to lay their eggs.

A long trough on the floor contained the chicken feed, or laying mash, as Mam called it. A round container that was upended into a tin tray held their water. Lizzie never could figure out how you could set that large container full of water upside down in the tray and have only a small amount trickle out at a time. Just enough came out to allow the chickens to have a satisfying drink of water but not so much that they could slop around in it.

Lizzie disliked milking, but she loved horses. For her, chickens fell somewhere between love and disgust. She liked to gather the eggs, as long as the chickens didn't have a crazy notion in their heads about hatching the eggs they sat on. Mam said that a "cluck" or a mother hen, had a natural maternal instinct to remain seated on the egg she had laid so it could hatch into a baby chick.

Thinking about the yolk turning into a baby chick was disgusting for Lizzie. But she loved to eat eggs—fried, scrambled, soft-boiled, just any which way, with salt, pepper, or ketchup. They were delicious. Mam often made an egg in a nest for Jason. She began with a slice of bread, cut the center out of it with a small drinking glass, buttered the "frame" of bread on both sides, and then laid it on the griddle. She broke an egg into the hole in the center, then fried it until the bread was browned and the egg set.

So Mam's chickens were a good thing, providing their family with fresh eggs every day, until egg production dropped drastically. When Lizzie brought in only five eggs from the flock of 21 chickens, Mam said it was time to butcher them. They would need to do the entire cleaning, laundry, and baking on Friday so that on Saturday, when all the girls were home, they could help butcher chickens in the morning.

Lizzie sat at the table, trying to get herself in gear for a job she dreaded. She was tired and discouraged as she thought ahead to Sunday. Her last weekend in Allen County had left her extremely irritable and insecure. She hadn't yet had the nerve or the energy to talk to Emma about things. Marvin was grouchy and slept, or pretended to sleep, the whole way home from the singing. So far, Lizzie was getting no real help in this whole business of how you went about finding a husband, especially one who didn't milk cows or wouldn't suddenly decide to move to another county. Her questions were totally unresolved.

Lizzie stuck the tines of her fork straight into a whole chocolate cake cooling on the kitchen counter and pulled on a small piece. She went back for another before Emma told her that if she wanted cake, she could cut a piece for herself, put it on a plate, and eat it.

Lizzie ignored her. When she heard Mam say that she was ready to start butchering chickens, she tried to ignore that, too.

"It's time you girls learned how to butcher chickens," she said, doing her best to get them all motivated. "You can't be a good wife until you learn," she said, smiling at Emma.

Emma beamed. "Of course, I want to learn," she said happily. "I would love to be able to butcher and can my own chickens."

"I'll have to teach you to make homemade potpie, too," Mam said.

Lizzie snorted but not loud enough for them to hear. Wasn't that just so Emma-ish? Planning all her cozy housewife duties a year or so in advance. She still loved old houses with homemade quilts and rag rugs, and baking bread and jelly rolls, and all sorts of other impossible things.

"I'm not going to help," Lizzie announced loudly,

pulling out another forkful of cake.

Mam kept washing dishes and without turning her head, said, "Oh yes, you are."

The emphasis was very strongly on the "Oh," so Lizzie knew there was no use arguing. She had often watched Mam butcher chickens, which was, in Lizzie's opinion, the most horribly unnecessary thing to do when you could go to town and buy chicken already butchered, quartered, cleaned, and sealed in a package.

Mandy didn't mind butchering. She had helped Mam take the insides out of a chicken once, and she said she found it quite interesting. Not Lizzie. So far, she hadn't been able to stay in the kitchen long enough to watch. The warm, wet chickeny smell sent her into the living room, swallowing desperately to keep from gagging.

But that Saturday morning Mam carried a kettle of boiling water out the door, and Emma carried another as Lizzie and Mandy pulled on shoes. Dat had already chopped the chickens' heads off neatly with a hatchet, and so the chickens were ready to be dunked into the boiling water. That step was to make the feathers easier to pluck. Lizzie started swallowing as she approached the chicken house, trying with all her being to help along with this gruesome task. Mam was already bent over the steaming water, holding waxy yellow feet as she swirled a dead, headless chicken in the hot water. Emma grabbed a chicken, held it by its feet, and followed suit.

"Here!"

Mam handed the gray, sodden, headless chicken to Lizzie, the water running off the ghastly-looking feathers as a sickening, steamy smell wafted toward her flinching nostrils.

She swallowed gamely and reached out for the scaly, yellow feet. Gingerly holding both feet with one hand, she started plucking the feathers a bit tentatively from one side of the bird. Blood dripped onto the snow from the severed neck. Lizzie held the gruesome thing as far away from her snow boots as she possibly could until her back started hurting.

"Why are you leaning over like that?" Mandy asked, plucking feathers with nimble fingers, blood splattering all over her shoes.

"Look at your boots!" Lizzie shrieked.

"It's only chicken blood. It's not going to hurt me," Mandy said sensibly.

So Lizzie knew for sure that she was all alone in hating this task. Mandy and Emma laughed and talked, Mam hurried into the house for more hot water, and no one seemed to be sharing her disgust for the dead chickens.

After the chickens were plucked, Lizzie offered to clean up the feathers, anything she could desperately think of to avoid going into the kitchen. She knew Mam wanted to teach her how to "dress" a chicken. In Pennsylvania Dutch, the process was called "taking it out." As Lizzie raked the feathers, she wondered why English people said "dressing" the chicken. Probably because they were more fancy than Amish people, they wanted to make it sound as if they were dressing the chicken up in a fine suit of clothes. Besides, if they would say "taking it out," someone might think they were going out to a fine restaurant with a chicken. But how did the term "dressing" ever get started? What they were doing was more like *un*dressing the chickens' feathers. The English language was strange, she decided, just like Pennsylvania Dutch was.

When she opened the kitchen door, her cheeks red from the cold, a small pile of raw, dismembered chicken pieces stood on the counter. Emma was holding a plucked chicken while Mam stood beside her, patiently instructing Emma in how to dress it. Mandy was looking over Emma's shoulder, her eyes wide, interested, and wanting to learn, Lizzie could tell.

"Lizzie, this slop bucket needs to be taken down to the fencerow," Mam said, swiping at a stray hair with the back of her hand. No wonder she uses the back of her hand, Lizzie thought, swallowing hard. She bent to pick up the stainless steel bucket of unimaginable objects with waxy feet floating around in it and carried it across the yard, down the field lane, and over another grassy area before heaving the contents of the bucket into the fencerow.

Dat had opened the garage door and was sweeping the forebay of the horse barn, pushing the wide broom in short little bursts.

He stopped, looked at Lizzie, and laughed when he saw her expression. Pushing back his hat, he called, "Are you happy butchering chickens?"

Lizzie gave him a withering look, and he laughed again, bending his back to resume his sweeping.

"Oh, Dat!" was all she said, hoping he knew she didn't find him or her job funny.

"I 'took out' a whole chicken," Mandy announced triumphantly when Lizzie returned.

"Good for you," Lizzie said dryly.

Mam was cutting the cleaned chicken into pieces and packing the pieces onto trays, which she then set out on the back porch to cool thoroughly before she started canning the meat. Lizzie carried the trays out to the porch, thinking about how the chickens had died with goose bumps all over their skin. They were probably so horrified at the massacre in the chicken yard as Dat started brandishing the hatchet, that they all broke out in goose bumps of pure terror. She had noticed that the eyes of the dead chickens were open extremely wide, which only underlined the fact that these chickens died a most awful death.

She pitied chickens anyway for having to sit in tin boxes and lay one painful egg after another. Then people came along and took away what the hens wanted to keep and what they hoped would hatch into children. She wondered if the clucks forgot about their eggs a few minutes after laying them. Were their brains developed well enough to wish they could have a whole family of baby chicks?

They couldn't be too smart, Lizzie thought, or they wouldn't eat bugs and worms or any insect they could catch. Chickens ate almost anything you tried to give them, even chewing gum that had already been chewed, so they couldn't be too bright.

"Someone has to guard that meat," Mam said. "I don't want the cats taking all this good chicken."

"I'll watch out for them," Lizzie offered.

That, plus having no enthusiasm for the job, was why she never took out a chicken, she guessed later. Between guarding the trays of chicken, taking the slop bucket to the fencerow, and caring for Susan and KatieAnn, Lizzie escaped touching the insides of the chickens that day. When there were only a few more to take out, Emma alerted Mam to the fact that Lizzie had not cleaned one bird.

Mam sighed and then looked at Lizzie and the remaining chickens.

"Mam, I'll learn next time, all right?" she said quickly.

"Lizzie, you should do at least one now."

"You're getting tired of it, and I don't know the first thing about it," Lizzie reminded her.

So Lizzie ended up not dressing chickens that day. Emma told her she didn't pity her if she couldn't make good chicken potpie or chicken corn soup after she was married.

"I'm not going to get married, so don't worry about me," Lizzie shot back.

Emma looked at her teasingly. "Didn't look like it Sunday evening!"

"What do you mean?" Lizzie asked, her face coloring to a deep pink.

"Oh, nothing," Emma said, turning to wipe down the counter.

"What? What?" Mandy asked, fairly hopping up and down.

Mam stopped dressing chickens long enough to raise her eyebrows at Lizzie. "You didn't say anything to us," she said, smiling.

And so, while they finished the job and cleaned the kitchen afterward, Lizzie let the whole story of her first weekend with the young people tumble out. All her feelings of insecurity and her real fears. She wondered aloud how she could play Ping-Pong with such a nice-looking boy one moment, and even go for a walk with him, and then be left set, "like...like chicken innards in the fencerow," she said as she finished her miserable outburst.

Mam looked genuinely surprised, shocking to Lizzie, and Mandy squealed, clapping her hands excitedly.

Emma looked at Lizzie with disbelief written all over her face. "Lizzie," she breathed. "I can't believe you're saying these things. You always seem so self-assured. You didn't even seem shy on Sunday evening. I wished I could have been so talkative on my first weekend. To tell you the truth, I was even envying your ability to make friends. Just like you were with Amos. I would never have talked to a boy that much my very first weekend. You just have a way of making up to people."

"E...Emma!" Lizzie burst out, incredulous.

"I really have a hard time believing what you're

saying, Lizzie! You certainly didn't act like you felt that way."

Mam smiled. "Lizzie, I hope you realize that the first time you're with the youth is only a very small step on a much longer journey. You know that I believe that God already has a husband picked for you. We just don't know who it will be yet. So certainly, one game of Ping-Pong…"

"Two!" Lizzie broke in.

Mandy giggled and Emma rolled her eyes as Mam continued. "Well, two games. That is certainly not going to have a big effect one way or another in your seeking for your life partner."

"See, Mam?" Lizzie said miserably. "Right there's the trouble."

"What?"

"'Seeking your life partner.' That's not the girl's job. We can't do one thing about it. We just have to sit around and act like we don't even care if we get a husband or not. The boys are the ones who can do something about it. If we'd ask a young man for a date, they'd all have a fit. I bet the whole church, or anyone who found out anyway, would have a fit. It's so one-sided it isn't even right."

Mam sat down, lifted her hands, and laughed, taking off her glasses and wiping them clean with the corner of her apron as she always did. "No, Lizzie, you certainly don't want to go ask Amos for a date," she said, still chuckling.

"Who said I would even want to ask him?" Lizzie retorted.

"Well, it sounds to me as if you'd like to. But you're going way too fast and haphazardly as usual. Just because a young man is handsome, and you feel attracted to him, doesn't mean that you need to know immediately, right this second, whether he feels the same, or if you're even suited for each other, or if it's God's will. You need to let feelings develop over time and learn to pray about it. Ask God to show you the way, Lizzie. You have to slow down. You're far too immature at this stage in your life to be choosing your husband," Mam said wisely, as usual.

"What does he look like, Lizzie? Is he cute?" Mandy asked, leaning toward Lizzie, her green eyes shining. "Does he like you?"

Emma looked at Mam and shook her head in disbelief as Lizzie punched Mandy's arm. "Stop it."

The really good thing about growing older, Lizzie decided that evening as she got ready for bed, was that Mam's talk about God's will made a lot more sense than it had a year ago. She had come to really believe that her future was not based on nerve-wracking life or death, right or wrong, decisions. She was beginning to understand that God had plenty of time to let you grow up in knowledge and understanding. You couldn't run ahead of him, trying to figure things out on your own, because that gave you the blues.

So she would try and calm down, enjoy her weekends in Allen County, and not insist on knowing right away who her husband would be. Mandy told her that she thought too much and tried to figure things out that were none of her business, which was true. But how could you stop thinking? It just happened.

And another thing. How in the world was God going to show her the way? Mam was just so much further advanced in knowing God than she was, that it wasn't even funny. How did God talk to a 16-year-old girl when that girl's thoughts of him were still not very clear at all?

God was supposed to be way up in heaven, and who even knew if he was there for certain? Nobody did. They just *hoped* he was or *believed* he was. They didn't know for sure.

Lizzie closed her eyes tiredly. She found the turmoil of a budding faith to be a bit too overwhelming. It was much easier just to have fun and be young and enjoy life than to become too serious too soon.

Mam, on the other hand, believed that Lizzie's thoughts were probably very much like the egg under the cluck. Her faith was being well cared for and nurtured into growth by a very loving heavenly father whom she did not yet feel very close to.

Chapter 37

Sunshine and warm breezes found their way into the house and barn. Clyde and Bess ran back and forth across the pasture. Milking cows wasn't even quite as distasteful on these lovely spring mornings.

When Sunday evening rolled around, Lizzie wore a new lavender dress, almost the color of the delicate crocuses bordering the porch. Emma looked very pretty in a shade of green which matched her eyes and made her hair appear darker still.

When the driver came to pick them up, Lizzie was surprised to see Stephen sitting in the back seat. His skin was already tanned to a dark shade of brown, and his hair was bleached lighter by the spring sunshine. He is certainly not unattractive, she thought.

After climbing into the van, Lizzie smiled back at Stephen and said, "Why are you going along to Allen County?" she asked.

"To run around," he told her abruptly.

Marvin laughed loudly at this, and Stephen looked at Marvin, his eyes twinkling. They made Lizzie feel as if she was an annoying little 12-year-old. She turned around and resolved not to talk to Marvin the whole way to Allen County. That Stephen. He may be nice-looking, but when he and Marvin were in one of their moods, they irritated Lizzie to distraction.

Well, she liked Amos anyway, so there was no real problem. As she looked out the window at the light green beginning to appear on the mountain, she was filled with the joy of springtime. No use being grouchy, she thought, as she observed the beautiful tulips, daffodils, and hyacinths growing in neat rows along the bases of the well-kept houses they passed. She loved looking at new homes, at their landscaping and green lawns cut so evenly that they looked like indoor synthetic green carpet. That's what my yard will look like when I get married, she thought happily. No old farm for me.

That Sunday, the day itself was as light and joyous as a feather. Not a heavy, white, waxy chicken feather, but a downy, light blue feather that floated to the ground from a bluebird's wing. The whole earth was full of color and joy, the warm breezes blowing the girls' hair loose from beneath their coverings.

They all decided to go for a long drive to a nearby lake before going to the regular Sunday supper. Marvin, Stephen, and Amos, with Mary, Barbara, Lizzie, and Ruthie, traveling in two different teams,

headed out Barbara's driveway and onto the highway. Amos had his hands full with his feisty little
horse who was clipping along at an alarming rate.
He didn't say much as he held onto the reins with
both hands, his arms outstretched in an effort to
hold him back.

Ruthie and Lizzie rode with Amos, while Stephen
and Marvin took the other girls with their team and
followed them. Lizzie was secretly a tiny bit disappointed because she didn't want Ruthie to go along
with her and Amos. She wasn't convinced that Amos
didn't like Ruthie. That was the annoying part of liking someone too much; there was always the chance
that he wouldn't like you back. What if she wanted
Amos to ask her out on a real honest-to-goodness
date, the serious kind, and then maybe in a year or
so he would ask her to get married? Of course, this
would have to involve living in Cameron County,
not Allen, and in a new house, not on an old farm.
But there was no use thinking too far ahead, not on
a day like today, Lizzie reminded herself.

Ruthie was sitting between Amos and Lizzie. The
only way three people could sit comfortably on a
buggy seat was for the person in the middle to sit
on the edge of the seat while the two others sat as
far back as they could. Lizzie had been a bit miffed
when Ruthie plopped herself beside Amos, where
Lizzie had already been seated. But if she leaned over
far enough, it seemed as if it was just she and Amos
driving together without Ruthie being there. That
was a mean thought, Lizzie knew, but she thought

it nevertheless.

"My arms are getting really tired hanging onto this crazy horse!" Amos said, laughing.

"I'll drive!" Lizzie blurted out.

"You!" Ruthie gasped.

"I love to drive! He can't be worse than our old horse Billy was when he was younger," Lizzie said, glancing at Amos.

"You want to try?" Amos asked, a bit incredulously.

"Sure."

They exchanged seats, which was no easy feat with Ruthie in the middle, squeaking and exclaiming about her apron getting wrinkled if they didn't settle themselves soon. Amos apologized profusely, which irritated Lizzie so much that she had a notion to loosen the reins entirely so the horse would run away and throw them all out into a field.

No doubt about it, this horse had a mouth of iron, as Dat described a horse that wanted to run too fast. Lizzie bit her lip and clamped her hands down hard on the reins. It felt so much like driving Billy in Jefferson County that she burst out laughing. This was an absolutely exhilarating feeling, with the powerful little horse lunging into his collar and the breeching across his rump flapping up and down with every frenzied step he took.

The warm breeze swooshed through the window of the buggy until Lizzie's hair flew across her eyes and her covering slid helter-skelter. She remembered the first time Dat had let her drive Teeny and Tiny, the miniature ponies. She had started to giggle when the ponies went too fast, just like now. There was something about a horse going this fast that made Lizzie laugh.

"What's so funny?" Ruthie asked.

"I always have to laugh when a horse runs too fast. It just gives me the giggles," Lizzie answered.

"It isn't funny, Lizzie. Let Amos drive."

"She can handle him," Amos said, glancing at Lizzie behind Ruthie's back. The twinkle in his eyes caught hers, and they looked at each other rather long, Lizzie thought. She could tell he admired her for driving his horse, or she hoped that's what he meant when his eyes smiled at hers.

Springtime was unbelievably wonderful. Lizzie's heart sang as the little horse kept up his rapid trotting for the next mile. Was it true that a young man's thoughts turn to love in the springtime? At least she was sure that she had impressed Amos by driving his horse, and that felt like butterflies flitting across her heart. She bet it wouldn't be long until he asked to come see her at her home like when Joshua came to see Emma.

When they stopped at the lake, Lizzie was awestruck by the weeping willows and their branches drooping at the water's edge. The softly moving limbs rustled gently while the water lapped at the new shoots of grass. Lizzie thought of Cinderella's long skirts that swayed whenever she danced with her Prince. She supposed God designed willow trees to be graceful and able to talk with the gently rippling water in the spring. God actually had lots of good spring-time ideas—butterflies, crocuses, baby birds, tulips.

Suddenly she realized that she had wandered alone to the far side of the lake. She turned around and hiked quickly in the direction of the hollering and laughing.

When Lizzie reached the group, Ruthie was clutching a tiny bouquet of purple violets and smiling up at Amos who was smiling back at her. Jealousy, unlike anything Lizzie had ever felt before, clamped its iron jaws around her heart until she thought she would suffocate like a mouse in a trap. She knew instinctively that her feelings were wrong. Mam had always taught the girls that jealousy came directly from the devil.

She turned away, detouring around Amos and Ruthie to find Barbara and Mary unhitching their horse, with Marvin still sitting in the buggy. They were laughing and teasing him, and Lizzie had to laugh in spite of trying desperately to fight off her jealousy of Ruthie. Marvin held a bag of potato chips and calmly munched on them, his feet on the dashboard as if he hadn't a care in the world.

"Marvin!" Lizzie called, laughing.

"What? Oh, Lizzie! How's my niecely?" Lizzie's heart grew warm with fondness for Marvin, for the pet name and for the genuine sense of safety he gave her, as well as the admiration and love she felt for him.

"Come join me, Niecely!"

Gratefully, Lizzie climbed into the buggy beside him, grabbing his bag of potato chips. "Share your chips, Marvin!"

"You want a Pepsi?"

"Do you have extra?"

"Sure!"

Lizzie took a long drink of the refreshing soda until her eyes watered, her nose burned, and she burped.

"You mean you still can't drink soda like a lady?" Marvin teased.

Lizzie hiccuped, smiled, and ruefully shook her head. "Nope, Marvin. You know I'm not used to drinking soda."

They sat in companionable silence, watching the little wavelets slapping themselves to nothing on the pebbly shoreline. The weeping willows danced gracefully above them, the sky full of puffy clouds as white as cottonballs against the blue sky. Out on the lake, two people pulled on oars, pushing their streamlined orange canoe against the little waves. It was all so peaceful that the perfect spring scene here by the lake brought a lump to Lizzie's throat. If she hadn't had these troubling thoughts about Amos, Stephen, and Ruthie, the day would have been wonderfully perfect.

"Marvin, do you think Amos likes Ruthie?" she asked, nervously toying with her Pepsi can.

Marvin looked at Lizzie, noticing the anxiety in her eyes. "Why should you care?" he asked bluntly.

"I don't," Lizzie said forcefully.

"You do!"

"I *don't*."

"Then why do you ask?"

That was as far as the conversation went before Amos came walking over to the buggy. There was a light in his eye and a real spring in his step as he approached them.

"Hey, this guy told me we can take his canoe out. Wanna go, Marvin?"

"Why don't you ask Lizzie?" Marvin asked. "I'm busy eating chips."

Lizzie looked at Marvin and then at Amos, becoming flustered immediately. "Well, I…"

"I can ask Ruthie," Amos said.

"No! I'll go. I just didn't want to go unless you wanted me to. I mean, you didn't ask me. Marvin just said I could go. If you'd rather ask Ruthie, please do. It's not like you have to ask me to go along." Lizzie stopped, noticing the strange look Marvin was giving her. His eyebrows were drawn down, and his eyes seemed to plead with her to be quiet. Why couldn't I just be quiet? Lizzie thought miserably.

The canoe looked awfully long and narrow. But after she was seated, she wasn't frightened because there was much more room than she first thought. Amos clambered in. He held onto the oars and tried not to rock too much before he found his seat, facing Lizzie.

"Ready?" he asked.

"Mm-hmm," Lizzie said, clamping her teeth down hard to keep her voice from shaking. She certainly hoped he had rowed a canoe before.

He lifted the smooth wooden oars into the oarlocks, set them evenly on each side, and pulled. The muscles in his strong, brown arms bulged as he heaved on both oars.

Lizzie's nervousness evaporated easily, and she laughed out loud at the thrill of gliding so swiftly through the clear blue water. Amos was adept at handling the oars, which propelled them along at a surprising rate. Lizzie put her hand over the side and found the water to be alarmingly cold. She quickly put her hand in her lap.

"Is it cold?"

"It's icy cold!"

"Can you swim?" Amos asked.

"Oh, yes!" Lizzie answered, hoping with all her heart that she had impressed him even more than when she drove his horse.

"Really? Come on! You can't!"

"Of course, I can swim."

Amos stopped rowing and they sat quietly, the canoe rocking gently from side to side. It was the single most blissful moment Lizzie had ever experienced. Here she was in the middle of a beautiful lake on this extraordinary day. With Amos. She had to admit to herself, too, that it was especially sweet because he was with her and not Ruthie. The only thing that bothered her was the fact that Marvin told Amos to take her canoeing. Amos had not actually asked her on his own.

When they got back to the lake's edge, Amos hopped out and held the canoe so Lizzie could step safely onto the grass. She felt warm and a little confused. And almost rapturous. She drifted off to catch her breath under a long-armed willow tree.

A moment later, she heard a step behind her and turned to find Stephen approaching her. How could he have crept up on her like that? He must be part Indian.

"What are you doing here by yourself?" he asked.

"I didn't realize I was by myself. I guess I just walked over here to look at the weeping willow branches hanging in the water. Aren't they the prettiest things you've ever seen?"

"No."

Lizzie looked at him, puzzled at his curt answer. She found Stephen's blue eyes looking intently into hers without a trace of laughter.

"You are," he said.

Lizzie was shocked. She was so surprised that she could say absolutely nothing. In fact, she couldn't look at him so she looked at her shoes, which felt much safer. And her shoes were really quite interesting. She tried desperately to think of a fitting comeback, even a joking one, but she was absolutely tongue-tied. When she looked up, he was gone.

She turned to walk back to the others, putting her hands up to her warm cheeks to cool them. Oh, mercy! Now Stephen had said that, and she liked

Amos. How complicated was this whole husband thing going to become? She didn't know Stephen liked her. Well, maybe he didn't. Maybe he just thought she was pretty, and it was very nice of him to say that. He did intrigue her, but...there was Amos.

Amos had taken her to the middle of the lake alone. Was that, she worried, so indescribably special mostly because Ruthie had to watch?

She would ask Emma to give her honest opinion about whether, when you sit in a canoe with a boy and feel absolutely joyful, you are in real love. And did Emma think she should learn to know the mysterious Stephen better? Who was he really and how could she find out?

Lizzie would have to relate this whole wonderful day, bit by bit, to Emma and Mandy. Thank God for sisters. And for interesting boys. Including Uncle Marvin, who may or may not be helpful.

❧

The Recipes

Lizzie's Favorite Recipes

WHOOPIE PIES   326

CREAMSTICKS   328

MOLASSES COOKIES   331

APPLE PIE WITH CRUMB TOPPING   332

CHICKEN STEW   334

BAKED MACARONI AND CHEESE   336

HOMEMADE BAKED BEANS   338

RED BEET EGGS   339

Whoopie Pies

Makes about 4 dozen whoopie pies

2 cups sugar
1 cup oil
2 eggs
4½ cups flour
1 cup dry cocoa powder
½ tsp. salt
1 cup sour milk
2 tsp. vanilla
1 cup hot water
2 tsp. baking soda

FILLING:
4 cups confectioners sugar, *divided*
2 egg whites, beaten
1 tsp. vanilla
1½ cups vegetable shortening

1. To make pies, cream sugar, oil and eggs together thoroughly in a large mixing bowl.

2. In a separate bowl, sift together flour, cocoa powder, and salt.

3. Add these dry ingredients to creamed mixture alternately with sour milk.

4. Stir in vanilla.

5. In a small bowl, dissolve baking soda in hot water.

6. Stir into batter until smooth.

7. Drop batter by rounded teaspoons onto cookie sheets.

8. Bake 8-10 minutes at 400°.

9. Remove from oven and allow to cool.

10. While pie tops/bottoms are cooling, make Filling.

11. In a medium bowl fold 2 cups confectioners sugar into beaten egg whites.

12. Stir in 1 tsp. vanilla.

13. Beat in shortening until smooth.

14. Beat in remaining 2 cups confectioners sugar until smooth.

15. Assemble pies by spreading a dab of filling over a cooled bottom and topping it with a second cookie.

Creamsticks

Makes about 2½ dozen doughnuts

PASTRY:
1 cup milk
1 cup warm water
2 pkgs. yeast
½ cup vegetable shortening
⅔ cup sugar
2 eggs, beaten
1 tsp. salt
6 cups flour
vegetable oil for deep-frying

FILLING:
3 tsp. flour
1 cup milk
1 cup vegetable shortening
1 cup sugar
1 Tbsp. vanilla
2½ cups confectioners sugar

TOPPING:
1 cup brown sugar
half a stick (4 Tbsp.) butter
⅓ cup milk
½ cup vegetable shortening
2 cups confectioners sugar

1. To make pastry, begin by scalding 1 cup milk. Allow to cool to room temperature.

2. In a separate bowl, dissolve two packages yeast in one cup warm water.

3. In a large mixing bowl, cream ½ cup shortening with ⅔ cup sugar, 2 beaten eggs, and 1 tsp. salt.

4. Combine cooled milk and dissolved yeast with creamed mixture.

5. Add flour 2-3 cups at a time (for a total of about 6 cups), and mix until you get a soft dough.

6. Cover and let rise in a warm place until double in size.

7. Roll out on a floured surface.

8. Cut dough into rectangular strips, approximately 4 inches by 1 inch. Place on baking sheets about 1 inch apart.

9. Cover and allow to rise again in a warm place until almost double in size.

10. Deep fry in vegetable oil.

11. Cool and cut slits in top.

12. While pastry is cooling, make filling.

13. Make a paste by combining 3 tsp. flour and 1 cup milk in a medium saucepan over medium heat.

recipe continues on next page

14. Stir continuously until mixture boils and becomes smooth.

15. Remove from heat and allow to cool completely.

16. Combine 1 cup shortening, 1 cup sugar, and 1 Tbsp. vanilla in a large mixing bowl.

17. When smooth, mix with flour and milk mixture until well blended.

18. Stir in 2½ cups confectioners sugar.

19. Force filling into creamsticks with a cake decorator or cookie press.

20. Make topping by combining 1 cup brown sugar, 4 Tbsp. butter, and ⅓ cup milk in a medium saucepan.

21. Bring mixture to a boil, stirring frequently to prevent sticking.

22. Cool.

23. Blend in ½ cup shortening and 2 cups confectioners sugar.

24. Spread topping over filled creamsticks.

Molasses Cookies

Makes 7-8 dozen cookies

3 sticks (1½ cups) butter, softened
2½ cups brown sugar
3 eggs
1 cup Bre'r Rabbit molasses
7 cups flour
2 tsp. cinnamon
2 tsp. ginger
1 Tbsp. baking soda
granulated sugar

1. In a large bowl cream butter and brown sugar together.

2. Add eggs and molasses.

3. Stir in flour, cinnamon, ginger, and baking soda to form a firm dough.

4. Pinch off about 1 rounded tsp. dough and roll into a ball.

5. Roll each ball in granulated sugar.

6. Place on cookie sheet and flatten a little to make a cookie shape.

7. Continue until all batter is used.

8. Bake 10 to 12 minutes at 350°.

Apple Pie with Crumb Topping

Makes 1 pie

FILLING:
- 1½ cups water
- 1 cup brown sugar
- 2 Tbsp. cornstarch
- 1 tsp. cinnamon
- 1 Tbsp. butter
- 2 to 3 cups grated apples

9" unbaked pie shell

CRUMB TOPPING:
- 1 cup brown sugar
- 1 cup dry old-fashioned, or quick, oatmeal
- ½ cup flour
- 3 Tbsp. butter, softened

1. Combine water, 1 cup brown sugar, cornstarch, and cinnamon in a large saucepan.

2. Heat over low heat to dissolve sugar and cornstarch. Stir frequently to prevent sticking.

3. Add 1 Tbsp. butter and grated apples.

4. Remove from heat.

5. Spoon filling mixture into pie shell.

6. Combine brown sugar, dry oatmeal, and flour in a good-sized bowl.

7. Cut butter into dry ingredients to create crumbs, none larger than pea-sized.

8. Sprinkle crumb topping uniformly over apple filling.

9. Bake at 350° for 45 to 60 minutes, or until well browned.

Chicken Stew

Makes 6-8 servings

3 cups cooked chicken, deboned and
  cut in chunks
1 qt. chicken broth
2 tsp. granular chicken bouillon
2 cups potatoes, cubed
2 cups peas
2 Tbsp. onion, chopped
2 cups sliced carrots
1 Tbsp. parsley
1 tsp. salt
pepper to taste
flour
water
1 box buttermilk baking mix

1. Put first 10 ingredients into an 8-qt. kettle.

2. Cover and bring to a boil.

3. Reduce heat. Simmer until vegetables are soft.

4. Thicken or thin with water and/or flour as desired.

5. Make dumplings according to buttermilk baking mix box.

6. Drop dumplings on top of cooked stew.

7. Simmer until dumplings are cooked through.

Baked
Macaroni and Cheese

Makes 4-6 servings

2 cups cooked macaroni
half a stick (4 Tbsp.) butter
3 Tbsp. flour
2 cups milk
2 cups cheddar cheese, shredded
½ cup white American cheese, shredded
½ tsp. salt
dash of pepper
3 Tbsp. butter
¾ cup bread crumbs

1. In a large saucepan melt half a stick butter.

2. Over low heat, stir in flour until sauce is smooth.

3. Gradually add milk. Continuing over low heat, cook and stir constantly for 2 to 3 minutes, or until sauce bubbles and thickens.

4. Stir in cheese. Continue heating until cheese melts and sauce is smooth.

5. Stir in salt and pepper.

6. Place cooked macaroni in a greased 9 × 13 baking dish.

7. Pour cheese sauce over macaroni.

8. In a small saucepan, melt 3 Tbsp. butter. Stir in bread crumbs.

9. Cover macaroni and cheese with buttered bread crumbs.

10. Bake uncovered 1 hour at 350°.

Homemade Baked Beans

Makes 20-25 servings

1 gallon Great Northern beans, drained
1 lb. bacon, cooked until crisp and drained
1 medium onion, diced
1 Tbsp. salt
¾ cup brown sugar
½ cup molasses
1 cup ketchup
1 pt. tomato juice
2 tsp. cinnamon

1. Pour beans into a six-quart roast pan.

2. Crumble cooked bacon over beans.

3. Add remaining ingredients and stir together.

4. Bake covered 2-3 hours at 350°. Stir at the end of each hour. Beans are done when they're heated through and are the consistency that you want.

Red Beet Eggs

Makes 24 servings

1 dozen hard-boiled eggs
1 qt. pickled red beets with juice

1. Cool eggs and peel.

2. Place in a good-sized jar or bowl.

3. Pour pickled red beets, including juice, over eggs.

4. Stir so each egg is surrounded completely by juice. Make sure eggs are fully submerged in juice.

5. Cover. Chill in refrigerator overnight.

6. Cut each egg in half lengthwise and serve.

The Glossary

Cape—An extra piece of cloth which Amish women wear over the bodices of their dresses in order to be more modest.

Covering—A fine mesh headpiece worn by Amish females in an effort to follow the Amish interpretation of a New Testament teaching in I Corinthians 11.

Dat—A Pennsylvania Dutch dialect word used to address or to refer to one's father.

Dichly—A Pennsylvania Dutch dialect word meaning head scarf or bandanna.

Doddy—A Pennsylvania Dutch dialect word used to address or to refer to one's grandfather.

Driver—When the Amish need to go somewhere, and it's too distant to travel by horse and buggy, they may hire someone to drive them in a car or van.

English—The Amish term for anyone who is not Amish.

Fadutsed—A Pennsylvania Dutch dialect word meaning plain.

Gros-feelich—A Pennsylvania Dutch dialect word meaning vain.

Lebbley—A Pennsylvania Dutch dialect word referring to a small piece of cloth, attached to the center back of the waist of a dress.

Mam—A Pennsylvania Dutch dialect word used to address or to refer to one's mother.

Maud—A Pennsylvania Dutch dialect word meaning a live-in female helper, usually hired by a family for a week or two at a time. *Mauds* often help to do house-, lawn-, and garden-work after the birth of a baby.

Mennonite—Another Anabaptist group which shares common beliefs with the Amish. The differences between the two groups lie in their practices. Mennonites tend to be more open to higher education and to mission activity and less distinctly different from the rest of the world in their dress, transportation, and use of technology.

Mommy—A Pennsylvania Dutch dialect word used to address or to refer to one's grandmother.

Ordnung—The Amish community's agreed-upon rules for living, based upon their understanding of the Bible, particularly the New Testament. The *Ordnung* varies some from community to community, often reflecting the leaders' preferences and the local traditions and historical practices.

Patties down—Putting one's hands on one's lap before praying, as a sign of respect. Usually includes bowing one's head and closing one's eyes. A phrase spoken to children who are learning the practice.

Running around—The time in an Amish young person's life between the age of 16 and marriage. Includes structured social activities for groups, as well as dating. Usually takes place on the weekend.

Vocational school—Attended by 14-year-old Amish children who have completed eight grades of school. These students go to school three hours a week and keep a journal—which their teacher reviews—about their time at home learning farming and homemaking skills from their parents.

The Author

Linda Byler grew up Amish and is an active member of the Amish church today. Growing up, Linda loved to read and write. In fact, she still does. She is well-known within the Amish community as a columnist for a weekly Amish newspaper. Linda and her husband, their children, and grandchildren live in central Pennsylvania.

Don't miss
books two and three in the
Lizzie Searches for Love series.

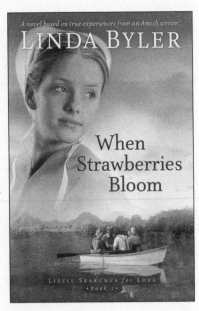

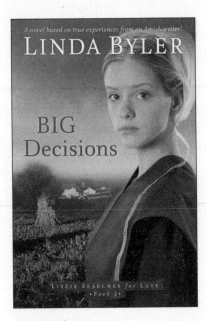

Book Two
978-1-56148-699-1
Coming in October, 2010

Book Three
978-1-56148-700-4
Coming in March, 2011

Good Books